P9-CEB-137

WITHDRAWN

Praise for *Biggest Flirts*,
the first book in the Superlatives trilogy

"Teen romance fans on the hunt
for a flirty fix will find plenty to enjoy
in this sexy, fun beach read."
—*Kirkus Reviews*

"Entertaining and engaging."
—*School Library Journal*

Also by Jennifer Echols

the superlatives

perfect couple

JENNIFER ECHOLS

Simon Pulse

New York   London   Toronto   Sydney   New Delhi

This book is a work of fiction. Any references to historical events, real people, or real places are used fictitiously. Other names, characters, places, and events are products of the author's imagination, and any resemblance to actual events or places or persons, living or dead, is entirely coincidental.

SIMON PULSE
An imprint of Simon & Schuster Children's Publishing Division
1230 Avenue of the Americas, New York, NY 10020
This Simon Pulse edition January 2015
Text copyright © 2015 by Jennifer Echols
Cover photographs copyright © 2014 (back) and 2015 (front and spine) by Michael Frost
All rights reserved, including the right of reproduction
in whole or in part in any form.
SIMON PULSE and colophon are registered trademarks of Simon & Schuster, Inc.
For information about special discounts for bulk purchases, please contact
Simon & Schuster Special Sales at 1-866-506-1949 or business@simonandschuster.com.
The Simon & Schuster Speakers Bureau can bring authors to your live event. For more information
or to book an event contact the Simon & Schuster Speakers Bureau at 1-866-248-3049
or visit our website at www.simonspeakers.com.
Cover design by Regina Flath
Interior design by Mike Rosamilia
The text of this book was set in Adobe Caslon Pro.
Manufactured in the United States of America
2 4 6 8 10 9 7 5 3 1
The Library of Congress has cataloged the paperback edition as follows:
Echols, Jennifer.
The superlatives : perfect couple / Jennifer Echols.
— First Simon Pulse paperback edition.
p. cm.
Summary: When yearbook photographer Harper and the star player of the high
school football team get voted "the perfect couple that never was" by their senior class,
the unlikely pair start falling for one another. But a handful of obstacles, including
Harper's boyfriend, stand in the way of their perfect ending.
[1. Dating (Social customs)—Fiction. 2. High schools—Fiction. 3. Schools—Fiction.
4. Photography—Fiction. 5. Popularity—Fiction. 6. Family life—Florida—Fiction.
7. Florida—Fiction.] I. Title.
PZ7.E1967Sup 2015
[Fic]—dc23
2014006872
ISBN 978-1-4424-7449-9 (hc)
ISBN 978-1-4424-7448-2 (pbk)
ISBN 978-1-4424-7450-5 (eBook)

the superlatives

perfect couple

1

FAMOUS PHOTOGRAPHS WALLPAPERED MR.
Oakley's journalism classroom. Behind his desk, Martin Luther
King Jr. waved to thousands who'd crowded the National Mall
to hear his "I Have a Dream" speech, with the Washington
Monument towering in the distance. Over by the windows, a
lone man stood defiant in front of four Chinese tanks in protest of the Tiananmen Square massacre. On the wall directly
above my computer screen, a World War II sailor impulsively
kissed a nurse in Times Square on the day Japan surrendered.

Mr. Oakley had told us a picture was worth a thousand words, and these posters were his proof. He was right.
Descriptions in my history textbook read like old news, but
these photos made me want to stand up for people, like
Dr. King did, and protest injustice, like Tank Man did.

And be swept away by romance, like that nurse.

My gaze fell from the poster to my computer display, which was full of my pictures of Brody Larson. A few weeks ago, on the first day of school, our senior class had elected the Superlatives—like Most Academic, Most Courteous, and Least Likely to Leave the Tampa/St. Petersburg Metropolitan Area. Brody and I had been voted Perfect Couple That Never Was. Brody had dated Grace Swearingen the whole summer, and I'd been with the yearbook editor, Kennedy Glass, for a little over a month. Being named part of a perfect couple when Brody and I were dating other people was embarrassing. Disorienting. Anything but perfect.

And *me* being named one half of a perfect couple with *Brody* made as much sense as predicting snow for Labor Day next Monday in our beachside town. He was the popular, impulsive quarterback for our football team. Sure, through twelve years of school, I'd liked him. He was friendly and *so* handsome. He also scared the hell out of me. I couldn't date someone who'd nearly lost his license speeding, was forever in the principal's office for playing pranks, and had a daily drama with one girl or another on a long list of exes. And he would never fall for law-abiding, curfew-obeying, glasses-wearing me.

So I hadn't gone after him as my friend Tia had urged me

to. I only found excuses to snap photos of him for the yearbook. For the football section, I'd taken a shot of him at practice in his helmet and pads. Exasperated with his teammates, he'd held up his hands like he needed help from heaven.

For the candid section, I planned to use a picture from my friend Kaye's party last Saturday. Brody grinned devilishly as he leaned into his truck cab to grab something. I'd cropped out the beer.

For the full-color opening page, I'd taken a close-up of him yesterday in study hall. His brown hair fell long across his forehead. He wore a green T-shirt that made his green eyes seem to glow. Girls all over school would thank me for this when they received their yearbooks next May. In fact, Brody had implied as much when I snapped the picture. He made me promise I wouldn't sell it to "a porn site for ladies," which was why he was smiling.

In short, he was the sailor in the poster: the kind of guy to come home from overseas, celebrate the end of the war in Times Square, and sweep a strange girl off her feet.

I only wished I was that girl.

"Harper, you've been staring at Brody for a quarter of an hour." Kennedy rolled his chair down the row of computers to knock against mine. I spun for a few feet before I caught the desktop and stopped myself.

Busted!

"You're not taking that Perfect Couple vote seriously, are you?" he asked. "I'll bet a lot of people decided to prank you."

"Of course I'm not taking it seriously," I said, and should have left it there. I couldn't. "Why do you think we're so mismatched? Because he's popular and I'm not?"

"No."

"Because he's a local celebrity and I'm not?"

"No, because he broke his leg in sixth grade, trying to jump a palmetto grove in his go-cart."

"I see your point."

"Besides, *we're* the perfect couple."

Right. I smiled. And I waited for him to put his arm around me, backing up his words with a touch. But our relationship had never been very physical. I expected a caress now because that's what I imagined Brody would do in this situation. I was hopeless.

I said brightly, "If I was staring at Brody, I was zoning out." I nodded to the Times Square poster. "I get lost in that image sometimes."

Kennedy squinted at the kiss. "Why? That picture is hackneyed. You can buy it anywhere. It's on coffee mugs and shower curtains. It's as common in the dentist's office as a fake Monet or a print of dogs playing poker."

Yes, because people loved it—for a reason. I didn't voice my opinion, though. I was just relieved I'd distracted Kennedy from my lame obsession with Brody.

When Kennedy had bumped my chair, he'd stopped himself squarely in front of my computer. Now he closed my screen *without asking*. I'd saved my changes to Brody's photos, but what if I hadn't before he closed them? The idea of losing my digital touch-ups made me cringe. I took a deep breath through my nose, calming myself, as he scrolled through the list of his own files, looking for the one he wanted. I was tense for no good reason.

I'd known Kennedy forever from school. We'd talked a little last spring when Mr. Oakley selected him as the new editor for the yearbook and I won the photographer position. Back then, I'd been sort-of dating my friend Noah Allen, which made me technically off limits. Kennedy was a tall guy who looked older than seventeen because of his long, blond ponytail and darker goatee, his T-shirts for punk bands and indie films I'd never heard of, and his pierced eyebrow.

Sawyer De Luca, who'd been elected Most Likely to Go to Jail, had taunted Kennedy mercilessly about the eyebrow piercing. But Sawyer taunted everyone about everything. I'd had enough trouble screwing up the courage to get my ears pierced a few years ago. I admired Kennedy's edgy bravery. I'd thought it put him out of my league.

We hadn't dated until five weeks ago, when we ran into each other at a film festival in downtown Tampa that we'd both attended alone. That's when we realized we were perfect for each other. I honestly still believed that.

I crushed on Brody only because of the Perfect Couple title, like a sixth grader who heard a boy was interested and suddenly became interested herself. Except, as a senior, I was supposed to be above this sort of thing. Plus, Brody *wasn't* interested. Our class *thought* he should be, but Brody wasn't known for doing what he was told.

"Here it is." Kennedy opened his design for one of the Superlatives pages, with BIGGEST FLIRTS printed at the top.

"Oooh, I like it," I said, even though I didn't like it at all.

One of my jobs was to photograph all the Superlatives winners for the yearbook. The Biggest Flirts picture of my friend Tia and her boyfriend, Will, was a great shot. I would include it in my portfolio for admission to college art departments. I'd managed to capture a mixture of playfulness and shock on their faces as they stepped close together for a kiss.

Kennedy had taken away the impact by setting the photo at a thirty-degree angle.

"I have the urge to straighten it," I admitted, tilting my head. This hurt my neck.

"All the design manuals and websites suggest angling some photos for variety," he said. "Not every picture in the yearbook can be straight up and down. Think outside the box."

I nodded thoughtfully, hiding how much his words hurt. I *did* think outside the box, and all my projects were about visual design. I sewed my own dresses, picking funky materials and making sure the bodices fit just right. The trouble I went to blew a lot of people's minds, but sewing hadn't been difficult once I'd mastered the old machine I'd inherited from Grandmom. To go with my outfit of the day, I chose from my three pairs of retro eyeglasses. The frames were worth the investment since I always wore them, ever since I got a prescription in middle school. They made me look less plain. If it hadn't been for my glasses and the way I dressed, everyone would have forgotten I was there.

As it was, my outside-the-box look and the creative photos I'd been taking for the yearbook made me memorable. That's why Kennedy had been drawn to me, just as I'd been intrigued by his eyebrow piercing and his philosophy of cinematography. At least, that's what I'd thought.

I wanted to tell him, *If this design is so great, tilt the photos of the chess club thirty degrees, not my photos of the Superlatives.*

Instead I said carefully, "This layout looks a little dated. It reminds me of a yearbook from the nineties, with fake paint splatters across the pages."

"I don't think so." Turning back to the screen, he moved the cursor to *save* and communicated how deeply I'd offended him with a hard click on the mouse.

I kept smiling, but my stomach twisted. Kennedy would give me the silent treatment if I didn't find a way to defuse this fight between now and the end of journalism class. Tonight was the first football game of the season, and I'd be busy snapping shots of our team. I was the only student with a press pass that would get me onto the sidelines. Kennedy would likely be in the stands with my other sort-of ex-boyfriend, Quinn Townsend, and our friends from journalism class. They'd all be telling erudite jokes under their breath that made fun of the football team, the entire game of football, and spectator sports in general. After the game, though, Kennedy and I would both meet our friends at the Crab Lab grill. And he would act like we weren't even together.

"It's just the way the picture is tilted," I ventured. "The rest of it is cool—the background and the font."

In answer, he opened the next page, labeled MOST LIKELY TO SUCCEED. I hadn't yet taken the photo of my friend Kaye and her boyfriend, Aidan, but Kennedy already had a place for it. He selected the empty space and tilted that, too, telling me, *So there.*

"When are you going to turn in the rest of these photos?" he asked me. "The deadline to send this section to the printer is two weeks from today."

"Yeah," I said doubtfully. "It's been harder than I thought. I mean, taking the pictures isn't hard," I clarified quickly, before he reassigned some of my responsibilities. "It's tricky to get out of class. We've had so many tests. And convincing some of our classmates to show up at a scheduled time is like herding cats."

"Harper!" he exclaimed. "This is important. You have to get organized."

I opened my lips, but nothing came out. I was stunned. I prided myself on my organizational skills. Kennedy should have seen the schedule on my laptop. My arrangements for these photo shoots were difficult but, in the end, impeccable. If the people who were supposed to pose for my pictures didn't meet me, how was that *my* fault? I couldn't drag them out of physics class by the ears.

"I need these shots on a rolling basis so I can design the pages," Kennedy said. "You can't throw them all at me on the last day. If you make us miss the deadline, the class might not get our yearbooks before graduation. Then the yearbooks would be *mailed* to us and we wouldn't get to *sign* them."

My cheeks flamed hot. What had seemed like a fun project at first had quickly turned into a burden. I'd been trying to schedule these appointments during school, around my classes. At home, I selected the best photos and touched them up on my computer. But I also had other responsibilities. I'd signed on to photograph a 5K race at the town's Labor Day festival next Monday. And of course I had to help Mom. She ran a bed and breakfast. I was required to contribute to the breakfast end of it. I didn't see how I could produce these finished pictures for Kennedy any faster.

"Is everything okay here?" Mr. Oakley had walked up behind Kennedy.

"Of course," Kennedy said. From his position, Mr. Oakley couldn't see Kennedy narrow his eyes, warning me not to complain. Mr. Oakley had said at the beginning of school that he wanted the yearbook to run like a business, meaning we students reported to each other like employees to bosses, rather than crying to him about every minor problem. That meant Kennedy had a lot more power than a yearbook editor at a school where the advisor made the decisions.

For better or for worse.

Mr. Oakley looked straight at me. "Can you work this out yourselves?"

"Yes, sir." My voice was drowned out by the bell ending the period.

As Mr. Oakley moved away and students gathered their books, Kennedy rolled his chair closer to mine and said in my ear, "Don't raise your voice to me."

Raise my voice? *He* was the one who'd raised his voice and caught Mr. Oakley's attention.

The bell went silent.

Kennedy straightened. In his normal tone he said, "Tell Ms. Patel I'll miss most of study hall. I'm going to stay here and get a head start on the other Superlatives pages, now that I know we're in trouble."

"Okay." The argument hadn't ended like I'd wanted, but at least he didn't seem angry anymore.

I retrieved my book bag and smiled when I saw Quinn waiting for me just inside the doorway. His big grin made his dyed-black Goth hair and the metal stud jutting from his bottom lip look less threatening. Most people in school didn't know what I knew: that Quinn was a sweetheart. We wound our way through the crowded halls toward Ms. Patel's classroom.

"I overheard your talk with Kennedy," Quinn said.

"Did you see his designs?" I asked. "I understand why he'd want to angle some photos for variety *if* the pictures themselves were boring. Mine aren't."

"He'll change his mind when he sees the rest of your masterpieces," Quinn assured me. "Speaking of the Superlatives, Noah said Brody's been talking about you."

I suspected where this was going. Noah and I hadn't been as tight this school year, since I'd started dating Kennedy. In fact, if I hadn't checked Noah's calculus homework every day in study hall, we might not have talked at all. But last spring when we'd gone out, he'd told me what great friends he and Brody were. Brody's dad had been their first football coach for the rec league in third grade. They'd played side by side ever since. Now Noah's position on the team was right guard. His responsibility was to protect Brody from getting sacked before he could throw the ball. Friends that close definitely shared their opinions of the girl one of them had been teamed with as Perfect Couple.

Brody must have told Noah it was ridiculous that he and I had been paired. He would never dream of wasting his time with a nerd like me. I should have told Quinn that whatever it was, I didn't want to know. And still I heard myself asking, "What did Brody say about me?"

"Yesterday in football practice," Quinn said, "Brody told

the team that you two aren't the Perfect Couple. You're the Perfect Coup*ling*. And then he expressed admiration for your ass."

"Oooh." I was thrilled at the idea of Brody noticing my body and wishing he could have sex with me. But I quickly realized I was supposed to feel insulted. I turned that "Oooh" into a more appropriate "Ewww. He shouldn't kid around like that. Somebody's bound to tell Kennedy."

"Yeah, but . . ." Quinn looked askance at me. "Do you care, after the way Kennedy treated you just now? Why don't you stand up to him?"

"Kennedy has a point," I explained. "He needs my pictures for the Superlatives. If I miss a deadline and make him miss his, it doesn't matter why. An excuse won't fix it. And he doesn't want me to argue with him in class, because it looks bad to Mr. Oakley."

We'd reached Ms. Patel's doorway and stopped outside to finish our talk. Sawyer was in our study hall. Sawyer and private conversations didn't mix.

Quinn put one hand on my shoulder, something Kennedy rarely did. "I've worried long enough about keeping up appearances. I'm done with that today."

I nodded. Quinn was making a big announcement at the end of the period.

"Come with me," he said. "Come into the light. Stop worrying about how things *look*."

I frowned. "We're not in the same situation, Quinn. And how things look—that's everything I care about."

"You'll be sorry." He spun on the heel of his combat boot and disappeared into the classroom.

Perplexed, I turned to frown at the end of the slowly emptying hall. My senior year was supposed to be the time of my life. Two weeks in, all I felt was anxious about my photo assignment. And thrilled that a random hot guy, who would never ask me out, had made a joke about hooking up with me.

Tia leaned against the lockers outside Mr. Frank's room next door. Will propped his forearm above her and leaned down to say something with a grin. She laughed. I was glad they'd gotten together earlier this week. Will had just moved here from Minnesota. After a rocky start, he seemed to be adjusting better. And Tia, a comedian, finally was genuinely happy.

She noticed me watching them and must have read the expression on my face. She stuck out her bottom lip in sympathy.

I shook my head—*nothing was wrong*—and dove into Ms. Patel's room.

"Hey, girlfriend." Brody grinned at me as I walked toward him between two rows of desks. His green eyes were bright, but the shadows underneath were visible despite his deep tan. He'd always had the circles under his eyes. When we were in kindergarten, Mom had wondered aloud whether he was getting enough sleep. In middle school, guys had teased him about being a drug addict. Now the shadows seemed like a part of him, permanent evidence of his rough-and-tumble life—and love life. He held up one fist toward me.

I fist-bumped him. "Hey, boyfriend." The way we'd reacted to our Superlatives title underscored how different we were, and how imperfect a couple we would have made. I never could have admitted this even to Tia or Kaye, but I'd puzzled endlessly over what our classmates saw in us that led them to think we'd be good together.

In contrast, Brody called me his girlfriend and teased me. The "Hey, girlfriend" and the fist bump had been going on for the full two weeks of school. Every time we did it, I was afraid someone would mention it to Kennedy. He would pick a fight with me because I looked like I was flirting behind his back.

Brody didn't seem concerned that someone would mention it to his girlfriend, Grace. The idea of me threatening their relationship was that far-fetched. Although—and this thought had kept me awake some nights—Brody never called me his girlfriend and fist-bumped me when Grace and Kennedy were around. He did it only in moments like this, a period without Grace, with Kennedy missing. Aside from twenty other students and Ms. Patel, we were alone here.

And if Brody had progressed to telling my ex-boyfriend, Noah, what he'd like to do with me when we were *really* alone, he was getting too close for comfort.

After dumping my book bag beside my desk, I asked Brody quietly, "May I talk with you?" I nodded toward the back of the classroom.

His eyebrows rose like he knew he was in trouble—but just for a moment. "Sure." He jumped up with a jerk that made the legs of his desk screech across the floor. Four people in the next row squealed and slapped their hands over their ears.

He followed me to the open space behind the desks, next to the cabinets. In the sunlight streaming through the window, I noticed his slightly swollen bottom lip and a faintly purple bruise on his jaw. He must have been hit in the mouth by another football player—or punched by an irate girl. Leaning against the wall with his arms crossed, he was back to looking as flaked out and heroin-chic as usual. I almost laughed, because he was so handsome and he'd said something so stupid to get himself in hot water—except that the person he'd said it about was me.

"I heard you were talking about me in football," I began.

He gaped at me. I couldn't tell whether he was horrified that I'd found out, or fake-horrified. He didn't say anything, though. He eyed me uneasily.

"What if Grace hears?" I asked.

He gave the smallest shrug as he continued to watch me, like he hadn't considered the possibility and couldn't be bothered to care very much.

Well, here was something *I* cared about. "What if Kennedy hears?"

This time I got the reaction I'd been dying for, though I would never admit it. Brody narrowed his eyes at me, jealous of Kennedy, frustrated that he couldn't have me for himself.

Of course, I could have been interpreting his expression all wrong. But in that moment, the rest of the noisy classroom seemed to fall away. Only Brody and I were left, sharing a vibe, exchanging a message. His green eyes seemed to sear me. He was gazing at me exactly the way I felt about him.

2

BUT THE NEXT SECOND, I DECIDED I'D BEEN mistaken. He blinked, and the mad jealousy I'd seen in his eyes looked more like sleep deprivation. He shrugged again. The move gave way to a stretch as he raised his arms behind his head and clasped both hands behind his neck.

He wasn't preening for me. Hot athletic guys purposefully showed their bulging triceps to cheerleaders like Grace, not geek bait like me. The message to *me* was, *If Kennedy confronts me, I will squash him like a bug between my thumb and forefinger.*

Frustrated, I whined, "Brody!" just like I had, and every other girl had in kindergarten, when he tickled us and made us giggle during quiet time or dabbed paint on our noses just before our dramatic debut onstage in the class play.

My protest snapped him out of his jock act. He held

out his hands, pleading with me. "Harper, I'm sorry. I didn't mean it. You know me. I just blurt shit out sometimes. Or, all the time. The guys on the team asked me about the Superlatives thing. In football, when somebody asks you how you feel, you answer with a sex joke."

"I see," I said. "What you told the guys was a more offensive, more personal version of 'I would totally hit that.'"

Grinning, he pointed at me. "Yes."

I tried an even better imitation of the assholes on the team. "'I would hit that *thang*.'"

He patted me on the head, possibly mussing my careful French twist. "The guys are pretty taken with you. They think the idea of you getting with an idiot like me is hilarious. They'll keep teasing me about you. I'll keep making sex jokes. I'm just warning you."

"Are you going to keep adding that bit about my ass, too?"

He wagged his eyebrows.

"Fine," I said over the bell that started our half-hour study hall. We headed for our desks. To keep up the facade that I thought the idea of us getting together was hilarious too, I made small talk. "Ready for the game tonight?" I hoped he wouldn't give me a detailed answer I couldn't follow and force me to expose my ignorance about football. I'd never been interested in sports. Over the last few days, Mr. Oakley had given me a crash course in what I hadn't absorbed while dating Noah, so I'd know enough about the rules to catch the important plays through a camera lens. Ideally.

But I did want to know how practice had been going for Brody, and how he felt about the pressure he must be under before the game. I'd been part of the crowd at parties at his house a couple of times recently, but we'd never had what I'd call an in-depth conversation. I knew more about his football career from the local newspaper than from him. Seeing the game through his eyes would help me capture a star quarterback's perspective and immortalize it in the yearbook.

Plus, I enjoyed the way he looked at me. I wished he would give me that narrow-eyed stare again, no matter what emotion was behind it. I might have had a boyfriend, he might have had a girlfriend, and the idea of us getting together under any circumstances might have been ridiculous, but I wanted his attention a little longer.

He stretched his arms way over his head again. Sitting this close to him, it was hard to get perspective on how much taller than me he was, but I never forgot. Then he settled himself across his desktop, arms folded, head down, and closed his eyes. "Don't I look ready?" Conversation over.

Ms. Patel eased into her chair at the front of the room and pulled a stack of papers out of her desk drawer. The people who'd been milling around the classroom slid into seats and hauled books out of their backpacks or, like Brody, settled down for a nap. Ms. Patel had said she didn't care what we did in study hall as long as we kept the noise down to a dull roar.

I pretended to check Noah's calculus homework while gathering the courage to ask Brody about our yearbook photo together.

I was on deadline. Taking the easy route would be smartest. I should schedule a meeting in the school courtyard like I'd arranged for most of the other Superlatives. I could set up a tripod and program a simple picture on a time delay, then dive into the frame with Brody before the shutter opened. But that wouldn't be cute. It wouldn't be original. It wouldn't contribute to the portfolio I needed to get into a college art program next fall.

And it wouldn't put me in proximity to Brody for as long as I wanted.

I raised my eyes from problem number five on Noah's homework and considered the close-shorn back of his head. If Brody and I discussed the photo here, Noah would hear me. I could say one wrong thing and let on that my weird pairing with Brody had developed into a crush, and Noah would make sure the whole locker room knew what was going on. That would *definitely* get back to Kennedy. Noah wasn't one to keep his mouth shut about other people's business. His own business, yes. Mine, no.

Quinn sat in front of Noah. He would overhear the conversation too. He wouldn't spread the gossip like Noah, but when Brody slighted me, Quinn would feel sorry for me, just like he had when Noah broke up with me. That would be worse.

And in front of Brody sat Sawyer. He didn't have it in for me, as far as I knew, but if he overheard my awkward request, he would retell the story in the funniest way possible, which would make my life a living hell. That's just how Sawyer was. He might have been asleep, though. His white-blond head was down on his arms, and he hadn't moved since I'd entered the classroom. As our school's mascot—he dressed up like a six-foot pelican at the games—his first act of bringing about student solidarity had been to pass out from heat exhaustion at a practice on the football field last Monday. He probably was resting for his debut at the game tonight.

And that meant at least *he* would nap through what I said to Brody. As for Noah and Quinn, maybe Quinn had been right: It was time I stopped worrying about how things looked. Once more, I rehearsed what I would say to Brody. *We need to take a yearbook photo for Perfect Couple That Never Was*, and *We need to think of an original way to pose for the photo*, and *What if we met off campus? Like on a date? We'd be a couple—get the joke? Not a real date, of course. We don't want Kennedy and Grace mad at us!* Feeling like I was about to fling myself off a cliff, I took a deep breath and turned to Brody.

He was asleep. In the thirty seconds I'd taken to steel myself, his hunched shoulders had gone slack. His upper body rose and fell with deep, even breaths. I was amazed he could relax amid the buzz of the classroom—but after all, *he* wasn't a geeky girl whose nerves were stretched taut to the point of snapping because the popular quarterback was an arm's length away.

With a defeated sigh, I faced the front and crossed my legs under my desk again.

"Is my homework that bad?" Noah asked, turning his broad body around. "I thought I actually understood this unit, for once."

"No, sorry, I've hardly started." I bent over Noah's work, checking his answers against mine.

My gaze drifted across the aisle to Brody. His handsome face was hidden: the high cheekbones, the expressive mouth. All I could see from this angle was the top of his head, longish light brown hair curtaining over his face, and one strong upper arm straining against the sleeve of his tight athletic shirt. He also wore long athletic shorts and flip-flops, as always. On the coldest day of the year, which admittedly wasn't very cold around here, he *might* add a hoodie. We'd been in various advanced classes together since middle school, but the way he dressed, he looked like he'd taken a wrong turn from the gym. That's how Brody had always been: grinning, a bit of a mess, and a world away from me.

Twenty minutes later, I'd checked Noah's homework. I hoped I had just enough time to finish my questions on the chapter in English so I wouldn't have to take my book home. Ms. Patel interrupted my thoughts. "Class, may I have your attention, please? Quinn and Noah want to make an announcement before lunch."

Sawyer stirred and raised his head from his arms. Brody couldn't even make that much effort. He kept his head down but shifted so he could see around Sawyer. He would be sitting up in a minute, though. Surely he knew what was coming. I put my hand on Noah's back as he stood. He smiled nervously at me before he and Quinn made their way up the row to stand in front of Ms. Patel's desk.

"We. . . ," Noah began, then folded his muscular arms. He was African American, with such dark skin that the fluorescent lights overhead highlighted the indentations of his huge muscles like he was a comic-book superhero. He'd also perfected a threatening scowl he used to intimidate other football players, but he wasn't wearing it now. It was strange to see him look nervous. He glanced over at Quinn.

"Tick-tock," Ms. Patel said. "The bell's going to ring. Better get it out."

Quinn wrung his hands in fingerless black leather gloves, an odd accessory during hot weather in Florida, even for one of *my* friends. Then he ran his hands through his black hair. Finally he burst out, "Noah and I are dating. Each other."

Silence fell over the classroom. It was so quiet that Mr. Frank's voice filtered through the wall from the next room. I wanted to jump up and pound on the wall to stop Mr. Frank, but I felt dizzy. That's when I realized I was holding my breath.

Brody started clapping.

The class burst into applause.

Sighing with relief, I clapped along, harder and harder as the weight of the last year lifted from my shoulders. I'd been so worried about Quinn and then Noah when they came out to me. This positive reception to their official, public coming out was a great sign for their future.

The door opened. Kennedy gave the noisy classroom a bewildered glance. Ms. Patel pointed to an empty desk near the door, indicating that he should park it rather than moving all the way back to sit behind me. As he slung off his backpack and slouched in the desk, Noah mouthed an explanation for the commotion: "We're gay." Kennedy blushed bright red.

Not the reaction I'd expected from Kennedy. He prided himself on being open-minded. I'd thought he'd be mildly supportive, or have no reaction at all.

The applause died down, and Noah cleared his throat. "Some of you may be wondering, 'Why now?' A couple of weeks ago, when we voted on the Senior Superlatives, I wrote in myself and Quinn for Perfect Couple That Never Was. I thought the student council would take it as a joke. Really it was just wishful thinking, I guess. I wasn't even sure Quinn was gay."

Quinn put his gloved hand on Noah's shoulder. "I did the same. Principal Chen called us both into her office and told us that if we had something to say to the school, we could go ahead if we did it in a way that wouldn't disrupt class."

My friend Chelsea raised her hand. "Those were secret ballots, I *thought*. How did Ms. Chen know they were yours?"

"Because she's *creepy*?" Quinn said.

"Careful," Ms. Patel spoke up.

"She's really old," Noah said with a sideways glance at Ms. Patel. "You know how she's always telling us in assemblies that we'd better not try to slip anything past her."

Ms. Patel bit her lip, trying not to laugh.

"Anyway," Quinn said, "we decided to do it here in study hall because we wanted to come out in front of the people who've encouraged us the most." He put his hand over his heart. "For me, that's Harper."

"Awwwww." A chorus of girls' voices echoed how I felt. I'd tried to support Quinn any way I could, but I hadn't expected him to acknowledge me in front of the class.

"And for me," Noah said, "that's Harper and Brody."

"Brody!" Sawyer yelled a raunchy, "Aoow!"

Brody thumped him on the back of the head.

Sawyer turned around and took a swipe at Brody. Brody leaned back in his desk to dodge the blow.

"We also wanted to come out in front of Sawyer," Noah said, "so we'd catch him off guard, before he had the chance to work up any jokes."

"Oooooh," said the class. All eyes were on Sawyer now. It wasn't often that somebody stuck it to Sawyer.

Quinn went on, "And of course, Sawyer is our study hall's student council representative. He can help us address our grievances to the school if anything bad happens."

Sawyer nodded. He must take his position seriously. I'd been as surprised as anyone when he nominated himself for student council representative at the beginning of the year. We'd elected him because nobody else ran. But it was nice to know he would step up for Noah and Quinn if they needed him.

Then he muttered, "I've got nothing. Good material takes time."

"Exactly," Noah and Quinn said together.

Their speech seemed to be winding down. Before anybody else could heckle them, I called, "Cupcakes!"

"Cupcaaaaaakes!" several people cheered.

As I slid out of my desk, Brody cracked a smile at me. "You made coming-out cupcakes?"

"Yeah. Wait till you see them."

"Do you need help?"

"No, thanks." There was only one container. I'd hidden it on the counter at the back of the room, underneath a huge folded poster of the periodic table.

I was halfway there before I realized that I'd just turned down an innocent excuse to interact with Brody. When it came to guys, I was a little slow on the uptake.

Brody was standing beside his desk now, stretching. I grabbed the container and brought it to him. "I mean yes," I said, "I need your help. Could you open these on Ms. Patel's desk?"

"Sure. What are you going to—Oh."

I pulled a camera out of my pocket, the small one I carried when I didn't have my expensive one, so I never missed a shot. "Say cheese," I told him.

"Cupcakes!" He held them up.

It was another killer picture of him, I realized with dismay. Brody was a little too photogenic. I wanted my best work to go into the yearbook, but I couldn't get away with slipping a photo of him onto every page.

I shot a few more candids of the class while I waited for him to deliver the cupcakes to the front of the room. Then I cornered Quinn and Noah against the whiteboard for the commemorative picture I really wanted. They put their heads close together and held up their cupcakes. I'd used rainbow papers, and each cake was topped with a plastic rainbow and a cutout photo of someone in the class. So Noah's cake had his face on top, and Quinn's had his. After we all three checked the camera display and laughed over that classic shot, I pocketed my camera and reached into the box for the Harper cake.

Brody held his cake, as if he was waiting for me to start eating. "This was why you went around the room yesterday, taking pictures of everybody."

"Yeah." That, and it had been another reason to take a picture of *him*. "I thought if I made cupcakes and put people's faces on them, involving them in the celebration, they'd be less likely to say something ugly once we get to the lunchroom."

"Smart," he said. "Do we have to eat our own cupcake?"

"That was the idea, yeah."

"Because some guy's going to ask if he can eat your cupcake, Harper."

I nearly choked on the icing. After swallowing, I said, "I figured Sawyer might say that. I've done some deep-breathing exercises, and I'm okay with it."

"Sawyer isn't the only person here with a dirty mind." Brody licked his icing. I watched his mouth.

Sawyer walked over. I'd stopped at the bakery that morning and bought him a vegan muffin, since vegan cupcakes were not in my repertoire. He was stuffing the last of it into his mouth. "Quinn," he called, "didn't you date Harper last year?"

"Here it comes." Quinn rolled his eyes. His thick black eyeliner made the whites of his eyes more pronounced.

"And, Noah," Sawyer continued, "didn't *you* date Harper last spring?"

"Fuck you, De Luca," Noah said softly enough that Ms. Patel couldn't hear by the window.

"What does that say about the guy Harper's dating now? What's his name, again, the one with the rad pierced eyebrow?" Sawyer snapped his fingers a couple of times close to Kennedy, who hadn't moved from the desk by the door. "I can't ever remember that guy's name."

"*This* is the joke you came up with?" Brody asked.

"I haven't had time!" Sawyer protested. "And *you*! Be careful about this Perfect Couple That Never Was thing, Larson. Harper obviously has a way with guys."

"Here's what I'm going to do to you in PE," Brody told Sawyer. "Should I say this now, or do you want me to surprise you?"

The bell rang.

Most of the class moved toward the door, their minds already off Quinn and Noah and on lunch. A couple of girls looked over their shoulders, smiling, and said a few encouraging words to Noah and Quinn, who were talking with Ms. Patel. Noah put his hand on Quinn's back. I couldn't hear what Noah said over the noise of everyone changing classes, but I read his lips as he asked, "Are you okay?" Quinn nodded and relaxed his shoulders, tension released.

Happy the announcement had gone well, I started to follow Brody back to my desk to pick up my stuff. Kennedy spoke over the noise. "Harper, I need to talk to you."

Uh-oh. I hoped he wasn't sensitive about what Sawyer had said. Heart racing, I sank down in the desk next to his. While we waited for Ms. Patel and the rest of the class to file into the hall, I did my breathing exercises and tried to center myself.

I managed to calm down quite a bit before Brody passed right in front of me, the last one out the door. My pulse raced again. He looked at me, brows knitted in concern, then at Kennedy, and back at me.

I gave him the smallest shake of my head, which I hoped Kennedy didn't see. My message to Brody was that everything was okay, even though I didn't believe it myself.

After he left, Kennedy got up, shut the door, and leaned against it with his arms folded, scowling at me. After all my efforts to appease him about my Superlatives photos and his yearbook designs, I was *still* headed for a weekend of the silent treatment.

To head him off, I said, "I understand why you're upset."

"I don't think you do," he said. "You dated Quinn, then Noah, and now they're *gay*? What does that say about *me*?"

I wanted to point out that Sawyer had said something similar to Brody, and *Brody* wasn't mad. Maybe Brody was more self-confident.

Maybe Brody wasn't my boyfriend.

"I realize it was a surprise," I said, "but—"

"You're damn right it was a surprise!" Kennedy seethed. "Why didn't you tell me?"

"I don't give away people's secrets," I said. "That's why Quinn and Noah confided in me in the first place."

"Yeah, well, it says a lot about your priorities if you put your two gay friends in front of your boyfriend."

"Kennedy," I said, "I'm not putting them in front of you. This has nothing to do with you."

"Really?" he asked. "You can't turn in your Superlatives photos to me, but you have time to bake cupcakes with pictures for *them*?"

"Um." I didn't have a response to that. The cupcakes had been important to me. I'd baked them with love for my friends' important day. Kennedy made them sound stupid.

"You bring rainbow cupcakes for your last two boyfriends, while your current boyfriend is sitting in the same class," he said. "Don't you see how that looks?"

"Yeah, I get it," I said softly, without really getting it. "I'm sorry."

He shook his head in disgust, focusing his gaze somewhere above my head instead of on me. Abruptly he jerked up his backpack by one strap and opened the door.

Tia was standing in the hall. Knowing her, she'd had her ear to the door. "Kennedy, we need a word with Harper," she said, pushing past him into the room.

"She'll catch up with you in a minute," Kaye added, walking in behind Tia.

"You can have her," Kennedy snarled. He stormed into the hall and slammed the door.

3

TIA AND KAYE STARED WIDE-EYED AT ME.
Finally Kaye said, "Brody came to our table in the lunchroom
and told us Quinn is *gay*? And Noah is *gay*? And Kennedy is
mad? Brody asked us to check on you."

Brody had asked my friends to check on me! If I'd been
by myself, I would have replayed this in my mind like the
best ending to a feel-good movie. As it was, I didn't want
Kaye and Tia to know how far gone I was for the unattain-
able Brody. I said only, "It's been an interesting study hall."

"Cupcakes!" Tia hopped up to sit on Ms. Patel's desk.
Crossing her long legs at the ankles, she reached into the
container.

"You can have those," I offered, as if I could have stopped
her anyway.

She held up the two remaining. "Harper, you made *coming-out cupcakes?*"

"You're adorable," Kaye said.

"I don't *feel* adorable," I grumbled.

"Do you want Kennedy or Shelley Stearns?" Tia asked Kaye. I'd forgotten Shelley had gone to her grandmom's in Miami for the long holiday weekend.

"Shelley," Kaye said.

Tia examined both cupcakes up close. "No, *I* want her," she said. "I don't want to eat Kennedy."

"It's only a cupcake topper," Kaye said.

"Then *you* eat him," Tia said.

Exasperated, Kaye flung out her hand for the cupcake. She examined the topper, murmured, "Cute," licked the icing off the pick, and tossed Kennedy into the trash can. She slid onto the desk beside Tia and elbowed her to make her scoot over. "So, Harper, you knew about Quinn and Noah all along? And you never told anybody, even us! You sneaky mouse."

I moved my own half-eaten cupcake to the far corner of my desk. I'd lost my appetite. "Remember I had a crush on Quinn last year? He wasn't dating anyone that we knew of, and we couldn't understand why he wouldn't ask me out. You both kept telling me to ask him on a date."

They nodded slowly. They didn't look quite as confident

as they had when they burst into the room. Obviously they were second-guessing their advice that I pursue Quinn.

"I did," I said. "I told you that part. Here's the part I didn't tell you. He came out to me. He wasn't ready to tell everybody. He was afraid of what his parents would do, judging from how they freaked when he dyed his hair black. But he knew some people at school were talking about him and wondering whether he was gay."

Tia nodded. Kaye said, "I'd heard that."

"Sawyer told me," Tia said.

"How did Sawyer know?" Kaye asked. "Surely Quinn didn't tell *him*."

"Sawyer just knows things," Tia said.

I explained, "Quinn asked me if we could go out a few times as friends but say we were dating, to get people off his back."

"And you said *yes*?" Kaye was livid. "Harper, we had that talk about people taking advantage of you."

"It was fine!" I exclaimed. "I didn't mind."

"And then you did the same thing for Noah?" Tia asked.

"No, Noah asked me on a date himself. Remember how excited I was? I'd wondered why a football player would want to date me. And *then* he came out to me."

"Oh," Tia and Kaye cooed sympathetically at the same

time. They were right to feel sorry for me. I'd been dev-astated when Noah told me the truth. In fact, I'd been so taken with him, and the feel of his huge arm curving around me, that he'd set the stage for my daydreams about another football player.

But this was exactly what I hadn't wanted. The more people felt sorry for me, the smaller I felt.

"And then you got the two of them together," Kaye said. "That's so sweet!"

"No," I said. "They both swore me to secrecy. Ms. Chen outed them to each other by mistake." I told Kaye and Tia the boys' story about the Perfect Couple vote. "I'm just glad they're happy."

"So why's Kennedy mad at you?" Tia asked. "Other than the fact that he's always mad at you lately?"

I winced. It was true, but coming from Tia, the truth was especially blunt.

"Sawyer made a joke about me dating gay guys. He said Kennedy must be gay too. Also Brody, since the school thinks we'd be perfect together."

"Oh my God!" Tia yelled with her mouth full. "Why did Sawyer say that? I'll kill him."

"Nobody cares what Sawyer thinks," Kaye said between nibbles. "Sawyer's a pothead."

"Not anymore," Tia corrected her. "He swore it off. He's turned into a health nut since he passed out on Monday."

Kaye tossed her cupcake paper into the trash and placed her fists on her hips, cheerleader style. "Why are you always defending him?"

"Why are you always so down on him?" Tia turned back to me. "And *that's* all Kennedy's mad about? Sawyer shouldn't have said it, but Kennedy's as used to Sawyer's inappropriate comments as the rest of us. There's no reason for him to be angry unless he was already sensitive about the subject in the first place. *Brody's* not mad."

"No, Brody's not mad," I acknowledged. "Brody and Noah are best friends, plus Brody's so happy-go-lucky. Brody . . ."

Tia and Kaye stared wide-eyed at me again. Any story including Brody was more delicious than cupcakes. I found myself telling them what Brody had said about me to the football team.

"Oooh, he's into you," Kaye said approvingly. She rubbed her hands together. "Intrigue!"

"Perfect Coupling?" Tia puzzled through Brody's joke. "Like you're a piece of PVC pipe and he's an elbow joint?"

"Yeah, I didn't think it was all that sexy either." Actually, I *did*, but I couldn't admit this. "I confronted him about it, and he said he blurted it out when the team teased him about the Perfect Couple title. Who'd *you* vote for?" I'd been wanting to ask them this for a while.

"I voted for you!" Kaye told me triumphantly.

"And Brody?"

"Oh, God, no! You and Evan Fielding. He looks so cute in his plaid hat, like an old man. You're both so retro."

Wearing an old man's hat was the most interesting thing I'd seen Evan do. He was in my journalism class, and when we brainstormed ideas for the yearbook, he never uttered a peep. I'd been partnered with him a couple of times and ended up doing most of the work myself because I'd expected he would let me down. This was the guy one of my best friends thought was my perfect match?

Kaye read the look on my face. "Only because of his hat," she backtracked.

"Why are you curious?" Tia asked me. "You're dying to know why so many people paired you with Brody, aren't you?"

"Nooooo." I tried to brush it off. "I have a boyfriend. Brody has a girlfriend. Being elected together is a big joke between us."

But joke or not, sometime in the next two weeks, we would have to take our yearbook picture together. And during that short interlude, at least on my end, our relationship would be dead serious.

*　　*　　*

I wished I could have hung with Kaye and Tia at the football game that night. But Tia stood next to Will in the drum section of the marching band. Kaye was on the sidelines with the other cheerleaders, including Brody's glamorous girlfriend, Grace. I braved the sidelines all by myself to shoot the game.

Though I was a bit unclear on the rules, I'd always enjoyed football games. I loved the band music, the screams of the crowd and the cheerleaders, and the charged atmosphere. And though I feared for my life a couple of times when huge guys in helmets and pads hurtled toward me, the danger seemed worthwhile after I got some great shots of our players.

That is, I got some great shots of *Brody*. In the third quarter, our defense recovered a fumble and returned the ball all the way to the end zone for a touchdown. I missed the entire thing because I was pretending to take pictures of our team watching from the sidelines. Really, I'd zoomed in on Brody, whose helmet was off. He'd pulled his long, wet hair out of his eyes with a band. And he had no idea he was in my lens. He focused on the action on the field and screamed his heart out for his friends on the defensive line.

In the fourth quarter, Sawyer, dressed as the pelican mascot, came marching jauntily toward me. He picked up his knees and big bird feet high with every step, swinging his feathery elbows. I hoped he hadn't caught me gazing wistfully at Brody. I wasn't sure how well he could see out of the enormous bird head he was wearing. If he'd noticed my moony stare, he would make fun of me for it.

He put his wing around me.

I glared up at him.

He turned his huge head to look at me, too. His fuzz-covered beak hit me in the eye.

"Get your wing off me," I said, moving out from under his arm.

He put his hands on his padded bird hips and stomped his foot like he wanted to know why.

"You have a lot of nerve, bird," I said. "Quinn and Noah were so brave today, but you *had* to take a jab at them, and at Kennedy and Brody and *me*. As if people can be turned gay! Now Kennedy is mad at me because of what you said."

Sawyer shrugged.

"I *know* you don't like Kennedy, but he's *my boyfriend*!"

He opened his hands, pleading with me.

"Sure, you didn't mean it. That's the problem. If a joke is funny, you'll go ahead and blurt it out, whether it hurts somebody or not."

He bowed his head, and his shoulders slumped. He was sorry.

"I don't care," I said. "Go away."

He got down on his knees and clasped his hands, begging me.

"No," I said. "You deserve to sweat it for a while." Instantly I felt bad for the way I'd phrased this. He *had* fainted from heat exhaustion four days earlier, and he was probably dying in that getup. The night was at least eighty degrees.

He didn't take offense, apparently. He wrapped both wings around my leg.

I tried to step backward, out of his grasp. He held on tightly. His wings were at my knee, dangerously close to pushing my dress up higher than I'd wanted to hike it in front of five thousand people.

I glanced up at the student section. Kennedy pointed at me and laughed to everyone around him.

Imagining the only thing worse that could happen, I looked over at the team. Sure enough, Brody was watching us too. Suddenly, his friends slugging it out on the defensive line weren't as interesting to him. Shouldn't he be watching the game?

He raised one eyebrow at me.

I protected myself with the only weapon I had. I leaned way back, focused my camera, and snapped a photo of Sawyer's looming bird head, with Brody grinning in the background.

The whole episode was so mortifying that I doubted I would find it funny by the end of the school year or when I was in college or by the time I turned thirty, but maybe I could laugh about it before I died.

"Hey!" Kaye came up behind Sawyer and slapped him on the back of his bird head. He spent PE with the cheerleaders. I guessed he and Kaye had been around each other enough, and he'd annoyed her enough, that she knew how to whap him in costume without hurting him. Or maybe she'd wanted it to hurt.

At any rate, he felt it. He let go of me and made a grab for her. She took off down the sidelines, behind the football team. He ran after her. All this happened so fast that I didn't even get a picture.

After we won the game, and the team and coaches and cheerleaders and Sawyer had surged onto the field for a group hug on the fifty-yard line, I watched Brody walk toward the stadium exit with Noah. The newspaper had said this would be a great season for the team and for Brody, but his talk with Noah looked way too serious for two friends who'd just won their first game.

I was thinking so hard about what could be wrong that it took me a few seconds to notice Brody was waving at me. By the time I waved back, he'd given up waggling his fingers and was making big motions with both arms like he was adrift at sea and trying to hail a Coast Guard helicopter. Then he resumed his solemn confab with Noah. I watched them until they'd wearily climbed the stairs and disappeared through the gate.

That was the highlight of my night. Afterward, I met my friends from journalism class at the Crab Lab, but Kennedy was still giving me the silent treatment. He didn't offer me an angry word or even look at me the whole time. He just sat in a two-person booth and had an in-depth discussion about yearbook design with the sports section editor. A couple of times I overheard him pointedly say that placing pictures at an angle was a great way to vary the pages.

He was leaving the next morning to visit his cousins in Orlando and wouldn't be back until Sunday night. I wanted to make up with him so the fight didn't hang over our heads and tarnish the Labor Day weekend. But since he was still ignoring me, I knew he wasn't ready to kiss and make up. I didn't order any food, and I left a few minutes later. I had a lot of stuff to do at home.

I worked most of Saturday and Sunday. My friends were tied up, anyway. Kaye had a family reunion. Tia's dad was about to buy a fixer-upper mansion, and she was helping him get the house they lived in ready to sell.

I wasn't lonely. I actually looked forward to two days almost totally by myself. I planned to process the remaining photos I'd taken for the yearbook but hadn't yet turned in to Kennedy. I would also get my website ready to showcase the pictures I'd take of the 5K on Monday. If I got caught up with this work, maybe I would feel less stressed about corralling my classmates—including Brody—for the rest of the Superlatives photos during the next two weeks.

Both days, I helped Mom serve breakfast. After that, she spent her time working on the B & B—cleaning the guest rooms and bathrooms and the common areas, then painting or replacing boards on the exterior that were rotting in the fierce Florida sun and rain. Most days if I didn't talk to her while she was making breakfast, I didn't talk to her at all.

I also took breaks from my computer to check on Grand-dad, who lived alone a couple of streets over. I'd been doing this every couple of days since he and Mom had argued a few months ago. Granddad didn't like it whenever Mom said she was willing to take my dad back.

After I made sure Granddad was okay, I walked the other way along the beach road until I reached the private strip of undeveloped sand that Granddad had inherited from his family. When my dad had been around, he used to complain that we'd all be rich if Granddad would give in and sell his beach. Stubbornly, Granddad had never put it up for sale or even built a house on it. He liked to go there by himself and paint the ocean.

I knew how he felt. That's where I'd fallen in love with photography, taking pictures of the palm trees, the sand, the boats on the water. Everybody saw the same thing, but a photographer framed it to focus on one object in particular, telling a certain story.

In fact, I was afraid I was a little too much like Granddad. Someday I would inherit his house on one side of downtown and his strip of beach on the other. Like him, I'd hole up with my art and resent having to interact with other people when I went to the grocery store once a week.

I enjoyed being alone on the beach, but sometimes I wished my friends were there. This weekend, the public beaches were crowded enough that I could hear families laughing through the palms. As I swam out into the warm waves, I could see kids splashing together over on the park side. A teenage girl hugged a guy in the water with her legs looped around his waist. He kissed her ear. They laughed and whispered.

Brody was probably over there too, with Grace.

Never mind. I had work to do.

*   *   *

Monday morning, I got up early, as if it wasn't a holiday, because it wasn't—for me. I chose a fitted blouse tucked into a trim pencil skirt I'd made, and my most professional-looking glasses. I pulled back my hair into a classy bun at my nape. Then I walked from the small house I shared with Mom, which had been converted from a coach house, over to the huge Victorian, her bed and breakfast. Mom was already there, cooking her boarders' one expected meal of the day. It was my job to help serve.

I hated doing this. Since my parents had separated two years before, I'd tried to be supportive of Mom, but the first thing she did to rebuild her life without my dad was to borrow money from Granddad and buy a B & B. She loved people. She thought living on top of a constantly rotating group of strangers was a fun way to spend her days. It was like a sickness. She'd dreamed of running a B & B in the beach town where she grew up. Obviously Granddad's introverted gene had skipped a generation. To me the B & B was a nightmare.

I stood outside the pink clapboard back of the house. Palmettos shaded me from the bright morning sun. My kitten heels ground the seashells in the path. I took a few deep, calming breaths. Then I opened the door into the kitchen.

"Good morning," Mom sang, pulling homemade orange rolls from the oven. She wore a long, flowing beach dress and feather earrings, and she'd put up her dark hair in a deliberate tousle. Her feet were bare. She liked to dress ultra-casual so her guests would feel at home with the beach lifestyle, but I was pretty sure serving orange rolls in bare feet was reason for an inspection by the Health Department.

She turned away from me to snag a bread basket from a shelf, but I heard her say, "You look [unintelligible]."

I didn't ask her to repeat herself. I'd heard all her comments about my fashion sense before.

She kept on me. Handing me a pair of tongs and the basket of rolls to pass out to guests in the dining room, she looked me up and down and said, "I thought you were photographing the 5K this morning."

"I am."

"You don't look comfortable."

Well, I *wasn't* comfortable *right then*, living out somebody else's dreams of owning a business. I didn't say this, because it wouldn't do any good.

"Smile," she said, touching my lips, possibly smearing my perfect red lipstick. Now I would have to check my face before I left the house. Then she tapped her finger between my brows, possibly transferring the lipstick up there, and reminded me, "Nobody likes a pouty B & B." She swung open the door into the dining room, where eight strange adults eagerly awaited me. They would ask me embarrassing, none-of-their-business questions they would never ask if they weren't on vacation, such as, *Do you have a boyfriend?*

Answer: I wasn't sure. Kennedy hadn't so much as texted me since Friday at school.

After the guests were served, Mom sat down to eat with them, putting on her best "colorful local character" act. She was their font of information on the best beaches and restaurants and sights in St. Petersburg and Tampa.

She set a place for me at the table too, but breakfast was the one time I suddenly took great interest in making sure the B & B ran smoothly. I always volunteered to stay in the kitchen and unload the dishwasher or watch the next batch of rolls. I was able to get away with this only because Mom's first rule was never to have an argument where the guests could hear. At the B & B, we were a hotel staff, not a family.

I wasn't trying to sabotage Mom and her business. The truth was, I couldn't stand to sit at the dining room table and talk to a new group of strangers each week as if it was a family meal. I didn't want to answer a million questions about my school and my friends and my boyfriend. It was too much like making get-to-know-you small talk every time Mom brought home some guy she was dating. Inevitably she whispered to me that *this* one was the one.

I supported her dreams. I only wanted her to leave me out of them.

This morning, I hid in the kitchen, periodically dropping a knife in the sink to make actually-busy-in-the-kitchen noises while I noiselessly opened the three-times-weekly local newspaper to the sports page. I expected a triumphant review of Friday night's game. Reading about Brody as a hero would give me the fan-girl fix I'd been bluesing for. Simultaneously it would remind me how out of reach he was.

But the headline was cruelty in six words: LARSON DISAPPOINTS IN PELICANS' FIRST WIN.

The article explained that Brody's signature as a quarterback was his willingness to wait until the last nanosecond to pass the ball. That increased the chances he'd be sacked—tackled, clobbered, hit incredibly hard by the other team, who wanted to take him out of the game so we'd have to rely on our second-string sophomore. Brody didn't care. He braved getting hurt, which gave him more time than quarterbacks normally had to choose a receiver for his long, accurate passes.

At least, that's what had happened in practice, and that's what sports reporters had been so excited about when they hyped the season. But the article went on to say that Brody had lost his mojo. During the game, he'd gotten rid of the ball as fast as he could, like an inexperienced quarterback running scared.

No wonder he and Noah had seemed so down after the game.

I couldn't imagine what had gone wrong.

Strangely, that one negative article about a guy I hardly knew threatened to ruin my whole holiday. That and Kennedy giving me the cold shoulder, and Mom's comment on my outfit. But once I'd passed the second batch of rolls around the table, shouldered the strap of my camera bag, and escaped from the B & B, my mood improved. Just around the corner, the town square had been blocked off to traffic. The sidewalks teemed with laughing people of all ages. They watched down the street for the first finishers of the 5K race.

I ducked under the retaining rope—not over, which would have been awkward in my tight skirt—and walked into the middle of the street, a few yards in front of the finish line. Mom had made me doubt the wisdom of what I was wearing. I guessed her opinion bothered me so much because I was afraid she was right. I was sweating already underneath my waistband and my bra. But dressing this way made me feel as beautiful as Lois Lane and as talented behind my camera as Jimmy Olsen, but with the strength of Superman. I had no identifying badge that said I belonged on the participants' side of the ropes, but nobody challenged me. I looked like I meant business.

Down the street, the crowd noise swelled and moved in my direction as the first finishers ran closer. I brought up my camera and prepared to focus. My goal was to snap at least one clear picture of every runner. I would use the runners' numbers pinned to their shirts to label the photos for purchase on my website. But that was a tall order: nearly perfect photos of hundreds of people in the space of a few minutes. I took a deep, calming breath.

The crowd noise spiked as the leaders of the race came around the corner and entered the town square. The thirty front-runners were experienced athletes, led by the owner of the running-shoe store who'd sponsored the race and arranged for me to photograph it. I needed a perfect picture of *him*, at least. I focused as well as I could and set the continuous feed to snap a number of frames in quick succession. As soon as the runners had passed, another wave bore down on me. I kept up as best I could, heart hammering in my chest.

And then, *oh*. There, centered in my viewfinder, was Brody.

4

TINGLES OF EXCITEMENT SPREAD DOWN MY
neck and across my chest before I even consciously understood I'd recognized Brody. And I *hadn't* recognized his
face. He was still too far away, even through my zoom lens.
I recognized his running stride. I'd been looking out the
window of English class, watching him run wind sprints
for football practice in the parking lot, *way* too often in
the past two weeks.

Remembering what I was standing in the road for, I
opened the shutter and snapped a picture of him shoving
the guy jogging next to him, who laughed and shoved Brody
right back. It was Tia's boyfriend, Will, I realized as they
came closer. I snapped photos of every runner I could see
clearly, then focused on Brody through my viewfinder again.

His sun-streaked brown hair, long enough to fall into his eyes, was held back with the same sort of headband he used on the football field. I watched the defined muscles in his legs move as he sprinted toward me at top speed. He wore red gym shorts and no shirt, showing off his six-pack abs. Strong as he looked, I was surprised at how thin he was compared with his apparent mass when he wore a football uniform and pads. After the newspaper's hype, I'd expected him to be more muscle-bound. Maybe all athletic high school boys looked like this, and they bulked up in college.

The number 300 was printed across his chest in marker—which meant he'd been the last runner to register, because that was the total number I'd been told to expect. But the 3 had smeared into more of an 8 during his shoving match with Will. The two of them galloped toward the finish, gaining speed, cackling as one and then the other got a long arm in front of the other's body.

Suddenly another runner broke from the pack behind them—Noah. His shirt was off too, and his body gleamed in the sunlight as he found an even faster gear and tore past them. Though they were still down the street from me and I was seeing all this through my telephoto lens, I could hear Brody's and Will's moans of dismay at being beaten.

And watching them, something happened to me.

I'd never thought of guys in the same way other girls seemed to. Kaye was devoted to Aidan, but we occasionally caught her following another guy with her eyes. She would let slip a remark about his fine ass that made clear she wasn't about to cheat on her boyfriend but she did appreciate the male physique. Tia offered a constant stream of the same kind of commentary. She was a sexual being and not the least ashamed. I admired her for this, though I didn't tell her. She certainly didn't need any encouragement. In comparison, I didn't consider myself sexual. I wasn't gay, I wasn't bi, I was just disconnected from the entire scene.

So out of it, in fact, that I was gay guys' go-to girl when they weren't ready to come out and wanted to put their friends off their trail a little longer. They figured I wouldn't mind too much because I wasn't that interested in the opposite sex anyway.

Until now. Maybe it was because I'd thought about Brody constantly and planned what I would say to him when I told him we needed to take our Superlatives photo. But I didn't think so. The pure sight of his beautiful body, shining with sunscreen and sweat in the morning sun, running toward me, made me realize I was a part of this scene after all.

A part of the scene that was about to get knocked on its ass. Since the first runners had approached, I'd trusted that my professional attire and large, expensive camera would warn the competitors not to run me down. But Noah galloped past me a little too close for comfort. Brody and Will were barreling straight for me, their shoes slapping the asphalt.

Brody turned away from Will. His eyes drilled straight through my viewfinder, into my eyes. He kept coming. He was about to hit me.

With a squeal, I spun to protect the camera if he elbowed me.

He passed so close, I felt the wind move against my back.

And then I was watching him raise both hands in victory as he crossed the finish line just ahead of Will.

Brody had forgotten me, if he'd even intended to pay me any attention at all.

Grumbling to myself, I turned back to the pack of runners and shot as many of them as I could, thankful I'd taken some of their pictures before I focused on Brody. I wondered if he knew or cared how close he'd come to making me drop my camera. But that was Brody. He was a daredevil who took crazy chances. Nothing bad ever happened to *him*, though. He always landed on his feet.

Except for that time on Fifth-Grade Play Day when he dove off the water slide and had to go to the hospital.

And another time, in second grade, when he wandered

away from the group during our class field trip to the children's museum in Tampa, and the teachers found him *inside* a priceless dinosaur skeleton.

In fact, now that I thought about it, I recalled that he'd wrecked his mom's car when he was fourteen . . . and I held on a little more tightly to my camera as the crowd passed me on both sides.

After another thirty runners, I spotted Kaye with two of her fellow cheerleaders, race numbers pinned neatly to their shirts, which matched their shorts. Kaye saw me first and yelled to the other girls. They waved wildly and mugged for the camera as they passed. At least one of them had her mouth open or eyes closed in each frame. The key to getting a great shot of all three of them, so flattering that they would swear forever I was the world's best photographer, was simply to set the camera on continuous feed to shoot frame after frame. If I took enough photos, one of them was bound to be good. Photographing crowds for pay involved more know-how and logic than art.

A few more small groups ran by me, and then Sawyer jogged into view. He might have made it through Friday night's game, but he should *not* have been running a 5K on a hot September morning a week past being hospitalized.

Sure enough, after three miles of running, his wet T-shirt

stuck to him, and his normally bright hair was dark, soaked with sweat. His exertion hadn't dampened his spirit, though. As I tried to center him for a good shot, he ran straight toward me with his hand out like a movie star trying to block the paparazzi. I got three brilliant shots of his palm.

"Sawyer, dammit!" I cried as he passed, realizing as the words escaped my lips that this was a common exclamation at our school. Sawyer's middle name might as well have been Dammit.

The groups of runners grew thicker now, and I struggled to keep up, taking at least one clear shot of every face. They still stuck together in packs, though. During a break in the crowd, I looked over my shoulder at the runners who'd finished—but *not* to locate Brody. Only to find Kaye.

The runner I saw instead was Sawyer, standing stock still and staring into space, his face so white he looked green.

Picking up the camera bag at my feet, I strode over and handed it to him. "Get my phone out of the front pocket, would you?" I couldn't watch him because I had to keep clicking away at the runners, but in a minute he was holding the phone in front of me. At least he could still follow instructions. I swept my thumb across the screen, punched in my security code, and handed the phone back to him. "Dial Tia."

When my phone appeared in front of me again, and there was another break in the runners, I spared Sawyer a glance. He was blinking awfully fast. I sandwiched the phone between my chin and my shoulder as I awkwardly peered through the camera and kept clicking.

"Hey there, Annie Leibovitz!" Tia chirped.

"Sawyer might pass out."

"I'll be right there." The line went dead.

I slipped the phone into my pocket. I didn't want to have to explain to the race sponsor, my boss for my first-ever gig as a professional photographer, that I'd missed capturing the last half of the race because my friend was going to faint. But I *would* have abandoned my job if Sawyer looked like he was about to hit the ground.

Before that could happen, Tia rushed over to him. I turned back to the runners. Tia and Sawyer were close enough to me that I could hear their voices above the noise of the crowd and the rock band starting up somewhere behind the finish line.

Tia: "Sawyer, dammit! Are you okay?"

Sawyer: "I will be. In a couple of years."

Tia: "What the fuck did you run this race for? You just got out of the hospital. Are you trying to kill yourself?"

Sawyer: "Not . . . actively."

Tia: "Jesus. Sit down. Sit down right here on the curb. Will!"

She sounded alarmed enough that I glanced over at them again. Will elbowed his way through, holding two bottles of water high above the crowd. Brody followed right behind him.

Tia: "Did you know he was running this?"

Will: "I tried to stop him. Sawyer, dammit, put your head between your knees."

Tia: "Help me take him to the medical tent."

Will: "There's no medical tent. It's a 5K."

Sawyer, muffled: "Fuck everybody."

Brody: "Shut up. Just enjoy the view."

Though I was in the middle of picking out faces from a huge group of slow runners, Brody's voice made me look over my shoulder again. He had his hand on the back of Sawyer's neck, pressing his head toward the pavement. Will was pouring water over Sawyer's hair. Now Kaye and her cheerleader friends circled him. Sawyer was in good hands. I tried to concentrate on the last fifty people crossing the finish line, some of them grimacing with the exertion, others giving me elated smiles and peace signs as they passed.

Finally the race seemed to be over. I watched downstream for a few moments, but the street in front of me was filling with pedestrians as if the police had signaled that no more runners were coming. I heaved a deep sigh, rolled my shoulders, and started scrolling back through the photos to one group in particular. I was curious whether my obsession with the beauty of Brody's body had been a product of my vivid imagination.

It was not. The image was tiny, but I ran my eyes over his shining muscles and his smeared race number, and looked forward to viewing the enlarged version on my computer.

"Whatcha looking at?" Tia asked, peering over my shoulder. "Got a Pulitzer winner? You seem very intent, even for you."

"How's Sawyer?" I asked.

"Oh, fine. Just stupid. Will's walking him home. Don't change the subject. Let me see what's so intriguing in there."

I handed the camera over to her and watched her look at the view screen herself. "I feel like a pervert," I said.

"You should. That is disgusting. Be sure to e-mail me a copy." She handed the camera back to me. "Have you scheduled your Superlatives picture with Brody?"

"I've been trying to find an in," I said. "Seeing him like this makes it harder. We were elected Perfect Couple That Never Was, and I'm thinking . . . in what universe would we be a perfect couple? I'm not built like a gymnast."

I looked down at the view screen and scrolled to the best photo of Brody alone. He was so beautiful, and he looked so happy running and shoving Will out of the frame, that my heart hurt. "Did you vote for Brody and me? You didn't answer me before."

"No," Tia said. "I wrote you in as Most Artistic and Brody as Most Athletic. For Perfect Couple That Never Was, I put a couple of nerds who giggle together at the back of my calculus class."

"So, you paired like with like," I said. "That's how I voted too. And of the guys at school, I think Kennedy is my perfect partner, but we're already dating."

"Yeah, you're such a perfect couple that you're not talking," she said.

"How do you know?" I'd texted her grumpily from the Crab Lab while Kennedy was giving me the silent treatment, but she and I hadn't caught up since. She had no way of knowing we *still* weren't talking.

"He does this to you every week," she said. "Every time you have a date planned."

I thought back over the weeks we'd been going out. Tia was right about the timing. Kennedy couldn't be picking a fight with me just to avoid spending time with me, though. Why would he do that?

The whole idea of him made me uncomfortable, so I changed the subject. "Do you think people elected Brody and me Perfect Couple because we have something in common that other people can see but I can't?"

"No," Tia said as Brody walked over. He must have poured a bottle of water over his own head. He was wetter than he'd been when he'd first rushed past me. His hair was dark and slick, still caught by the headband. He stood so close to me, and his green eyes were so intense, that I looked away shyly. I found myself staring at the dent in his upper arm where his deltoid disappeared underneath his biceps. This was the first time I had ever used eleventh-grade anatomy in real life.

I forced my eyes up his taut pectoralis major, all the way to his face. He seemed to be staring at the barest shadow of baby cleavage in the open neckline of my blouse. Then he saw I was watching him and cracked a guilty grin.

"Later," I heard Tia say, but I was so focused on Brody that it took me a few seconds to realize she was talking to me.

"Later," I responded faintly after she'd already walked away. I was sweating as much as Brody was now. I could feel drops rolling down my cleavage. Holding his gaze had gotten so uncomfortable that I glanced down at my old standby and savior, my mechanical wingman, the camera. "Brody, there's a picture I wanted you to see." I handed the camera to him.

The view screen was paused on the best photo I'd taken

of the race: Noah in the foreground, slightly blurry, looking back over his shoulder, while Brody and Will were in sharp focus in the sweet spot of the frame, a third from the top and a third from one side. They'd just realized Noah was beating them, and their outrage was hilarious. Their bare chests weren't bad either. I figured the perfection of the photo was so obvious that even a layperson like Brody would see it. He wouldn't think my admiration for his body was gratuitous. No, that wouldn't be obvious unless he scrolled through my camera and saw all the other photos I'd taken of him.

He peered at the view screen and burst into laughter. I watched his mouth. His bottom lip wasn't swollen anymore, and the bruise on his jaw had faded. When he laughed that hard, the dark circles under his eyes disappeared too. He wasn't some older, intimidating bodybuilder. He was seventeen, like me.

With as deep a calming breath as I could draw without him noticing, I gathered the courage to ask, "Would you mind if I tried to sell this picture to the newspaper?"

He eyed me mischievously and asked, "Are you going to pay me?"

I smiled. "No."

"Are you going to pay me half?"

"No."

He tilted his head, perplexed. "Are you going to pay me a fourth?"

"No." His interrogation had gone on so long that I wondered if he really didn't want me to sell the picture. That was fine. It was his image, after all. I was profiting from his free services as a model. But I'd thought he was so happy-go-lucky that he wouldn't care.

"Harper!" he burst out. "I'm kidding."

"Well, I couldn't tell!" I took the camera back from him, my mind spinning. I wanted to get Will and Noah's permission too. Will was gone and I hadn't seen Noah since the end of the race. I'd never find him now in the milling pedestrians. I could text them both later and then e-mail the photo to the local paper.

All that was easier to work through than one tall guy standing in front of me, too easygoing for me to decipher.

Brody wasn't mortified about our misunderstanding like I was, though. He was still grinning as he said, "I guess you're going to take our photo for the yearbook sometime soon, like you took Will and Tia's."

"Right, like Will and Tia's," I echoed faintly. When I'd shot their picture for Biggest Flirts, they'd shared an unplanned kiss, which had gotten Will in trouble with his sort-of girlfriend Angelica. It had all worked out in the end. Will and Tia were dating now.

I stammered, "Um, I mean . . ." I lost my verbal abilities because I was at eye level with his nipples. This was distracting.

I forced my eyes up to his face. "We have to take the photo," I said. "We need to take it soon, because Kennedy's deadline for the whole section is in a week and a half. He kind of jumped down my throat about it Friday."

Brody raised his eyebrows at the idea of Kennedy scolding me. He'd been trying to flirt with me, and I'd ruined it by bringing up my boyfriend.

Exactly. "Setting up the picture is touchy when we're both dating somebody," I muddled through. "I've been taking photos in the courtyard at school because it's convenient and the light is good, but anyone can look out of the classrooms and see us. I found that out the hard way when I took Tia and Will's Biggest Flirts photo and there was a big fight and a fallout. Also, I don't have an inspiration for how we'd pose. Do you?"

"I was planning to do what you told me."

"Oh, *really*?" I exclaimed, stressing my excitement. This was my only success at flirting for our entire conversation. And when his mouth curled into a sly smile, my heart sped up.

"Here's a thought," I ventured. "I know the football team

is practicing a lot, but if we could figure out a time . . ." I sounded like I was trying to get out of our meeting before I even proposed it.

He watched me like he was thinking the same thing.

I made myself continue, ". . . we could go on a date and take a picture of ourselves. It would be ironic, see, that we're the Perfect Couple That Never Was, except we *would* be a couple for the photo. It will be hilarious to, like, the five or six of our friends who would actually give a shit."

He laughed so hard that he took a step back. The space between us was wide enough that a couple of little kids dashed through, chasing each other.

Laughing uneasily along with Brody, I said, "Well, I didn't think it was *that* funny. Maybe seven or eight friends."

He stepped toward me again. "No, it's just funny to hear you say '*shit.*'"

"Oh." Tia had told me this before. I was so prim and proper, apparently, that a curse coming out of my mouth was as charming as a potty-mouthed toddler on a viral video. I felt myself blush as I always did when people said that kind of thing to me, like I wasn't a real person but a wholesome caricature.

Not knowing or caring that he was poking me in the tender parts of my psyche, Brody said, "I like this idea. Would we be going on a real date, or a fake date just for the photo?"

Well, of *course* it would be a fake date, and of *course* he knew this. We were both in other relationships. But the very idea of us going on a real date was so deliciously outrageous that I heard myself saying, "Whatever."

"I'll be at the beach with some friends this afternoon." He nodded toward the curb where Sawyer had sat, as if his friends were standing there, but I didn't see anyone I knew.

A lot of my friends, including Tia and Kaye, would be at the same beach. I was supposed to join them. I'd been thinking I should stay home instead and upload the race photos to my website. A delay was okay—the runners wouldn't expect their pictures to be available instantly—but I needed to get them online a.s.a.p. so I could turn my attention back to the yearbook photos.

Suddenly, Labor Day spent in front of the computer seemed like the world's saddest pastime compared with going to the beach with Brody. Or, not with Brody. The same beach as Brody. A photo of a fake date with Brody, more fun than any real date I'd ever been on with Kennedy. I said, "I'll be there too."

"So, I'll catch up with you there?"

"Okay."

"See you then." He walked toward the curb.

I enjoyed basking in the afterglow of his attention—for

about one second. My ecstasy was over the instant I recognized one of the friends he was probably meeting at the
beach. I heard her before I saw her. Grace had a piercing,
staccato laugh, like a birdcall that sounded quirky on a nature
walk and excruciating outside a bedroom window at dawn.
Boys had been making fun of her laugh to her face forever—
but Grace was so pretty and flirty that they only teased her
as a way in.

She stopped laughing to say, "Sorry I missed your race,
Brody! You know me. I just rolled out of bed."

The crowd parted. Now I could see her better. Just rolled
out of bed, my ass. She stood casually in a teeny bikini top.
At least she'd had the decency to pull gym shorts over her
bikini bottoms so she didn't give the elderly snowbirds a
heart attack. But her hair and makeup didn't go with her
beach look. Grace's long blond hair rolled across her shoulders in big, sprayed curls, the kind that took me half an hour
with a curling iron and a coat of hairspray. Her locks were
held back from her pretty face by her sunglasses, which sat
on top of her head. Her eyes were model-smoky with liner
and shadow and mascara. She was ready for an island cast-
away prom.

"Did you win?" she asked Brody.

He chuckled. "No."

She led him away by the hand. And that was that.

I watched him go. I *needed* to watch him *walking away with his girlfriend*, so I could get it through my thick skull that he was taken. Brody and I had exchanged some friendly jokes and agreed to fulfill a school obligation—at a gathering we'd both already planned to attend. He'd seen his girlfriend and forgotten about me. I didn't even get a good-bye, not that I should have expected one. The "Never Was" part of our title was a lot more important than the "Perfect Couple" part.

Then he looked over his shoulder at me. Straight at me—no mistaking it. His green eyes were bright.

My heart stopped.

Still walking after Grace, he gave me a little wave.

I waved back.

He tripped over an uneven brick in the sidewalk but regained his balance before he fell. He disappeared into the crowd.

"That was smooth," Tia said at my shoulder.

Kneeling to pick up my camera bag, I grumbled, "Shut up."

"Does this mean you're going on a real date or a fake date?" she asked. "It wasn't clear from where I was eavesdropping."

I gave her the bag to hold while I snapped the lens off my camera and stuffed the components inside. "I don't know."

"Does this mean Brody's previous plan and your previous

plan to go to the beach are actually the date in question, or is there another fake or real date after that?"

Exasperated, I gave her a warning look.

"Sorry," Tia said. "I know. I shouldn't be criticizing your romantic life. Before Will, my dating scene pretty much began and ended with giving Sawyer hand jobs behind the Crab Lab." Several elderly men walking past turned to stare at her as she said this. She winked at them.

"I'm too polite to bring that up," I said.

"Do you want me to get Will to ask Brody, then report back . . . to . . . you?" Her words slowed as my expression grew darker.

"Thanks but no thanks," I said. "This is already embarrassing enough. No reason to take us back to the fifth grade."

Her mouth twisted sideways in a grimace as she handed the camera bag back to me. Tia clearly wanted to help but didn't know what to say. There *was* nothing to say, because my situation was so hopeless.

"It's okay," I assured her. "I have a boyfriend. This is just a yearbook picture. I'll see you at the beach."

"Later," she said, but she looked uncertain as she wound her way up the street toward the antiques store where she and her sister worked.

Tia was tall. It took a few minutes for me to lose the back

of her shining auburn hair on the sidewalk now crowded with shoppers. I should have turned for home, e-mailed Noah and Will for permission to send my shot of them to the newspaper, and started uploading my race photos.

But now that Tia was gone and Brody was gone and I stood alone in the middle of the street, I was aware of the happiness all around me for the first time that day. The rock band had launched into another song. Families stood in line outside the ice cream parlor, even though it was nine a.m., because regular meal times meant nothing and calories didn't count on holidays. Kids giggled as they tumbled out the door of an inflatable bouncy castle. I pulled my camera out of my bag again, attached the telephoto lens, and snapped a few shots of the kids' flip-flops and sandals lined up on the street.

I glanced down at my own kitten heels with their shiny, black-patent pointed toes.

In the midst of all this carefree joy, I looked like a mutant. A mutant on a job interview.

I thought ahead to my meeting with Brody at the beach. He would be shirtless, again, and irresistible, again. I would be wearing my 1950s-style, high-necked, one-piece maillot. If an item of clothing had a French name, it probably wouldn't leave much of an impression on a Florida jock. At least, not the impression I wanted.

Last spring I'd been ecstatic to find a bathing suit made specifically for my retro style. Kaye and Tia had told me it was adorable. But next to Grace, I would look like I was wearing a hazmat suit.

Ten minutes later, I found myself in the dressing room at a surf shop, staring at myself in the mirror, guessing what Brody would think when he saw me in a red bikini.

5

I MUTTERED TO MYSELF, "I HAVE AN ILLNESS."

"What'd you say, sugar pie?" the lady who owned the store called through the curtain. "Do you need a different size?"

I raked back the curtain to show her the bikini.

"You do not need a different size," she declared. "Maybe an extra bottle of sunscreen to protect all that lovely skin you're showing, but not a different size."

I paid for the bathing suit. The shop lady put it in a pretty bag with color-coordinated tissue paper fluffing out the top. But on my walk home, I felt like I'd stolen it. It was as if everyone at the street festival watched my escape. I was so self-conscious about the bikini in my bag that I stowed it in my room, at the back of my closet, where Mom wouldn't see it. If she asked me about it, I'd never wear it. I would chicken out.

I went to find Mom. She was upstairs in one of the B & B's guest bathrooms, on her hands and knees, scrubbing the grout on the floor underneath the sink. After I located her, I backed out of the bathroom, tiptoed down the stairs, and then stomped back up so she'd know I was coming and wouldn't bang her head against the sink at my sudden appearance. I had found out a lot of things the hard way.

When I entered the bathroom again, she was sitting cross-legged, waiting for me. "Survived the heat in that outfit?"

I skipped right over that one and asked, "Where are the guests?" This phrase was our code to make sure we were alone before we said anything private. Mom had taught me it was more out of courtesy to the guests than to us.

"They're all out enjoying the day," she said.

"Do you still have my prescription for contacts?" Every time I got my eyes checked, I wanted only a glasses prescription. Mom asked the optometrist to give me a prescription for contacts, too, in case I changed my mind.

"You changed your mind!" she exclaimed.

I shook my head. "I just want to try them."

She raised her eyebrows at me. "After five years of me begging you? What happened?"

I would rather have given up on the idea of contacts than tell her about Brody, Grace, Kennedy, Sawyer, Noah,

Quinn. . . . I couldn't even reconstruct how the wild ride of the last few days had dumped me off at a place where I never wanted to wear my adorable glasses again, or kitten heels, or a pencil skirt. And even if I could have verbalized my mindset, I didn't want to share it with Mom, who would pass my teen angst around the B & B's dining table tomorrow morning like a basket of orange rolls.

I said, "You don't have to stop working. Just tell me where the prescription is."

She lowered her brows and opened her mouth, ready to put up a fight. But her cell phone was ringing in the hall on her cart of cleaning supplies.

"Get that, would you?" she asked. "If it's your father, tell him I'm unavailable."

Not *that* fight again. I didn't want to get dragged into it. And I didn't want to get dragged into a personal one with *her*, either. I repeated, "Where's my prescription?"

Because she didn't want to take a chance on missing a call from a potential boarder, she quickly told me which office file my prescription was in. After that victory, I dashed into the hall, my heels clattering on the hardwood floor, and scooped up the phone, hoping it *was* my dad. I didn't want to get in the middle of my parents' fight, but I hadn't talked to my dad in a month or seen him in three. I glanced at the screen. Mom had been right. I clicked on the phone and said, "Hi, Dad!"

"Hey there, Harper," he said. "Is your mom around?"

My stomach twisted into a knot. I didn't think about my dad a whole lot because he wasn't home and didn't have much to do with my life anymore. But I wanted him to *want* to talk to me. I said stiffly, "I'm sorry, but she's unavailable."

"Unavailable how?" he asked, suspicious.

I couldn't lie to my dad, but I didn't want to say Mom was just scrubbing the floor and refusing to talk to him either. I swallowed.

"Harper," he said firmly. "Give the phone to your mother."

Funny how his tone of voice could send my blood pressure through the roof, even over the phone. "Just a minute," I whispered. With my temples suddenly pounding, I walked back into the bathroom, extending the phone toward Mom. "It's Dad."

She started upward and banged her head against the sink.

"Ouch," I said sympathetically.

Dropping her scrub brush and pressing both rubber gloves to her hair, she glared at me with tears in her eyes. Ever so slowly, she reached for the phone. "Hello."

In the pause as my dad spoke to her, I escaped. But her

next words followed me, echoing out of the cavernous bathroom, into the wide wooden stairwell, and down the steps: "I told Harper to say that because we're going to court next week. You're supposed to leave me alone until then. *Leave me alone.*"

Inside the house was cool and dark with a faint scent of age and the sound of Mom's angry language. As I shut the heavy door behind me, outside was bright and smelled like flowers. Tree frogs screamed in the trees. I skittered back to our little house and dug through Mom's office files until I found my prescription, wondering how I'd ever thought I could spend the hot holiday at home.

The locally owned drugstores in the old-fashioned downtown around the corner from the B & B couldn't help me today. To get my contact prescription filled on Labor Day, I needed the discount store with the optical shop out on the highway. And that meant I needed Granddad's car.

I knocked on the door of his bungalow, just as I had yesterday and the day before, holding my breath until he answered. He drove to the grocery store once a week, and sometimes he swung by the art supply store to pick up more oil paints. As far as I knew, those were the only times he left the house where he'd lived forever and where Mom had grown up.

Granddad and Mom argued a lot. She told him she

wanted to make sure he was happy and safe, and he said she was being a nosy busybody. He told her she needed to get rid of that no-good cheat of a husband once and for all, and she said he was being an overbearing jerk. They were both right. In the middle of these fights, I was the only one checking on him. Sawyer lived next door, and Granddad paid him to cut the grass, but I doubted he thought to conduct a welfare check when Granddad didn't leave the house for days on end. That took a certain level of granddaughterly paranoia.

I'd be the one to bang on Granddad's door someday, grow suspicious when he didn't answer, force open a window, and find him dead—though if he was dead already, I wasn't sure why this idea made me so anxious. It wasn't like finding him dead an hour earlier was going to help.

I knocked harder. "Granddad!" I yelled. "It's Harper." It couldn't be anyone else, since I was his only grandchild.

I sighed with relief when I finally heard footsteps approaching. Even his footfalls sounded misanthropic, soft and shuffling, like he'd rather wrestle snakes than let his granddaughter into his house.

He turned the lock and opened the door a crack—not even as wide as the chain would allow. At a quick glance, I couldn't see any reason for his secrecy. He looked the same as always, with his salt-and-pepper hair pulled back in a ponytail, and a streak of yellow paint drying in his beard. "I'm fine," he said.

"Would you open the door?" I pleaded. "You didn't let me in the house on Saturday, but at least you opened the door for me. You opened it only a crack on Sunday. This is a smaller crack. I can't tell whether you're less glad to see me or you're trying to disguise the fact that you're getting thinner." He'd already started to close the door completely. Apparently he didn't think I was as funny as I did. Quickly I asked, "May I borrow your car?"

"No." The door shut.

"Granddad!" His footsteps didn't retreat into the house, so I knew he was still listening. "Why not?" And why was I so determined to borrow his car? Why couldn't I drive to the discount store to get contacts another day?

Because I was on a mission to be bikini clad and glasses free when I met Brody at the beach. And I was damned if this was the one day out of the year Granddad decided I couldn't borrow his car.

"I don't have to tell you why not," he said through the door, which was the adult version of me changing the subject when Mom asked why I wanted contacts.

"You said when I turned sixteen that I could borrow your car whenever I wanted. That was your birthday gift to me.

You wrote it on a scrap of paper and wrapped it up in a box." If he didn't remember that, we needed to have a talk about what he *did* remember, and what year it was, and whether he should be allowed to live alone and own a microwave oven.

"That was a fine idea of mine," he said, "when you didn't want to borrow my car."

I demanded, "What are you doing with your car today?"

"I don't have to tell you that, either. I'm sixty-eight years old."

And you're acting like you're two, I thought, but that was Mom's line. Really, he was acting like *me*. I took care never to be as mean as he was, but I wanted to be by myself a lot, and people probably took it as meanness. Tia had asked to hang out with me at my house in the past, and I'd told her no. She was so extroverted that after a few hours with her, I needed to be alone with my art. And I'd ruined some fledgling relationships back in ninth and tenth grade by complaining when guys with boyfriend potential called me and texted me and interrupted my thoughts. They were insulted when I turned my phone off.

Granddad was just dishing out the same antisocial behavior to me, and I couldn't take it.

"All right," I called through the door. "I'll come back to check on you tomorrow." The way things were progressing, he probably wouldn't even open the door for me then. I would have to wave to him through the window. I turned for the stairs off the porch.

The lock turned. The door opened. He stuck his hand out with his car key dangling from one finger.

"Thank you," I said, sliding the key ring off his pointer before he changed his mind. "I'm going shopping out on the highway and then to the beach. You can call me on my cell if you need the car back."

Instead of answering, he shut the door and locked it.

A few hours later, I parked Granddad's car way back from the beach in the nearly full lot and lugged my bag and cooler out of the trunk. I always brought thermoses of water so my friends didn't have to throw away plastic bottles, which was bad for the environment. The smooth cooler felt strange on my bare tummy. In my teeny bikini, I struggled to haul my load onto the sand, across the beach, and around families and motorcycle gangs and groups of elderly drunken rabble-rousers. Finally I spotted the cluster of towels and umbrellas where my friends had settled.

As I walked, I squinted at the ocean. Compared with my glasses, my new contacts made the sun almost unbearably bright. But I recognized Aidan and Kaye in the waves. Her hair in black twists was easy to pick out. Then I saw the drum major of the marching band, DeMarcus, and his girl-friend, Chelsea, and the cheerleaders who'd run the race with Kaye that morning. Noah and Quinn and Kennedy sat in the sand with the tide flowing over their feet.

Obviously Kennedy wasn't as worried about being associated with Quinn and Noah as he'd been when he'd sneered at me in Ms. Patel's class on Friday. Maybe Tia was right: He picked a fight with me only when we had a date planned.

Off to themselves in the water, Brody held Grace. I could tell he was supporting her in deep water because she was higher than him. Her sunglasses still balanced on top of her head, and her bouncy curls were dry. In fact, he might have been holding her out of the water specifically to keep her hair dry, which was the dumbest thing I'd ever seen at the beach, and I'd lived here almost my whole life.

"Howdy," I said, plopping down my ice chest and bag near Tia, Will, and the huge dog Will borrowed from the shop where Tia worked. The three of them lay on towels in the shade of an umbrella. Will still had trouble staying in the Florida sun for long.

He and Tia stared at me for a moment. Then he exclaimed, "Oh, Harper! I didn't recognize you without your glasses."

"I didn't recognize you in a bikini," Tia said. "Look at that bod! You could crack pecans with those abs. What gives?"

I spread out my towel next to them and lay down. "I don't know if you heard Sawyer this morning," I said, "but when he was sitting on the curb about to pass out after the race, he said, 'Fuck everybody.' That's pretty much how I feel."

The more I thought about it, the more sense it made. Sawyer had been angry that he couldn't run a race like everybody else. I was sick and tired of trying to make a statement with my look, and sabotaging myself in the process.

As usual, Tia didn't press me for details. "Well, you look super cute in that bright red 'fuck you.'"

"I'm not complaining either," Will said. Tia snagged an ice cube from her cup and placed it in his belly button. He jumped, grabbing his stomach like he'd been shot. Then he dropped the ice in *her* belly button. She shrieked. The dog jumped up. The ice slid off Tia's tummy and onto her towel, where the dog ate it.

"Is Kennedy still maintaining radio silence?" Tia asked me.

"Yeah."

"Wait till he sees you."

"You look hot, Harper," Will said.

Tia told him, "There's 'Thanks for being nice to my friends,' and then there's 'You can stop being nice to my friends now.'"

She turned back to me. "Let's go hang with girls. You can walk slowly by Kennedy like your very own Labor Day parade. Brody's going to be pleased by your ass, too." She stood and held out her hand to help me up. The dog lay down in her place.

We shuffled across the beach. The sun was really doing a number on my contacts. I squinted and followed the blur of Tia. It wasn't until we'd reached the water that I realized she'd led me on a roundabout path that veered much nearer Kennedy than necessary.

I didn't look toward the boys, but I recognized Noah's wolf whistle.

Quinn said something under his breath that ended in "Harper."

"What?" Kennedy asked. "Oh."

Now that Quinn had drawn his attention to me, Kennedy must have been watching me pass. But I forgot all about them when I saw Brody coming toward me from the ocean, stepping over the waves—without Grace.

He put out his hand. Tia slapped it as she passed.

He kept holding it out for me. I slapped it. But before I could pass him, his hand enclosed mine. We both stopped calf high in the surf.

"I thought you weren't coming," he said. I couldn't see his

eyes behind his sunglasses, which made him somehow sexier. He was so near, and—like that morning—so nearly nude, with almost every inch of his tanned skin showing over tight muscles. I imagined I could smell him over the salt air and sunscreen. Suddenly my entire body was glowing.

Then my brain kicked in. What did he mean by "I thought you weren't coming"? He'd been out in the ocean with Grace because he assumed I wouldn't show up? It didn't matter anyway. We had a date for a picture *only*. I said, "You thought wrong."

"I sure did," he said. "See you in a few." He let my hand go. We walked on.

I hazarded half a glance behind me and caught *him* looking back too, at my butt.

And beyond him, Kennedy sat in the surf with his knees drawn up and his arms around them, watching us. Kennedy was a big guy, but this position made him look like an unsure kid.

Another day, my heart would have gone out to him. He was my geeky soul mate, the boy I belonged with. So what if he wasn't a muscle-bound hunk ready to challenge Brody when he brazenly eyed me? As an independent woman, I didn't need a protector. I wanted a sensitive guy with a great sense of humor and a fresh view of the world.

But today, my heart was cold to Kennedy. For the first

time, I felt a pang of distaste when I looked at him. My skin tingled, wanting Brody to touch me again.

I sloshed after Tia until we'd waded shoulder deep where the other girls bobbed in the surf. Grace had joined them. They were all giggling at something one of them had said. Grace's staccato laugh was easy to pick out among the others. But when she saw me coming, she called, "It's Miss Perfect Couple with My Boyfriend."

"Girl, I told you the Superlatives are whack," Kaye said. "There's no telling why the class votes like it does." This was directly opposed to the way Kaye had acted when she was elected Most Likely to Succeed: like it was the most important award of her life. And I was surprised to hear she'd talked Grace down about my title with Brody. Kaye hadn't mentioned this to me. She must have been worried I would worry. She confirmed this by grimacing sympathetically as I swam up.

"Happy Labor Day!" I sang.

Grace glared at me. The other cheerleaders laughed uncomfortably. One of them, Ellen, exclaimed, "Harper! I didn't recognize you without your glasses."

"I got contacts today," I said.

They ooohed and cooed over me and told me how good I looked and how pretty my eyes were, which they'd never noticed before—all except Grace, who stared me down with a look that said, *Oh, you got contacts so you could come to this beach to seduce my boyfriend, eh?* At least, that's how I interpreted it.

At my first chance, when the conversation turned to Chelsea's story about fighting with a stranger over a pimento cheese sandwich at Disney World yesterday, which was the sort of thing that happened to Chelsea, I ducked beneath the surface to wet my hair. That would convince Grace I had no designs on her boyfriend. My hair was long and dark and board straight anyway, whereas she was still sporting her big blond curls. They were wilting a bit, though, now that Brody wasn't holding her out of the surf. Her hairdo was wet around the edges, like a sandcastle nipped by waves.

As soon as I surfaced, I was sorry I'd gone under. My eyes stung. I hadn't opened them in the water, but as I wiped away the drops, I got salt and sunscreen in them. I wiped them again, which made the stinging worse.

"I'm going down the beach," I heard Grace say. "I saw some guys I know who are home for the weekend from Florida State. I'm scoring some beer. Tia, come with."

"No, thanks," Tia said.

"Why not?" Grace insisted. "You're always drunk."

"I am not *always* drunk," Tia said self-righteously. "I am

drunk on a case-by-case basis. And not on Labor Day. The beach is crawling with cops."

"Ellen," Grace said, "come with. Cathy?"

The other cheerleader, Cathy, giggled nervously. "Wish us luck!" The three of them waded toward the promised land of beer and college boys.

Kaye called after them, "If you get caught, do *not* admit you're cheerleaders for our high school. We have standards." She said more quietly to the rest of us, "Let's wait five minutes and then go after them. We'll watch from the water and intervene if they get in trouble."

"Or we can just enjoy the show when they do," Tia suggested.

By now I could hardly see through the slits that my stinging eyes had become. "I'll catch up with y'all," I said. "Back to the towels for me. I'm having contact problems." Amid the chorus of "Oh, no!" and "Poor baby!" and "Do you need help?" I explained what had happened. "If I can wipe my eyes and run fresh water over my hands, I think I'll be okay."

I sloshed toward shore. But as I reached dry sand, I was anything but okay. My left eye stung. My right eye was worse. When I opened it, all I could see was blur. The beach was as bright as another planet with no atmosphere to filter the sun. I could hardly see my way back to the island of umbrellas and towels I'd come from. When I finally made it, I tripped over several boys and landed on the dog, who didn't budge.

"Move, dog," I said rudely. She got up, sticking her sandy butt in my face as I opened my cooler for a thermos of water.

Kennedy was telling the other guys about the indie film we'd seen at the Tampa Theater downtown last weekend. They were laughing uncontrollably. Kennedy was brilliant and had great comedic delivery. He would be perfect someday as the vastly intelligent, super dry commentator on a political comedy show. His shtick was as much about what he left out as what he said. At the moment, he was strategically omitting that we'd had an argument in his car on the way to the movie and that he still hadn't been speaking to me by the time he dropped me off at home afterward.

"Right, Harper?" I heard him ask. He wanted me to verify some funny point in the movie—something he hadn't discussed with me one on one, because we'd hardly talked since then.

This was his way of making up. After our fights, he ignored me until he just decided not to anymore. He asked me a question and I responded, and then it was like nothing had happened between us.

This time, instead of answering, I poured freezing water over my hand and wiped at my eye. Now it felt like I'd gotten sand in my eyeball. I tried to shift the offending particle into the corner where my tears would flush it out. That was a mistake. The stinging was intense.

I tried to open my eye. I couldn't. My upper eyelid felt wedged shut by my contact. Was it possible that my contact had drifted that far back? Could it float even farther and get stuck on my optic nerve? *Where was my eleventh-grade anatomy knowledge when I needed it?*

"Guys," I called. Kennedy kept up his blasé movie commentary while I went blind in one eye. Tears streaming down my cheek, I said more loudly, "Guys, do any of you wear contacts? I need help. I think my contact has shifted into the back of my eye socket."

"Harper," Kennedy said, "only you."

I took in a deep breath to calm myself, but I was on the verge of panic. These boys were not going to help me. Kennedy would make fun of me while this piece of flexible plastic sliced its way into my brain and gave me a lobotomy. The girls would help me, but they were too far away to hear me yell over the surf, and I couldn't open one eye, and now I couldn't see out of the good eye because of the tears. I felt like screaming.

Strong hands framed my face. One thumb pulled at my lower eyelid. I was surprised Kennedy had relented and come to my rescue. My hero said, "I wear contacts, and I know all about this, unfortunately. Let me help."

But it wasn't Kennedy's voice. It was Brody.

6

"OPEN YOUR EYE," BRODY SAID.

"I can't." I was almost sobbing.

"Noah," Brody said, "kneel here in front of her so the glare from the beach isn't in her eyes. Will, pour some water on my hand."

"It's not sterile," Kennedy pointed out from a distance.

"It's a beach," Brody said, sounding irritated. "Nothing is sterile. At least get the sand off."

I heard water hiss in the sand and tried to be patient. So much moisture was coming out of my eyes that the contact should have washed out already, but I could feel it still lodged somewhere it should never have gone.

His hands were on my face again. He pulled at my eye. He was closer to me than he'd ever been, his skin only an inch from mine, but I couldn't enjoy it with all these guys watching us and my eye falling out. "Harper, relax," he said.

Relax? Impossible. I had a boyfriend and a crush on another guy. I'd given myself a mini-makeover to impress my crush, and now he was trying to help me through my mortifying comeuppance, my punishment for trying to attract him. I felt like a spy who had to stay undercover after she'd been shot.

I sucked in another deep breath, counted to five in my head, and exhaled. I relaxed under Brody's hands.

He opened my eye. The huge blur of his finger came at my eyeball, but I managed not to flinch as he manipulated the contact. And suddenly—*ahhh*. My eye still stung, but I could tell the contact was back in place.

"Thank you so much," I said, cupping one hand over my eye. I kept the other shut too, because that felt better. I couldn't see Brody in front of me, but I felt his warmth there. I said, "It was burrowing into my sinuses and wanted to come out my nose. Is it supposed to do that?"

"No," he said. "You must have rubbed it really hard. Maybe you should take it out."

"I wouldn't have anywhere to put it."

"You're supposed to carry a small bottle of contact solution with you everywhere," he said, "and a contact case, and a spare pair of glasses."

"Do *you* carry all that stuff?" I asked.

"No, I'm a guy. Are your contacts expensive? Maybe you should just throw it away."

"They're expensive," I said, "and I can't see without them, and I have to drive home."

"I could drive you home," he offered.

"Did you get it?" Kennedy called from behind Brody—still several towels away. He hadn't bothered to come any closer to help.

Maybe he wasn't even asking about my contact. The film conversation had continued despite my medical emergency. He could have been asking Quinn if he'd gotten a ticket to next week's indie. At any rate, Brody ignored Kennedy. He asked me quietly, "Did you bring sunglasses?"

"I don't have any," I said sheepishly. "I couldn't wear them before because I've always worn glasses."

"Contacts make the glare worse, so sunglasses are more important. You can have mine." He pulled up my free hand and gave me what I assumed were his sunglasses.

"No, you need them."

"I've got another pair in my truck." I heard him rattling the ice in the chest again. "Lie down."

His voice had a bossy edge. I kind of liked it. I did what he said and lay down on the towel.

He handed me a cold, wet bundle. "Press this to your eye, but not hard. Take a time-out. You'll feel better in a minute. Your eye will re-lubricate or whatever."

"Thank you."

I lay on my tummy in the hot shade, breathing deeply and evenly, willing my eye to feel better. The boys were talking about TV shows now and had obviously forgotten I was there, because they were repeating the kind of jokes boys didn't usually tell when they knew girls were listening. I didn't hear Brody's voice, but I assumed he'd moved back into the group with the rest of them.

Then a warm, comforting hand settled on my back. My mind spun with who would be so kind to me. Definitely not Kennedy. Possibly Quinn or Noah. They could get away with it because Kennedy would have no reason to be jealous. Probably Brody, and then Kennedy would be jealous. Or *should* be. Maybe Kennedy couldn't see his hand on me.

I tried to enjoy the camaraderie, but I couldn't stand the suspense any longer. I lifted my head and squinted across my body with my good eye.

It was the dog, lying right beside me with her chin on my back. Now that I knew it was her face and not a boy's hand, I recognized the feel of her hair and the trickle of her slobber.

I put my own head back down.

After a few minutes, the guys' voices moved away one by one. I heard them shouting out in the water. Only Kennedy and Quinn were left, making fun of Mr. Oakley, which I kind of resented because I liked Mr. Oakley. When I'd told him I wanted a press pass to photograph the football games, he'd set out to give me a football lesson rather than rolling his eyes like Kennedy had. I felt so distanced from the fun I'd come here to have, wrapped up in my own resentment and pain, that I almost jumped when Kennedy spoke just above me. "Harper, are you okay?"

"I'm better," I said without moving. *I am shocked that you give a shit*, I thought.

"We're going to the snack bar," he said. "Want anything?"

"No, thanks," I said.

Alone under the umbrella, I spent a few more minutes trying to chill. I let the cool cloth soothe my eye. Finally I took it off and blinked. My eye worked, and my contact stayed in place, thanks to Brody. I unbundled the cloth and looked at it. It was a huge T-shirt emblazoned with PELICANS FOOTBALL. Brody's last name was written in marker on the hem.

I placed his sunglasses on my nose and slowly sat up, tumbling the dog off me in the process. I was ready, however reluctantly, to rejoin my safe and small and constantly disappointing world.

Brody sat back on his elbows one towel over, watching me.

"Feel better?" he asked.

"Yes, thanks." I squinted at him, feeling my face slowly flush. I wondered what was keeping him here. Not me.

"I went to my truck to get my other sunglasses," he said, peering at me over the top of them. "When I got back, everybody was gone. Kennedy left you by yourself?"

"Just to go to the snack bar."

Brody glared in the general direction of the snack bar far down the beach as if he disapproved. I would have thought his concern was silly, except that my eye did still burn every time I blinked.

"Do you know where the other girls have been gone so long?" he asked.

"Mmmm," I said, which meant *Yes* and *If I tell you, I will seem like the scheming bitch I am becoming.*

He gave me a knowing look over his shades. "Did Grace go try to get beer from those college guys?" When I didn't answer, his shoulders dropped in frustration.

"Why don't you stop her?" I asked. "Or . . . help her?" Stopping her was what I would have tried to do if I'd been her friend, but helping her was probably more up Brody's alley.

He wasn't the class party animal. That would be Sawyer—at least, before Sawyer changed his ways last week, according to Tia. But the gatherings at Brody's house when his mom was out for the night weren't dry.

He smiled at me. "The first rule of breaking rules is that you take some basic precautions not to get caught, right?"

I didn't answer, because I wouldn't know. It *did* sound a lot like Tia's opinion on the subject.

"It's Labor Day," he said, "it's daylight, it's a public beach, and the cops are all over the place. Grace is being stupid. Besides, I think she's getting more than beer from one of those guys."

"Oh." I puzzled through what this meant. He didn't sound upset that she might be cheating on him. But inside, he must burn with jealousy. That's why he'd been paying so much attention to *me*. Grace hadn't been around to see, but he'd hoped it would get back to her.

This didn't explain why he was still here, alone with me.

"Let's see that eye," he said.

Again, I got a little excited at his bossy command. In the last half hour I'd come to think of him as the best candidate to get me to the emergency room if my eyeball popped out. I sat up on my knees. Just as before, our bodies almost touched. He took off his shades, slid the ones I'd borrowed from my face, and placed his pointer finger gently on my lower eyelid. "It's still a little red, but not nearly as bad as it was." He nodded down the beach. "Why don't we go to the pavilion and take the picture for the yearbook? That will get you out of the glare."

"Okay. Let me get my camera out of my car."

"I'll go with you."

I held out my hand. "Sunglasses, please. Definitely. Thank you."

We headed for the parking lot, leaving the dog behind. She made no move to follow us. I supposed she would be okay by herself. Our town didn't have a leash law because the hippie city government thought animals should run free like the wind. Someone needed to relay this to the dog, who rolled over on her back, watching upside down for Will to return.

As Brody and I walked together across the melted asphalt lot, I said, "Sorry, my car's all the way back here."

"We could have gotten in my truck and driven to your car."

"And then driven around the parking lot for the rest of the day after someone stole your space." I laughed.

"That doesn't sound too bad," he said.

Was he implying he'd enjoy driving in circles with me? He kept saying things like this, or I kept interpreting them that way. I had to remind myself the only concrete evidence

I had that he liked me was a cold compress he'd constructed from his T-shirt. Lately my brain had turned into a multiple-choice "Does he dig me?" quiz from *Seventeen*.

He snapped me out of it by exclaiming, "A 1990 Dodge Charger! This is you?"

"Yeah," I admitted as we stopped behind the trunk. "Granddad bought it when he was in his midforties. Grandmom had just left him and moved across town with my mom to live with *her* mom. The car was his consolation prize, I guess."

Brody put his hand out to stroke the red metallic paint. He snatched his hand back when the hot surface burned his fingers. "You're driving your granddad's midlife crisis?"

"He lets me *borrow* his midlife crisis." I unlocked the stylish (not) louvered hatchback and pulled out my camera case.

Brody reached up and closed the hatchback for me. "I hear these things are pretty fast. What have you gotten it up to?"

"Thirty."

He gaped at me, horrified. "You've never taken it out on the interstate to see what it can do?"

"Nope."

He grinned and raised his eyebrows. "Do you want me to try it?"

"I heard you were one point away from getting your license revoked because of all your speeding tickets."

"True. See? That's why I need you, Harper."

I looped the strap of my camera bag over my bare shoulder. As we turned for the pavilion, I said casually, "I've been reading about you in the newspaper."

"Yeah." He smiled wryly. "That's taken some getting used to. You have to keep it in perspective. In a town this small, high school football is entertainment. The only alternatives are the beach and a theater showing two movies. Unless, of course, you drive to Tampa with Kennedy to see the latest indie."

A little sarcasm? His tone wasn't sarcastic, but his message must be. Maybe he liked me after all. But I wouldn't let him change the subject, because I wanted him to explain something to me. "I was curious about this morning's newspaper article. I couldn't believe they were so down on you—and after you won the game!"

His smile faded. Though we were walking leisurely across a parking lot, his whole body took on a guarded look like he was about to get tackled.

"I just wondered whether they were making that up to sell newspapers," I said, "or if there was really something wrong with you at the game."

He watched me silently. Not a muscle moved in his face.

I asked him, "Are you having problems with somebody because Noah came out?"

"No," he said firmly. "Are you?"

I shrugged. "Kennedy was mad about what Sawyer said at the end of class."

Brody nodded. "I felt bad about leaving you alone in Ms. Patel's room after that. I couldn't tell whether you were upset. You never look like anything bothers you."

"I don't?" I asked, genuinely surprised.

He shook his head but watched me through his shades. As a result, I began to feel very hot and bothered. Heat crept up my neck and along my jawline.

"Now you *do* seem upset," he said. "Kennedy has no right to be mad at you because of something Sawyer said. If he was man enough, he'd take it up with Sawyer."

The idea of this made me uncomfortable. Kennedy was much bigger. Sawyer was more cunning and perhaps a little evil.

We reached the edge of the parking lot and the wooden stairs down to the pavilion. I called over my shoulder, "If it's not Noah, what was bothering you at the game? Or was there anything at all? You won, so the newspaper critiquing *how* you won seems kind of harsh."

He laughed shortly. "I wish the newspaper would hire *you*."

That was a good one. It was all I could do to keep track of which direction the ball was going on the field. I asked, "*Is* there something wrong?"

The pavilion was a large octagon with a vaulted wooden ceiling and thick stucco walls built to withstand tropical storms. Windows cut in all sides gave us a view of the beach. The sound of the ocean echoed inside. Beachgoers tended to use the pavilion as a lunchtime picnic area, or a shelter from the midday sun. In the late afternoon, it was empty.

The shelter was so dark in contrast to the bright day that I had to take off Brody's sunglasses to see. I hung the earpiece on the side string of my bikini bottoms, which I meant to be provocative but probably carried all the sexual overtone of a pair of pliers in a tool belt.

Brody removed his shades too. The shadows overhead descended across his face. The circles under his eyes seemed darker. He blinked and took a long breath. Something *was* wrong.

He set one shoulder against the wall. "Don't tell anybody," he said. "Only Coach knows."

I backed to the stucco beside him. "I'm good at keeping secrets," I promised.

He watched me for a moment and slowly raked his hair out of his eyes. "I got hurt," he said. "That part's not a secret."

"When?" I asked sharply. "It may not be a secret, but *I* didn't hear about it." If I had, I wouldn't have been able to think about anything else. "Are you okay?"

"Don't I look okay?"

"Brody!" I wailed, fed up with his teasing. I didn't want to joke about this.

"Yes, yes, I'm okay," he assured me, waving my concern away. "It happened before school started, in practice. I got dinged."

"Dinged," I repeated. "What's that mean?"

"I got my bell rung."

"Your *bell*," I puzzled. Was that a euphemism for an injury to the jockstrap area? Even Brody would have turned way redder in the face if he was admitting that.

"I got knocked out," he explained.

"Oh!" I gasped. "Brody!"

"It wasn't that bad," he said nonsensically. "It was an accident. The thing is, usually the quarterback doesn't get hit in practice. The whole team is relying on the quarterback during games, so we don't take chances in practice. We just got tripped up this time. We were running a new play. Somebody shoved Noah off balance. He couldn't catch himself, and he elbowed me. *Hard*. I don't know if you've noticed Noah's bony-ass elbows. I fell straight back"—he lifted both forearms and fell back a little to show me—"and landed right on my helmet." He cradled the back of his head in one hand. "At least, that's what they tell me."

"You don't remember?"

"No."

"You had a concussion?" I'd known football was rough, but I couldn't believe I hadn't heard this story before. Why hadn't somebody told me?

Of course, there wasn't a reason for anybody to tell me. Brody and I had had no link with each other until the yearbook elections on the first day of school. And even now . . . a very choice set of circumstances had placed us alone in the beach pavilion.

"Yeah, a concussion. But I recovered quickly, and the doctor was impressed," he said, like he was trying to talk me into something. "The doctor lectured my mom about it, though. A second concussion could be serious. If that happens to me, my mom's pulling me out of football completely. Don't tell anybody, because that's my secret. Only Noah knows." He shrugged. "If my mom nixed my high school career, I could still walk onto a college team, maybe, but my chances of starting would be pretty much over."

"Would you even *want* to play college football if you'd already had two concussions?"

He threw up his hands. I took this to mean that after a second concussion, every possible choice would suck.

I nodded. "The reporter wasn't imagining things. You're being more careful."

"I have to be. When the newspaper said I was so daring and fun to watch, it's not that I had any great talent. I just wasn't scared. And now I am. I don't care about getting hurt, per se, but I don't want my football career to end. It has to end someday, sure, but not *now*." He looked past me, across the pavilion and out a window to the ocean.

"You're talking like you're about to get a second concussion," I pointed out. "How long have you played football? Since your dad started coaching you in third grade, right?"

He blinked at me, surprised.

"That's what Noah told me," I explained.

"Yeah," Brody said slowly, "third grade."

"You've played football since *third grade* without a head injury. Then you get one as a result of a freak accident. There's no reason for you to be playing like you're about to have another."

"Yeah."

"I mean, I don't want you to get a concussion either. That would make it difficult for us to take our Superlatives photo for the yearbook, and I have a deadline!"

He grinned, which made me smile too.

I said, "But if worrying about a concussion makes you lose your magic, your football career is going to be over soon anyway. Might as well play like you mean it."

He nodded, then thought better of it and shook his head. "I don't know how to unworry about it." He tilted his head to one side, considering me. "A few minutes ago when I was trying to look at your eye and I told you to relax, you did, pretty much instantly. You just took a deep breath and did it."

"I have a lot of practice," I said. "It's a coping mechanism. I'm super high-strung."

"*You?*" he asked in disbelief. "You're always so calm."

"Me?" I laughed. "No, I'm not. I was able to relax when you told me because I trust you."

He watched me solemnly as he said, "You shouldn't."

Maybe he meant *You shouldn't trust me with your eye* or *You shouldn't trust me with your granddad's car.* But he was so near, I could only interpret his words as innuendo. *You shouldn't trust me when I'm alone with you.*

I gave him a sexy smile. I didn't have a lot of experience with this, but I attempted it anyway. I said, "Between you loving football and Mr. Oakley trying to explain it to me so I can take pictures of the games, you make even *me* want to play."

Brody raised his eyebrows. "That could be arranged." He glanced around the pavilion. "So, will this place work for our yearbook picture?"

I'd been hoping he wouldn't bring that up, because I didn't want our conversation to end. But maybe *he* did.

"Now that I look at it," I said, "no, it won't work. There's not enough light. We can't take the photo on the beach right now either, because it's too bright. All that white sand tends to mess with the camera's light meter."

Brody widened his eyes at me in fake exasperation. At least, I hoped it was fake. "Don't you have a night setting on your camera?"

"Yeah, but that slows down the shutter speed to let more light in, which means I would need my tripod. The shutter's open too long to keep the camera still if someone's holding it. The picture will be blurry. We should try again on the beach at sunset. The light will be perfect then."

"Does that mean you want to go back to the others?"

I asked, "What else would we do?"

He shrugged dismissively. But he held my gaze as he said, "Get to know each other better. We were voted Perfect Couple. I feel like I hardly know you, even though the senior class thinks you're the love of my life."

7

BRODY'S WORDS SET MY HEART BEATING
rapidly, but I threw back my head and laughed like nothing
was wrong. "You've known me since kindergarten."

He shook his head. "Not really. You look completely different today."

"You mean I look like everybody else," I said ruefully.

"No, ma'am," he said firmly, "you do not."

Speechless, I stared at him. His eyes flicked ever so
briefly to my bikini top, then back up to my face. My chest
and upper arms burned in a delicious way, a feeling I wasn't
ready to give up just because I hadn't brought a tripod.

Now that Kennedy had made motions to forgive me, he
would miss me. He would look around the beach for me. He
would give me the third degree when I eventually returned

to our home base on the towels. But I didn't care about that while Brody was gazing at me.

I was alone with him. Neither of us was going anywhere for a while if we could help it, but I couldn't think of a thing to say to him—which underscored why we were a terrible match in the first place. I wondered if he felt the same way about the title we'd been elected to. I said, "I've been racking my brain about this. Why do you think the class chose us for this?"

"Well, our study hall also chose Sawyer as our representative on the student council, so a good portion of our school is obviously on crack." When he saw my face fall, he said, "The good kind of crack."

"Crack—you know, the nutritional kind."

"Yes."

"Sawyer was the only candidate," I reminded him. "We had no other choice, except to elect nobody. Though come to think of it, maybe that would have been better."

"Look," Brody said, almost impatiently, "here's what I really think about the Superlatives, if you want to know."

"Of course I want to know." He was acting like people usually *didn't* want to know what he thought, which was sad.

He searched my eyes for a moment. Not glancing at my ass or sliding his gaze to my cleavage, but measuring me, as if deciding whether he could trust me on another level.

He said slowly, "I think it's pretty strange for the school to tell students we can't kiss and we're not supposed to hug each other in the halls, then make us vote on two people who should date but don't. I mean, the other titles are bad enough. If you get a good one, like Most Athletic, you feel like you have to live up to it. That's why I'm glad I didn't get something like that."

I wondered if he was telling the whole truth. I bet he would have appreciated getting Most Athletic. It would have caused him a lot less trouble than Perfect Couple That Never Was. I saw his point, though. He was already stressed out about being quarterback. Getting named supreme athlete of the school would have set higher expectations for him and hiked his stress level even more.

He went on, "And what if you got a bad one, like Most Likely to Go to Jail? That's just mean to Sawyer."

"Aw," I said. "It's sweet of you to care. Who did you vote for?"

"I voted for Sawyer, obviously, but it's still mean. I'm predicting the school won't vote on these titles much longer. Somebody's going to sue."

"I don't think so." Most of the titles weren't insulting, and most parents had no idea their kids had received them unless they looked through the yearbook when school was almost over.

"Oh, yes," Brody said, nodding. "The first thing they'll

sue about is a couples title like ours. The rule is that it has to be a girl and a guy. Why not a guy and a guy, or two girls?"

His words floored me. This was the sort of philosophical discussion I would have with Quinn or some other free thinker in journalism class or art class. I wouldn't have predicted this devil's advocate position to come from the mouth of the quarterback.

I shrugged my camera bag off my shoulder, set the case on the floor at my feet, and leaned against the pavilion wall again. "How long have you known about Noah?" I figured that's who we were really talking about.

"Forever," Brody said. "I mean, he actually came out to me in middle school. But we'd been good friends since we started football together in third grade, like you said. I wasn't surprised when he came out."

"Did he ever . . ." I wasn't sure how to ask this, or whether I even should, but I was dying to know. "Were you ever the object of his affection?"

"Why do you ask?" Translation: I shouldn't have asked.

Heart palpitating again at the idea that I'd offended Brody, I hurried on, "You've been super accepting of the whole thing."

He laughed long enough that the tension between us disappeared. Then he said, "Well, middle school is just difficult."

"Yeah."

"Back in middle school, Noah and I did have an uncomfortable five-minute conversation," he admitted. "But you know, I distinctly remember having a crush on Tia back then."

"Tia!"

"Yeah. I think all middle school guys—the straight ones, anyway—fantasize about getting in good with the wild girl. But I realized someday a couple of her boyfriends were going to duel each other in the parking lot. I didn't want to be one of them."

That sounded about right—at least, for the Tia I'd known forever. Tia had turned over a new leaf in the past couple of weeks, since she started dating Will. I asked, "You don't think Will's going to suffer that fate, though, do you?"

"No, opposites attract," he said. "Opposites may repel at first, but in the long run, they're the best thing for each other." He shrugged. "Anyway, I don't think the school should officially pair folks up. People don't naturally operate as permanent couples. You get married and swear that you're one body, operating as one unit. Half the time you unswear it a few years later and swear it again with somebody else. Everybody in my family is divorced. My parents, my grandparents, *everybody*. Christmas day might as well be Halloween, because it's like we're going from house to house, trick-ortreating. People stay individuals as they move through life, in and out of relationships. Being a couple is temporary, like cars in a train. They're detachable so you can switch them around. I'm not saying that's how it *should* be. I'm just saying that's how it *is*."

If Brody had said this to me when we first entered the pavilion, I would have been crushed that he wasn't coming on to me after all. These were not the words of a guy who was interested in a girl and wanted her to be interested in him, too. But we'd been talking for so long, and our conversation had delved so deep, that I no longer thought he was measuring every word against whether it would advance his cause with me. Now he was just telling me the truth.

I said, "My family is like that too."

His mouth twisted. He nodded.

And then, I couldn't let it go, could I? I couldn't just embrace the moment and my newfound, genuine friendship with Brody. I had to bring it back around to my superficial problem, the one that had kept me awake at night for the past two weeks, ever since the Superlatives elections. I asked, "Have you discussed this with Grace?"

He nodded. "I have. I've said all kinds of things to Grace. But did she hear me? I don't know. She has this laugh. Heh! Heh! Heh!"

I knew the laugh. I hated the laugh.

Brody said, "At first you think it's a cute, nervous laugh. Except that's her response to *everything*. She can't possibly feel the same way about *everything*. Or can she?"

My natural inclination was to smooth over arguments. Kaye had scolded me about this numerous times, and I had smoothed over her scolding. My automatic reaction was hard to turn off, obviously, even when I was smoothing over my crush's problems with his girlfriend. Stupidly I suggested, "Maybe it's you, not what you're saying. You make Grace nervous."

"Why would I make her nervous?" Brody grumbled.

Say it. Say it. Say it. Tell the truth. I felt like I was jumping off a cliff as I said it: "Because you're so attractive. Maybe when you get as close to her as you are to me right now, she forgets what she was talking about." It was a big, brazen mouthful, and after I'd gotten it out, I felt my cheeks turn bright red in the heat. I stared up at the vaulted ceiling as if it was very interesting.

Something touched my neck. I nearly put up a hand to brush away a bug. But the touch was Brody's fingertips smoothing along my skin, back and forth across my collarbone.

I hardly knew how to process that he was touching me. I spent more time listening to my brain than paying attention to my body. I was all mind, and my body was just a vehicle to get me from home to class and back again, like my bike or Granddad's car or the public bus. Sure, I put my look together carefully in the morning, and throughout the day I checked the neatness of my clothes and hair. Other than that, I never gave much thought to my body.

Brody reminded me that I was made of bones and skin and muscle. He was connecting my body back to my brain in a way I'd never experienced. I flattened my hand against the rough stucco wall. My palm turned sweaty. His fingertips felt so good stroking me in—let's face it—a first-date, innocent way.

"Is everything okay, Harper? Now you seem tense again." As Brody said this, he massaged my shoulder with a pressure so strong that it fell just short of hurting. It was intense enough, and good enough, that I wished he would do that to me everywhere.

But after a few strokes of his hand, his fingers followed the strap of my bikini, trailing fire, down to cup my breast. He wasn't technically touching me anymore since my bathing suit top separated his skin from mine. But I could feel the pressure of his hand, and the heat of it. Never mind what I'd thought about the innocence of his touch. Electricity arced from his body to mine.

If he felt the same way I did as he slid his thumb back

and forth across my breast, he didn't let on. In the darkness of the pavilion, I couldn't see the green of his eyes, but the shadows underneath were deep. He looked older than me, and serious.

I giggled.

"What's so funny?" he whispered.

"Um, where do I start? Most guys, if they were touching a girl's collarbone and noticed she was acting tense, would take their hands off her before asking after her health, rather than touching her breast." The last word came out as a sigh. I was pretty proud that I'd produced a joke under the circumstances, but inwardly I cringed as I heard myself. I sounded like I wanted him to stop touching me. I didn't.

Incredibly, he was unfazed. "Most guys?" he asked, raising his eyebrows. "You do this enough to have a test group?"

"It's all in the name of science," I said faintly.

"No means no," he said. "They lecture us about this endlessly in PE. Do you want me to stop?"

I shook my head.

"Me neither." He moved toward me. He was about to kiss me.

The nearer he came, the more scrambled my brain got. His lips were so close to my ear that his breath feathered across my cheek.

Suddenly he'd backed away from me. No! I wanted him to kiss me. Hadn't I made that clear?

He nodded toward the nearest arched doorway to the beach. Halfway understanding his message, I jerked my camera bag up by the strap just as Kennedy burst in.

"Harper!" Glancing from me to my camera bag and back to me, he let me hear all the accusation in his voice. "I've been looking everywhere for you."

I smiled. "Sorry. I was right here."

His angry eyes cut to Brody. A breeze from outside caught his wet ponytail and flopped it forward over his shoulder.

Brody didn't do much. He gave Kennedy a subtle look down and back up. I wasn't sure, but I thought this meant, *Come at me, bro, because I can take you.*

Amazingly, I might have been right. Kennedy seemed to get the same message. He didn't engage with Brody. He turned back to me and demanded, "What are you doing?"

I held up my camera bag. "The light's bad, but we were attempting to get our yearbook Superlatives picture out of the way."

"Because her deadline is coming up," Brody chimed in. He said this without a trace of sarcasm. Brody didn't really do sarcasm. But I heard the private joke in his words: Kennedy had been on me to meet this deadline. In a roundabout way, *he* was the one who'd convinced us to stand in a shadowy beach pavilion alone together. *So there.*

Kennedy's burst of anger seemed to have drained away. We'd managed to talk him down, just as I had in journalism class.

Except this time, he had reason to be jealous. Brody was toying with me.

Kennedy told me quietly, "Come on back."

"I will."

He paused a moment more, seemingly weighing the idea of insisting that I come back with him *now*. But he didn't press it. He walked out of the pavilion.

My feelings were a confused tangle, but Brody and I were casual acquaintances indulging a passing flirtation. I knew how this would play out. We would make a little joke about Kennedy and part ways.

"What did I tell you earlier?" Brody asked. "If you're going to break rules, you need to make sure you can get away with it." He stepped toward me. He glanced out the doorway as if to gauge how clearly someone standing outside could see him. Satisfied, he braced one forearm against the wall above my head, exactly how I'd seen Will standing with Tia in the hall at school on Friday. He slid my camera bag strap off my shoulder and set the bag on the tile floor again. He leaned down.

My body knew what he was doing before my brain did. I was still puzzling through his motives. I'd felt guilty enough about flirting, and letting him touch me inappropriately. This was worse. Actually *kissing*, when I had a boyfriend and he had a girlfriend, was officially cheating. Every bit of this spun through my mind as I closed my eyes and lifted my chin. My lips met his.

His mouth was warm and soft. He kissed me gently, his lips brushing along mine, pressing. When I'd pictured making out with Brody—and I had—he'd come at me forcefully, like an athlete battling to win a game. It surprised me that this tough-guy football player could be so tender.

But admittedly, I didn't have a lot of knowhow for a senior in high school. I'd kissed Kennedy, of course, and Noah, and Quinn when he wanted us to be seen, and a few guys before that when they'd brought me home from a date. I'd never had a long, intense session of experimenting with a boy's mouth, though, the kind I'd seen in movies and read about in books, the kind Tia and Kaye had with their boyfriends every weekend.

Afraid I would mess it up and Brody would figure out how naive I was, I let him take the lead. The tip of his tongue teased my lips apart. He swept inside. For long minutes he held my chin cupped in his hand and kissed me harder, deeper. I kissed him back. Finally he kissed his way across my jawline to the side of my neck. I shivered.

His thumb brushed my nipple again.

That's when everything changed for me. A current of electricity shot from my breast straight down to my crotch and pulsed there. He'd been toying with me before. I'd teased him back. Now he knew I wanted him, and so did I. In that one slight touch, every longing rushed back to me for boys who didn't like me as much as I liked them, every regret that other girls had boyfriends who were into them while mine weren't. Brody supplied me with more heat through the pad of his thumb than I'd experienced in my lifetime.

I set my hands on his hips, which were hard as rocks underneath his bathing suit, and pulled him closer.

"Mm," he said against my neck. The syllable sent tingles down my arms. He lifted his mouth. His breath felt so good in my ear that I could hardly stand it—and that was before he touched the tip of his tongue to my earlobe. I gasped.

He slid his entire hand across my bikini top to cup my breast. Then one finger slid underneath the fabric. I shuddered.

"Okay," he said, backing up again and chuckling uncomfortably. "That's as much as we can get away with here."

I stood there stunned for a moment, trying to make sense of what he'd said, as if it hadn't been in English. He was backing off because Kennedy had already checked on me. Since there was no door, we couldn't lock Kennedy out. If he didn't catch us, someone else would. It was a public beach. Right.

I just hadn't thought ahead to how this tryst with Brody would end. We'd fooled around because the school had made us curious about each other. And now he would go back to Grace, and I would go back to Kennedy.

Only, I didn't want to go back to Kennedy. I wanted to stay here with Brody. He was brilliantly lit now, the sun slanting over the planes of his athletic body. The darkness in the pavilion had lifted. Either my eyes had adjusted or the sun had sunk lower to peek directly into the windows. Or maybe my pupils were dilated, which happened to people who were sexually aroused. My knowledge of eleventh-grade anatomy had returned with a vengeance.

"Are you taking your camera back to your car?" Brody asked.

"Yes," I said, kneeling to pick up my expensive, beloved camera that I had completely forgotten about.

"I'll wait here a minute and walk back on the beach so as not to arouse suspicion." He said this in imitation of a spy movie, but he lacked Kennedy's dry sarcasm. With Brody, I was never sure whether he was kidding.

"Okey-doke," I said like a dork. "See you around." Which was worse. I hurried out to the parking lot, unfolding Brody's shades and slipping them on as I went.

"Hey," Brody called behind me, but I'd had enough. I needed to get over my obsession with him. Spending time with him wouldn't help. The more I knew about him, the more I realized he was *not* the guy of my dreams.

He was better.

And he wasn't mine.

8

I CROSSED THE PARKING LOT, LESS STEAMY now that the sun had relented. As I walked, I felt strangely taller, with bigger breasts. I returned my camera to the trunk of Granddad's car, then pulled out my second cooler full of water bottles and lugged it toward the beach.

Along the path, I stopped short and set the cooler down when I saw Will. He lay with his knees bent on a concrete bench that wasn't long enough for him. His body was dappled in shade from the palm trees and scraggly vines that liked to grow in sand. Where the sun found a way through the foliage to him, his skin glowed with sweat. The dog lay beside him. Presumably she would have gone for help if she'd smelled death. But Will was so still.

"Are you okay?" I asked, alarmed.

He opened one eye to peer at me over his shades. "Yeah, just hot." He eased up to sitting, his stomach muscles bunching into hard knots. Like Brody, this boy knew his way around a sit-up.

I refrained from commenting, *I'll say.*

He asked, "Does your eye feel better?"

"I'd forgotten about my eye," I said truthfully, "so it must be okay." Actually, now that he mentioned it, it still stung a little when I blinked.

He asked, "How about the rest of you? Kennedy said he found you and Brody taking your Superlatives picture at the pavilion."

"Was he mad?" I asked quickly.

"He didn't sound particularly mad," Will said. "I just wondered, because you were gone a long time. And I know how being voted something like Perfect Couple can mess with your head."

With a sigh, I sat down beside him and handed him a thermos of water from the cooler, my head spinning all the while about what to say. I was so confused. My lips still tingled from kissing Brody, and a fresh chill washed over me every time I thought about what had happened. Will had become good enough friends with Brody that he might be able to give me some insight—if I could phrase the question in a way that didn't expose me as Brody's wannabe girl-friend.

I asked, "Did you know Brody got knocked out in foot-ball practice?" Brody had said his mom would make him quit if he got another concussion. That was the secret. The fact that he'd gotten hurt in the first place was public knowledge. But *I* hadn't heard this until he told me, and I felt offended that the public had been keeping me in the dark.

Will was in the process of swallowing half the thermos of water in one long pull. Still drinking, he opened one eye and gave me a small nod. He wiped the wet bottle across his forehead. "Before school started, right?"

"Yes."

"But he was okay."

"I guess. Football players may be used to that kind of thing, but as a non–football player, I'm shocked that people get knocked out, the doctor okays them to play, and they're back at practice the next day. Aren't you?"

"No," Will said, "I play hockey. So, you're worried about Brody?"

"I'm more surprised that the class voted Brody and me Perfect Couple and then nobody thinks to tell me that my phantom boyfriend got knocked unconscious in football practice."

Will's brows knit behind his sunglasses. "That happened at least a week before the election."

"Yeah." I supposed I was just fishing for Will to confirm some connection between Brody and me that wasn't even there. "Who did *you* vote for?"

"Nobody," he said. "The election was the first day of school. I couldn't remember anybody's last name except Tia's. And, of course, Sawyer had made an impression by then too."

Of course. "Well, knowing us a little better now, would you put Brody and me together?"

"The way you look and act at school, no. But I'll say this. Brody likes pretty girls. Today, you definitely fit into that category. Not that you weren't pretty before, but now, wow. I don't want to get in trouble with my girlfriend, but you look beautiful."

"That's the nicest thing anyone's ever said to me, Will."

"You're not hanging around the right people."

"Okay." I laughed.

"Seriously, you're not. I think you and I are a lot alike. You're good at school. You get used to praise from teachers and your parents about your academics. Sometimes you forget about the rest of your life."

I took a long drink from my own thermos of water. "Yeah."

"Then you get elected Perfect Couple, and you realize that other people see you as something more than a walking, talking brain. Or, something *different*. That's how I felt when I was voted Biggest Flirt. I mean, hello? I was so worried about what my parents would think. I wanted a title that said 'Achievement.'" He spanned his hands in front of us, like framing his title in lights on a movie marquee. "Not . . . I don't know."

I framed my own movie title. "'Social Life.'"

"Yeah. I wasn't known for that at my old school. So I understand if you're kind of . . ." He trailed off, afraid of offending me.

I helped him out. "Obsessed with it."

Clearly that was the word he'd been too polite to use first. "Obsessed," he repeated. "I'll tell you, Brody was thrilled about getting paired with you."

"He was?"

"Yeah. And today . . ." Will gestured to me. His hand stopped in midair, roughly on a parallel with my stomach. I wasn't sure what he meant by this until he said, "Brody was happy to see you. And he was even happier to see you looking like you do today."

"Ah."

"And I know this is none of my business, but he has a girlfriend."

I took another sip of water and said slowly, "I know."

"I don't think Brody takes any of this seriously," Will

said. "Not the elections, not dating. You take it *very* seriously, like I do. That was my whole problem at first with Tia."

"I get it."

He drained the rest of his water and handed the thermos back to me.

"Here." I dug another bottle out of the ice for him and pointed toward the pavilion. "Go lie down in there, where it's actually cool. I'll tell Tia where you went."

"Thanks." He stood and turned down the sandy path. The dog jerked to her feet in one motion and followed him.

"No, thank *you*." As I watched Will go, I heard my own nonsensical words. *No, thank* you *for telling me the guy I have a crush on has no real interest in anybody, including me.*

Except that Will had compared Brody and me to Tia and himself.

And he and Tia were now together.

Did I have a chance with Brody?

No, that was ridiculous. To accept that interpretation of what he'd said, I would have to ignore his whole exposition on *Brody already has a girlfriend and it isn't you.*

Frustrated with myself, I stomped back to the towels, kicking up more sand than necessary, and threw myself down next to Tia.

"What's wrong?" she asked with her eyes closed. She

didn't even look over to see who'd collapsed next to her. Tia was laid back, and I envied her.

"This is not what's wrong," I said, "but I sent Will to the pavilion because he was melting."

"He claims he's normal and Floridians are made of asbestos. What's wrong with *you*? Does your eye still hurt? Will said you had a real problem with your contact and Brody came to your rescue while Kennedy just sat there."

"My eye is better." Then I said flatly, "And I went to the pavilion and made out a little bit with Brody."

Instantly she rolled over on her side. Her dark eyes were wide. "You don't make out a little bit. The definition of 'making out'— Where's my phone?" She felt underneath her towel. "Without even looking it up, I can tell you that 'making out' means you're hot and heavy. You can't do it halfway."

I told her solemnly, "So I made out with Brody."

"You're turning into me," she breathed, pretending to be horrified.

"No. You've made out with random people, and Sawyer. But you never had a boyfriend before Will, so you were never cheating. I'm a cheater." Honestly, I didn't care about this as much as I should have.

She shrugged as best she could while lying on one arm. "Brody's a cheater too."

"Yeah," I said, looking down the beach for him. He'd stopped about halfway from the pavilion with his back to me and his hands on his hips. Grace, Cathy, and Ellen walked toward him, presumably victorious after their foray for beer. Ellen staggered a little.

Tia still watched me. "Will told me he was going to warn you about Brody."

"He did, after it was too late." I looked around us to make sure nobody had plopped down near us on the towels. Then I admitted, "Brody felt me up a little."

"Oh, good Lord!" Tia cried.

"Oh, you can't get felt up halfway either?" I asked quickly. "Then Brody felt me up a *lot*. Don't tell Kaye. Grace is sure to ask her what she knows. Kaye can't spill it if she doesn't have the info."

Tia propped herself up on one elbow. "Can I just ask what the *fuck* you think you're doing?"

I gasped. "Are you *judging* me?"

"Of course I'm not judging you!" Tia exclaimed. "I'm just wondering what's gotten into you. The day of the elections, I told you to go after Brody, and you just reminded me you already had Kennedy. Today you're setting up clandestine meetings and letting Brody grope your bosom."

I laughed so hard at her phrasing that I sucked in some

sand and spent the next minute spitting it out and wiping it off my tongue. Continuing to giggle didn't help this process.

Finally I sighed and said, "This whole election has shaken me out of my comfort zone. I thought all I wanted was to spend a little time with Kennedy, and take pictures, then sit at home by myself and tweak them on the computer. But if this is supposed to be the most exciting time of my life, I'm wasting mine. The rest of the United States comes to Florida for adventure. I actually *live* here and I don't have any fun at all."

"You started taking pictures *because* it was fun," she pointed out.

"True." Tia and I hadn't worked through any of my problems, but I felt better talking to her. She was so upbeat about everything. My mood had improved. I sat up on my towel, half expecting the beach to hold wondrous surprises for me after all.

Cathy was still walking and Ellen was still staggering in our direction, but Grace had stopped where Brody stood. His head blocked her face from view. I couldn't tell what they were saying or how intense it was. All I saw was that he had one hand on either side of her bikini bottoms. And the pavilion where we'd just spent a very interesting half hour together was in his direct line of sight. That's how much our meeting had meant to him.

"Fuck everybody," I murmured to Tia, "and that's not a quote from Sawyer. Catch you later. I'm going swimming." I jumped up, ran across the sand, and plunged into the water, swimming way out and diving deep. This had been my coping mechanism for countless school gatherings and birthday parties when interacting with others became too much for me. None of that—really nothing about me—had changed just because I'd made out with Brody.

I floated on my back in the warm ocean. Here on the Gulf, the waves weren't high like they were on the Atlantic coast. Occasionally a big one would crash over my face and I'd snort salt water, but mostly the tide rocked me, lifting my head and then my toes like I was a strand of seaweed or a kid's floating toy.

After a while, I turned on my stomach and did the dead man's float—or dead chick's float, in this case—and tried to return to the me I'd been this morning before the race, the one who wanted nothing more than to dot *i*'s and cross *t*'s with nobody bothering her. *That* me wouldn't mind when Brody had his hands on Grace's bikini. *That* me would accept Brody returning to Grace as the natural order of things. *That* me would know his kiss with me had been an impulse, like his four speeding tickets last year, and another ticket for toilet papering the football coach's yard. My stomach hurt.

I felt something flutter against my stomach. This time I wasn't fooled. It was no fish brushing against me. A boy had crept up on me and thought it was funny to pretend to support me as I levitated in the water. I knew it wasn't Brody, who didn't do anything halfway. He would have wrapped his whole arm around my waist and scooped me up. This touch, so light I could barely feel it, was Kennedy.

I surfaced, letting the water stream down my face, careful not to rub my eyes. Kennedy smiled smugly in front of me like he'd *really* surprised me that time! I laughed drolly just to keep the peace.

I wouldn't have felt so indifferent about him last week. One interlude with Brody had ruined my relationship with Kennedy—without Kennedy even finding out!—and I wasn't sure I cared.

"Do you want to leave?" Kennedy asked.

Together? I almost asked in an astonished voice. But I wasn't going to prolong my argument with Kennedy when Brody was all over Grace. I hadn't glanced toward the beach since I entered the water, but I imagined Brody had taken her into the pavilion. That was a euphemism all Brody's love interests could use, the Brody's Fling Club. *Did he take you to the pavilion?*

"This isn't fun," Kennedy said. I'd gotten so lost in my

own thoughts again that I'd almost forgotten he was there, complaining. "Funny how one jock turns the entire vibe into a fraternity mixer."

There were two jocks here, counting Noah—three if you counted Will, even though our school didn't have a hockey team. I assumed Kennedy was referring to Brody.

"No, I'm not ready to leave," I said. "The sun hasn't even set."

"We have school tomorrow," Kennedy said. "Are all the Superlatives pictures ready for me?"

"Not yet."

"I need them."

"It's a holiday, and we still have a week and a half until the deadline."

"What's the matter with you?" Kennedy asked. "You're so crabby. Do you have PMS?"

I whirled to face him. The movement of my shoulders made a spiral wave like I was a hurricane. The wave sped toward him and hit him in the mouth as I said, "Listen. Never ask a girl that. It's offensive."

"That answers my question," he said.

A female could never win this argument. I said anyway, "I don't see how you can claim to be such a progressive thinker but make that kind of comment to a woman."

"Sor-*ry!*" he exclaimed.

"You know what?" I asked, my voice rising over the noise of the surf. "You offended me Friday with your meltdown about my friends and my *cupcakes*, for God's sake. Now you've decided I've been punished enough, and you're not mad at me anymore. Well, maybe *I'm* mad at *you*. And I deserve an apology. Not a 'sor-*ry!*' but a real one."

He gaped at me. I stared right back at him. A large wave smacked me in the back of the head and threatened to knock me down. I dug my heels into the sand and held my ground.

Kennedy sighed. "I wasn't saying anything against gays, just that I'm not one. I hear my dad in my head a lot. You haven't met my dad."

I shook my head.

"My dad doesn't approve of my piercing, and he doesn't like my hair." He reached back to grip the ponytail at his nape. "Or enjoy indie films. You should hear what he calls me."

I nodded. I didn't have to meet his dad to identify the type. Plenty of men with this attitude had made their beliefs known during breakfast at the B & B, assuming everyone else agreed with them. Little did they know that gay couples had slept in their beds a few days before.

"At our age," Kennedy went on, "what your dad says should roll off you, right? But for me, it doesn't."

"Me neither," I said. I meant my mom.

"I probably won't get to go to film school," he said. "I might not make it to college at all. My dad doesn't understand why I can't stay here and take over the plumbing business, since the money's good."

In a matter of minutes, Kennedy had transformed in front of me. Knowing what he was dealing with at home clarified why he acted the way he did, and where his anger came from.

But understanding him better didn't help me like him. I should have encouraged him to go to film school no matter what his dad said. At some point, I had stopped caring. I pictured him in ten years, a long-haired plumber claiming he could have gone to film school if he'd wanted, and making bitter comments about blockbuster movies that everyone else loved.

Instead of comforting him about his home life, I surprised myself by saying this: "You can't give me the silent treatment anymore."

"What?"

"The silent treatment. You get mad at me and stop speaking to me for days. I can't stand it, and I'm not going to put up with it. My mom and dad did that to each other when my dad still lived at home."

Kennedy stared at me across the water, like *he* was now having a revelation about *me*. A wave hit him in the chin, then another. Still he watched me.

Finally he said, "Me! *You* give *me* the silent treatment."

"I certainly do not," I said.

"You never say anything."

"I'm saying something right now. I hear myself speaking."

"You're excruciatingly quiet. Dating you is like being given the silent treatment *all the time*."

Well, maybe he shouldn't date me, then, if it was such torture. Maybe we should break up. These words were on my lips as I glanced toward shore.

Damn my contacts, giving me excellent distance vision. Against my will, I focused on the island of our towels and umbrellas. Grace and Brody were sitting up, facing us, her body tucked between his spread legs. He massaged her shoulders.

Instead of breaking up with Kennedy, I grumbled, "Why don't we ever make out?" If I was trying to prove to him that I was sane and logical and *not* on my period, the question wasn't going to help. At this point, I just wished I could put on a show for Brody akin to the one he was putting on for me.

"What are you talking about?" Kennedy asked. "We *do* make out."

Something told me the way we'd kissed wouldn't meet

Tia's standards for "making out," even a little. I asked, "Do you ever want to get down and dirty?" I sounded like an ad for an Internet porn site. I wasn't sure how else to phrase it. A guy like Brody wouldn't have cared how I put it. He would have accepted the invitation without question.

"That just seems cheap," Kennedy said. "It doesn't even sound appealing."

"I'm kidding," I said. "You're right—the whole day's had a fraternity mixer vibe. I guess it's rubbing off on me."

"Do you want to leave?" he repeated.

"I'm not ready to leave," I repeated.

"Let's get out of the water, at least," he said.

Sitting next to him on a towel, listening to him make jokes, wouldn't be any more titillating than standing next to him in the ocean, listening to him make jokes. But there was no way I would refuse his company after what I'd seen Brody do with Grace.

We sloshed toward land. Grace lay on a towel now, with Cathy and Ellen beside her. Brody was tossing a football with Will—"tossing" in this case meant he was bulleting it fifty yards. He wasn't touching Grace anymore, but I'd seen what I'd seen.

As a last-ditch attempt at not resenting Kennedy so much, I gave him an opening to make me feel good about myself. He didn't even have to make up a compliment. I saved him the trouble. I shouted over the noise of the surf, "Do you like my new bikini?"

"You look like a lifeguard," he said. It was like the time I'd worn a cute, structured blazer to a party and he'd said I looked like a man, and the time I'd worn a gauzy black mini-dress and he'd said I looked like a wiccan.

After we reached shore, he patted a place for me on his towel—*gee, thanks!*—and we settled side by side, not touching. Sitting next to each other on a towel was his idea of serious physical involvement. What if he made it to film school after all, and we were still dating in college? Would we sit next to each other on a blanket spread out on the quad? Was this how snarky intellectuals got knocked up?

"Ladies and gentlemen." Brody stood at the edge of the towel island, bouncing the football back and forth between his hands without looking at it. The ball was so familiar to him that it might as well have been part of him. "It's time for football. Touch football, so girls can play too."

Grace sat up and raised both hands. "I'm on your team, Brody!" she slurred.

"Drunks can't play football," Brody said. "Seriously, you'll get hurt. But you can cheer."

The drunk cheerleaders high-fived each other in response. Cathy called, "Can we cheer sitting down?"

Disgusted, I closed my eyes and lay back on my towel.

"Brody," I heard Noah call, "if you get hurt, Coach will kill you."

"He won't get hurt," I said to the air. "Just don't fall on him, Noah."

"Ooooooh," everyone around me moaned.

"Ha, good one," Kennedy commented.

Hooray, I'd qualified for the Snark Olympics. I hadn't meant what I'd said to be that funny. I hoped Noah wasn't mad. I opened one eye to look for him.

He was crawling across the towels toward me. When he reached me, he leaned so far over me that I felt a little uncomfortable. Out of the corner of my eye, I saw Kennedy leaning back to get out of Noah's way.

Noah rubbed the tip of my nose with his, just as he'd done when we dated. And weirdly, though I knew he wasn't attracted to me, butterflies fluttered in my stomach the way they had before he came out to me. He growled, "You know I'm going to get you during this game, don't you?"

I giggled. Kennedy scowled beside me. Noah had taken this flirtation too far, and I had let him. If I didn't end this, Kennedy would start giving me the silent treatment again, and I Just. Could. Not. Take it. I turned to Kennedy and asked, "Want to play?"

"Want to drive some bamboo under our fingernails later?" Kennedy asked.

"I'll take that as a no." I told Noah, "I'm not playing." I hoped Brody heard me.

After Noah walked off, Kennedy told me, "Sit up. This should be pretty good. Football oafs, the band's drum major, girls, a dog, the student council president, and a gay Goth in hand-to-hand combat? If only the drunk cheerleaders were allowed in, we'd really have a show."

I did think it would be a show. I also thought it would be infinitely more fun to be part of it rather than watching it, but I wasn't going to play when Brody was the one organizing. Obedient to Kennedy, I sat up and watched the teams gathering and dividing themselves.

Brody jogged out of the crowd. He reached our towel and held out one hand to me. "I thought you wanted to play football."

I stared way up at him. His green eyes sparkled in his tanned face. He beckoned to me like the devil. I wanted *so badly* to play. But I knew taking his hand would be a slap in the face to Kennedy. And there was no sense in goading Kennedy to give me the silent treatment over a football game at the beach, when there was nothing waiting for me as a consolation prize. Brody was just toying with me again.

I opened my mouth to say no. Instead, a yelp escaped

from my lips as I was grabbed around the waist from behind. Noah had disrespected the towel island by tracking sand right through it. He hoisted me onto his shoulder.

I told him to put me down, my voice lilting in time with his footsteps across the beach, but I didn't protest too much. I wanted Brody to know I was mad at him for having his hands all over Grace, but I *did* also want to play football. This was the kind of Florida fun I was sick of missing out on. Noah was getting me where I wanted to go, in a way that Kennedy would have no reason to complain about later. As Kennedy sat alone on his towel, I felt incredibly lucky to have a gay ex-boyfriend. Noah set me down gently on my bare feet in the middle of the huddle.

Brody, bent over with one hand on his knee and his other holding the football against his hip, was lecturing the teams. He stopped in midsentence. "Harper. Thanks for joining us finally." He stared at me and I stared back, acknowledging the heat between us.

"As I was saying," he continued, "this is two-hand touch football. No tackling. If somebody gets two hands on you, consider yourself down. How else should we change the rules while ladies are playing?" He paused and squinted into the sun, thinking. "No nudity. If you pull off someone's bathing suit, that's a penalty. Like, a one-yard penalty."

"I don't know," I spoke up. "If you manage to get some-body's bathing suit off, I think you should gain a yard, because that would be pretty difficult and you should get a reward."

"Harper," Brody said over the laughter, "you are my kind of girl. You're on my team, by the way."

Across the huddle, Kaye raised her brows at me.

"Wait a minute," Aidan said. "I missed something. How are we choosing the teams?"

Everyone in the huddle seemed to move a fraction of an inch backward. Aidan was the student council president, and he liked to govern *everything*.

"The teams should be equally weighted in terms of foot-ball experience," Aidan said, "and . . . I don't know. Height?"

"Watch it," Tia said.

"I wasn't talking to you," Aidan said.

"Parliamentary procedure," Kaye spoke up, because she was the student council vice president and had twice as much sense as Aidan. "Who thinks we should re-divide the teams con-sidering football experience, height, and whatever else Aidan deems worthy? This will take roughly six hours. All opposed?"

"Nay," said everyone.

"Aye," Aidan said testily.

"Ready?" Brody asked quickly, before Aidan could make a more detailed argument.

"Break!" all the guys said, clapping their hands and moving away, while most of the girls were left wondering what had happened. Kaye grabbed Aidan and used two fingers to curve the corners of his mouth up into a smile. Silently I wished her luck with that, because Aidan didn't like it when she usurped his authority. I hurried after Brody.

I'd assumed this would be a pretty boring game: Brody scoring for his team, Noah scoring for his, and the rest of us standing around watching. But the two-hands-and-you're-out rule made the competition exciting. Girls really could play. Tia got good at sidestepping Will and slapping two hands on Brody, sacking him. Other tackles weren't so clear cut. Did your hands have to be flat on the person you were tackling? Did one hand plus one pinkie count? After a couple of scores, we'd had so many arguments about the rules that Will asked Kennedy to referee. Of course he said yes to *this*. The job massaged his ego and met his need to feel superior.

His first ruling came when Brody tossed me the ball and I ran for the goal line. Noah stopped my run by picking me up with one arm around my gut—oof!—and setting me down facing the opposite direction, making the whole game with girls into a joke. I promptly spun and ran, not stopping again until I crossed the line.

"Score!" I hollered. "Noah didn't touch me with two hands."

Noah's side yelled, "Booooo." My side yelled, "Ooooh." Brody dashed across the sand, picked me up, and twirled me around in victory. I wasn't sure how much of this Kennedy saw. Six people already stood in front of him, arguing for their sides. I knew I'd won the point when my team cheered and Noah cried, "Damn it!" with his hands on his head.

"It has to be a two-hand touch!" Kennedy defended his call.

"You're just letting your girlfriend's team win!" Aidan exclaimed.

Kennedy shrugged and said slyly, "Privilege of being a referee." He winked at me.

Clearly he *hadn't* seen Brody twirl me around. I knew my current limbo between boys wasn't what healthy, wholesome relationships were made of, but at the moment I didn't care. I was mostly naked and testing my body along with lots of other mostly naked friends on a hot evening. Sand stuck to my skin with sweat. I tingled with exertion and the knowledge that two guys desired me. Whatever happened tomorrow, this was the night of my life.

"Pretty sunset," Kaye called.

We all stopped and looked out over the Gulf. Daylight had faded. The change had been so gradual that I hadn't noticed. Now the bottom edge of the orange sun balanced on the rippling surface of the ocean, then disappeared.

As the light grew tawny and soft, Will walked up behind Tia. He wrapped one arm around her. She backed against him until their bodies tucked neatly together as they watched the sunset. He kissed her neck.

I burned with jealousy—not of Tia, but of the sweet relationship she had with Will. In contrast, I was caught between dating Kennedy in name only—he held his ground on the sidelines of our game and hadn't bothered to come any closer to me during this time-out—and making out with Brody, who was more attached to Grace.

At least Brody wasn't enjoying the sunset with *her*, either. After the drunk cheerleaders' boast, I hadn't heard a single "Get fired up!" out of any of them. They lay on the towels and might have been asleep.

Once the sun started sinking below the horizon, it slipped behind bright pink clouds and into the ocean in a matter of minutes. "That's it for me," Brody announced. "It must be almost eight, and I have homework."

"Homework?" someone shouted. Another guy said, "Traitor!"

Brody held up his hands. "What can I say? I'm the school's scholar-athlete."

"You have, like, a three-point-one," Noah grumbled. "But I have to go too, or my mama will kill me."

Everyone else murmured their good-byes. We reluctantly disassembled the towel island. Gathering my towel and bag and two ice chests, I was surprised when Kennedy came up behind me. "See you in class," he said.

"Okay," I said brightly, as if I looked forward to it.

"And I need more of those Superlatives photos so I can work on the section," he added.

"Gotcha." That meant I would be up past midnight to put together something to show him, after I worked on the race photos. I watched him walk toward the parking lot, laughing with Quinn. I wondered whether the holiday had been worth it.

I'd hugged Tia and Kaye good-bye and had just realized with dismay that I would have to make two trips to lug the ice chests all the way to my car, when I saw Brody sauntering toward me with his towel around his neck. All the men in fashion magazines would be wearing the bulky terry-cloth scarf as haute couture on the runways next season. Brody made a beach towel look that good.

Yes, my holiday had definitely been worth it.

9

BRODY GRINNED AT ME. "HOW'S YOUR EYE?"

"Perfect," I lied. It still stung whenever I blinked. Probably I should wear my glasses to school tomorrow. Probably I wouldn't.

I wished Brody and I could pick up where we'd left off in the pavilion, but I wouldn't give him the satisfaction after he'd let Grace hang all over him. And I couldn't help but throw a little barb at him. "You're not driving Grace home, even though she's been drinking? Are you trying to get rid of her?" That would be the meanest joke if she lost a battle with a live oak tonight, but I couldn't imagine he'd really let her get behind the wheel.

"The drunks all rode here with Kaye."

He certainly seemed dismissive of his girlfriend, placing her in the collective of "drunks." He hadn't seemed so dismissive of her when he was holding her hips, or rubbing her shoulders while she sat between his thighs.

Without asking whether I needed help, he picked up one of my ice chests. "You haven't emptied this?" He pulled the plug in the bottom to let the water out.

"No!" When he looked up at me in surprise, I explained, "You're wasting water. If you're going to empty it, at least do that where the plants get watered." I nodded toward a palm grove.

"Anything that needs watering isn't native to the area," he said.

I laughed before I remembered I was supposed to be mad. "Brody Larson," I scolded him, "are you trying to out-environmentally conscious me?"

"No, ma'am." He turned his head and eyed me slyly. "Well, maybe. Come on, let's water your aspens or Rocky Mountain firs or whatever."

We dumped the water on some obviously nonnative flowers, then carried the coolers back to Granddad's car. As Brody shut the hatchback, he asked, "So, what about our yearbook picture?"

"It's too late now," I said solemnly. I meant for the picture. I meant for us, too.

His face fell. "Is it?"

"Yep," I said firmly. Then I sighed and looked up at the twilit clouds, which were rapidly fading into the night. "Seriously, it's too dark. The picture won't turn out. I still need to take it for my deadline, though." At the thought of all the photos looming, dread formed a knot in my stomach.

"That's okay. We'll just have to try again," Brody said happily.

"Yeah." After today, I knew I should take this picture with as little fuss as possible before I fell farther for him, or *went* farther *with* him. But if he suggested a new meeting place, I wasn't going to say no. "We could go back to my original idea of taking it in the school courtyard, just to be done with it. It's going to be hard to get what we want with a lot of other people watching, though."

"You're right about that." He almost sounded like he meant something else. Something more personal. Something very private.

He cleared his throat. "I have football practice every night this week, and when it's over, my mom wants me home. For some reason, she makes me do my homework."

"How odd."

"I still like your fake-date idea, though," he said, "and we have to eat. What if we met at the Crab Lab for dinner tomorrow? We could make that look like a date."

"We *could* make that look like a date," I agreed. And I would look forward to it like a date. I knew this was a bad idea, but today I'd found out how much fun Brody's bad ideas could be.

The next evening, I stepped out of the house wearing high-heeled sandals, shorts, and a pretty, flowing top. I knew I looked stylish. But I *felt* dressed down to the point of ridiculous, like Tia occasionally wearing her pajamas to school, with or without a bra, when she woke up late. I told myself I was uncomfortable only because I was used to wearing the 1960s-style high-necked trapeze dresses I'd made. Showing a normal amount of skin made me feel like I was letting it all hang out.

The last thing I needed was a commentary from Mom. But there was no getting around her. She was replacing the flowers at the base of the sign in the front yard of the B & B.

"Look at you!" she called. "Without the glasses, I hardly recognize my own daughter. Don't you look cute!" She wanted me to tell her that she'd been right about my contacts, and I'd been wrong.

Walking over, all I grumbled was "Thanks."

"Meeting Kennedy for a date?" She eyed the camera bag slung over my shoulder.

"No, I have to take some photos. I'm just grabbing dinner while I'm there."

She sat back on her bare heels and pushed her hair out of her eyes with one dirty garden glove. "I don't like you spending so much time on these photography jobs you're inventing for yourself."

She made my work at the 5K yesterday sound imaginary. It was hopeless to argue with her, though, so I only said, "It's not a job. This is for school."

"But you're going to all that effort at the yearbook to get into a college art program, right?"

"Yes," I said carefully, wondering where she was going with this. The way she phrased it, an art degree was a bad thing.

"I just think you're wasting a lot of time on this," she said, "working your fingers to the bone for nothing. You don't have to go to college. You can run the B & B with me, right here. Stop making work for yourself, and use your time to help me. I need you."

"No, thanks," I said faintly, even though I got the impression she was telling me, not asking me. "I've never wanted to run the B & B. I've always wanted to be an artist."

"You could still be an artist," she said. "You can take pictures in your spare time, just like you do now. Why would you need to go to college for that? Your grandfather never went to college, and look at the beautiful paintings he produces."

"Granddad was an insurance salesman," I reminded her. "He didn't need an art degree because he never tried to make a living as a painter. In fact, I think that's what drives him to paint so much now. He never took a chance and studied what he wanted for all those years, and now he's making up for lost time." I didn't add, *That's probably why he's crazy.*

She shook her head. "Painting gives him an excuse to lock himself in his house and never talk to anyone. But you and I have the perfect life over here. Business is getting better. Our finances would be better if you took on more of the work so I didn't have to hire so much out. And, Harper, the snowbirds would go *crazy* over a mother and daughter running a B & B. They would flock here."

"I have an appointment," I said. "Let's talk about this later." I hurried away as fast as I could in high heels on the soft earth, crossing my fingers this would be one of those weeks my mother was too busy for me.

I clopped down the brick sidewalk into town and swung open the door to the Crab Lab. Inside was dark. At first all I could see were the white lights strung over and around the old crab traps high on the walls. Over the doorway to the kitchen hung an antique diving suit with a picture of the University of Florida Gator mascot taped behind the mask. After my eyes adjusted to the dim light, they skimmed over the other diners and fell on Brody in a booth for two in the back corner. He was watching me.

He stood. His hair was damp from his shower after practice, and long enough that it curled at the ends. Instead of his usual all-purpose gym clothes, he wore khaki shorts and a green striped button-down shirt that made his eyes look even greener. When I reached him, he took me gently by the elbow and said, "You look nice," in my ear. He kissed my temple—which struck me as something adult friends would do when they met in public and were pretending not to have an affair. Something my dad must have done a million times.

We sat down. "Sorry," I said. "Am I late?"

"I'm early," he said quickly, sounding almost nervous. He lowered his eyes as if he was embarrassed. Brody Larson, nervous and embarrassed around a girl: me! Surely I was reading him wrong, but in my fantasy he was affected by my presence, which was adorable.

Then I noticed the long splint on the middle finger of his left hand. A metal brace kept his finger straight, forcing him to shoot the bird perpetually.

"Brody! Did you break your finger?"

"Oh." He looked at it like he hadn't noticed. "Maybe. Probably not. I'm supposed to have it x-rayed tomorrow."

I gaped at him. "Does it hurt?"

He shrugged.

"Well, excuse my concern," I said, laughing. "I tend to overreact. I thought I was going to die from a contact lens gone haywire yesterday."

"You were really in pain, though," he said. "It's hard to think about anything else when you can't open your eye."

"True," I admitted, instantly feeling fifty percent less stupid. Brody did that for me a lot—made me feel less stupid rather than more. It was a strange sensation after weeks and weeks of Kennedy.

"Anyway," Brody said, "the hurt finger isn't on my throwing hand, so who cares?"

"Right!" I said with gusto. "How did practice go—besides possibly breaking a bone, but not a bone you care about?"

He shrugged again, and his mouth twisted sideways in a grimace.

I was afraid I knew what his expression meant. I asked, "Still being too careful when you play?"

"Yes," he said, "but we're also having the other problem you asked about yesterday. Guys on the team are being dicks about Noah."

"Yeah." I couldn't imagine having to put up with teasing or worse from a bunch of ultra-macho guys with something to prove.

"If Noah and I weren't friends," Brody said, "I might be the one being a jerk. I feel like a terrible person."

It took me a moment to decipher what he meant. "I feel like a terrible person" coming from Kennedy would have been sarcastic, but Brody didn't play that game. As I worked through his words, I murmured, "You honestly feel bad for something you *didn't* do?"

"No, I said if Noah and I weren't friends—"

"But you *are* friends," I said. "I mean, this kind of self-flagellation is what *I* do. But in your case, it makes zero sense. You *are* friends with Noah, and you've had his back. When he and I went out last year, he talked about how supportive you've been. *That's* the type of person you are."

Maybe it was just the dim restaurant lighting, but the shadows under Brody's eyes looked darker than ever as he said, "You always make me feel better." He said this seriously, like it was a bad thing.

"That's exactly what you do for people," I said. "You make everybody feel more comfortable."

"No, that's what *you* do," he said.

He was right. I wasn't sure I *did* make people feel more

comfortable, but I tried. Maybe Brody and I were a lot more alike than I'd thought.

"You're an advocate for Noah," I assured him. "You don't have to give a speech about it or scold anybody. All you have to do is stand by him, because guys look to you as an example. You're the center of attention and the anchor of the team. You're so all-American, you might as well have the US flag tattooed on your forehead."

"Really?" he asked so sharply that I automatically responded, "No, of course not."

He eyed me. "You're saying I'm so unpredictable that I'm predictable. A football player who's everybody's friend, and who gets in a little trouble, but has a heart of gold."

I was shocked. That was *exactly* what I meant. And I could tell by his tone that he took it as an insult.

"I was kidding."

"It is what it is," he said. "That's not how I feel, but that's how people see me, and I have no argument with it, really." He spread his hands. The splint on his finger clicked against the tabletop. "Your observations about people are interesting. You don't have to back off just because I question you. I'm not Kennedy. I don't have to win the point every time."

I opened my mouth to respond, but I didn't know what to say. I'd resented Kennedy's power trip yesterday, but I'd thought I was just in a bad mood, crushing on Brody after he brushed me off. I hadn't realized my interaction with Kennedy was obvious enough for someone else to take note.

And I was *very* interested that Brody had noticed.

"Do you think I'm too quiet?" I asked timidly. "Kennedy tells me I hardly say anything, like I'm giving him the silent treatment."

"You speak when you have something to say, unlike Kennedy, who mouths off about movies nonstop until somebody tells him to shut up. Then he sulks and refuses to talk."

He had *that* right. "How do you know?" I asked. "I didn't think you and Kennedy were friends."

"I've had PE with him since kindergarten."

Sawyer appeared beside our booth with a tray. He wore a Crab Lab T-shirt. A white waiter's apron was tied around his waist. His blond hair seemed even brighter than usual in the dimly lit restaurant. He set a diet soda in front of me and a glass of iced tea in front of Brody.

"Thanks," I said. "We missed you at the beach yesterday."

"You could have found me right here." He moved to the next table.

Brody squeezed a lemon wedge into his tea. "Did Sawyer take our drink orders?"

I thought about it. "I guess not. I always get a soda, though." I tasted it. "Diet."

"And I always get tea." Brody tasted his. "Sweet tea. I guess he's cut out the taking-your-order step."

"Does that make him a good waiter or a very bad waiter?"

We both laughed. When we couldn't sustain that anymore, we both looked toward Sawyer as if he would give us something else to say. Especially after I'd shared how self-conscious I was about being quiet, I couldn't run out of words now! I wanted to talk about Kennedy some more, and then again, I didn't.

Suddenly I was aware of how Brody and me sitting together in this dark booth would look to anyone else from school. I reminded myself that we had a perfectly legitimate excuse to be here together.

I dredged up the courage to say, "I wish I'd applied for yearbook editor."

"Really?" Brody asked.

"Yeah . . ." I examined the paper placemat. "Maybe Kennedy would have gotten the position anyway, but I avoided even trying. It would be torture to have to tell people what to do and deal with them if they didn't."

Brody nodded. He knew plenty about that from being quarterback.

"But I didn't apply," I said. "And now Kennedy is in charge of the yearbook. He's in charge of *me*. I thought he had an eye for design, which is what made me like him in the first place. It turns out that he just talks the talk. I cringe every time he sets one of the photos I worked so hard on at some weird angle, or makes it so small that the detail is lost, or so large that the resolution won't support the image."

"I don't know anything about that stuff," Brody said, "but even I can tell you're great at what you do. Everybody is saying you take terrific photos for the Superlatives. You have a reputation for making people look better than they do in real life."

I laughed. "It's called lighting."

"You shouldn't downplay it," he said. "People will keep these yearbooks. When they show them to their kids in twenty years, they may not recall posing for the photos, but they'll see your results. You're framing how they'll remember themselves forever."

You always make me feel better, I thought.

"I guess you're majoring in art in college," he said.

"That was my plan," I said. "My mom told me a few minutes ago that I should drop my photography jobs, forget college, and help her run the B & B."

"No," Brody said in the authoritative tone that was becoming familiar.

"'No' what?" I asked.

"No," he said, "that's all wrong for you. People who cater to tourists around here are outgoing. You like meeting people, but only from behind a camera lens. You don't want to interact with strangers constantly. That would be a nightmare for you."

I laughed at how right he was. "My mom says it would look quaint, just what Yankees are looking for, a mother-daughter B & B."

"Who cares how it looks?"

"She does," I said. "And, hey—speaking of how things look—that shot I snapped of you and Will and Noah at the 5K will be on the front page of the local paper tomorrow."

"Wow!" he exclaimed.

"Yeah! I'm sure it's because you're a local celebrity."

He gave the restaurant a parade wave.

"But I was so much prouder of that picture than I've ever been of some sweet beach scene. I've studied form and color and setting up the perfect static shot, but what really excites me is catching people in action, the way a photo can tell the story of who they are. Maybe I shouldn't go into art after all. I could try photojournalism."

He opened his hands. "That would be great. Why don't you do it?"

I shrugged. "You have to be brave to do that. You can't stand on the sidelines. You wade into the thick of things. Otherwise you won't get the picture. Tia says I have an adventurous spirit without any wiles. I have the instinct to get myself into trouble, but not the courage to stay there or the wherewithal to get out."

"*Tia* said that?"

"Well, not in so many words."

He sat back. "That doesn't sound like something Tia would say to you. It sounds really discouraging."

"Oh, you're right. She just laughs at me for being adventurous, or for *wanting* to be adventurous. But I'm not daring like her."

Sawyer reappeared beside us with an even bigger tray than before. He set my plate in front of me—a green salad with shrimp, avocado, and mango: *yum*—and served Brody a huge fish sandwich with grilled vegetables. There was no "Does everything look okay?" from Sawyer. He tucked his tray under his arm and headed for the kitchen.

"Wait a minute," Brody called after him. "We didn't even order. What if we'd wanted something different from our usual?"

Sawyer marched back to our table and gave Brody a baleful look. "Did you want something different?"

"No," Brody said.

"See?" Sawyer started to move away.

"I did," I said, raising my hand.

Sawyer turned back to me. His eyes were crossed. "The only reason you're *saying* you want something different, Harper, is that I pointed out you always want the same thing." He walked toward the kitchen without giving us another chance to complain.

"That's *not* the only reason I want something different," I murmured in the direction of the kitchen door, which swung shut behind him.

"Very, very bad waiter," Brody muttered, picking up his fork.

We ate in silence for a few minutes. The wait staff was cranky, but the Crab Lab's food was delicious.

Finally Brody said, "You'll have a big adventure next year. You'll major in photojournalism at Harvard or Oxford or somewhere a million miles away."

I shook my head. "Try Florida. I'm on my own to pay for college. Mom says she doesn't have the money. She already borrowed money from Granddad to buy the B & B."

"Yeah." Brody nodded like he understood. I figured he was on his own too.

"My grades are good," I said. "I'll get an academic scholarship. It won't pay for everything, though, so I've been working on getting my photography business off the ground. That's why I photographed the 5K yesterday. And if I had a killer portfolio to show an art department—or a journalism department—I might get another scholarship from them."

Brody nodded. "You've got it figured out. I wish I did."

"You make good grades too," I reminded him.

"I'm in the college-track classes," he said, "but my grades aren't great. They're okay, but not scholarship level."

"You'll get a football scholarship," I said.

He shrugged.

"What would your major be?" I asked. "Or what would you do instead if you didn't go to college?"

He swallowed a bite and said, "Coast Guard."

Oh. He'd been so positive about my dreams that I didn't want to be negative about his, but I couldn't help the wave of nausea that washed over me. I pictured him in rescue gear, headed across the tarmac at Coast Guard Station St. Petersburg to a helicopter that would lower him over a compromised ship in rough seas.

If that was the life he wanted, I could never be with him.

10

BRODY PAUSED WITH HIS FORK HOVERING over his plate. "What's the matter?" he asked. "You look sick all of a sudden."

"Nothing." The nausea passed, along with the heat that had rushed to my face. My skin was left cool. A line of sweat had formed at my hairline. I took a deep breath through my nose, exhaled, and forced myself to take another bite of salad. "You know, my dad is in the Coast Guard."

Brody frowned at me. "Really?"

"Yep."

"Is he stationed down at St. Petersburg? How does he run the B & B?"

"It's just Mom," I explained. "My parents have been separated for a couple of years."

"Oh." Brody lifted his chin, puzzling out my words. "Are they getting back together?"

"I hope not. Um . . ." I racked my brain for a way to describe the situation.

"I'm sorry," Brody said. "You don't have to tell me."

"No, it's not a touchy subject, just complicated." I put down my fork. "See, my dad cheated on Mom. Often. She finally kicked him out and filed for divorce. But ending a marriage in Florida isn't that simple. One of two things has to happen." I touched my first finger. "One of you has to be crazy. Actually, both my parents would be good candidates there, but they would have to be proven crazy separately in court."

Brody chuckled like he was familiar with this feeling, then took another bite of his sandwich.

I touched my second finger. "Or, the marriage has to be 'irretrievably broken.' That's the wording. Mom had her day in court. My dad told the judge that the marriage wasn't irretrievably broken. Instead of giving Mom a divorce, the judge sent my parents to marriage counseling. Mom went to the first appointment. My dad didn't show. The judge held my dad in contempt of court."

"Oh, shit," Brody said.

"It gets better," I said with a lot more bitterness than

I'd known I felt. "My dad came crawling back to Mom. She comforted him, if you know what I mean. He moved back in. A few weeks later he cheated on her again. She kicked him out and filed for divorce. This has happened, I don't know, maybe four times in the past two years. It's about to happen again, because Mom has another court date next week."

Brody wasn't laughing like he was supposed to. He didn't make a snarky comment about Mom like Kennedy had when I told him this story. Granted, Kennedy's words had hurt my feelings, but I was used to his sarcasm. I couldn't get a handle on Brody's silence. Maybe my description had been too convoluted—too much like my own family life had felt for the past two years—and I needed to clarify.

"My dad wants to cheat on her and keep her too," I explained.

As these words were coming out of my mouth, I realized I was describing Brody when he made out with me, then ran back to Grace. I honestly hadn't made the connection earlier, but now it seemed embarrassingly obvious. And Brody must have been thinking I'd mentioned my dad specifically to make a point.

Brody watched me silently for a moment. He was quiet long enough that I believed he got my ugly unintentional message.

I laughed uncomfortably. "So, I'm the only minor in the state of Florida who actually *wants* her parents to get divorced."

If Brody had taken offense, he let it go. He moved on, because that's what Brody did. "I didn't want my parents to get divorced," he said. "I thought it was the end of the world."

"Yeah," I said gently.

"I don't miss my parents fighting, that's for sure," he said. "I miss my dad, though. I miss him so bad sometimes that it hurts, like, in my chest." He sat up and put one hand on his striped shirt, somewhere between his heart and his throat. Then he took a bite of vegetables, chewed, swallowed. Without looking up at me, he said, "We used to play a lot of football together."

"I'm sorry," I said.

He shrugged. "At first I thought it was so awful, but I can see how your parents' situation is worse because it's one-sided. At least my parents were both cheating on each other. My mom acts like it's a huge relief to be available again. Maybe your mom needs to date."

"She's in a serious, committed relationship with a bed and breakfast."

"Is that her only job?" Brody asked.

"Yeah, and it's full-time, when you count keeping up with the repairs. Actually, I think we'd be doing okay financially if it weren't for the two-year-long divorce. She might as well be standing on the front porch and tossing cash to the lawyers like Will throws treats to his dog. *The* dog. Whoever's dog it is."

Brody finished the last of his vegetables. He'd wolfed down his entire sandwich and had even vacuumed up any garnishes that might have been on his plate. I'd hardly touched my salad. I'd gotten lost in my own sad story. Vowing to act more sane and less troubled for the rest of dinner, I took another bite.

"My dad doesn't want me to go into any of the armed services because I won't be able to choose where I live," Brody said slowly. "But your dad never got moved. You've lived here forever."

Between bites I said, "We lived in Alaska when I was little."

"You did?" Brody sounded impressed. "No, we were in kindergarten together."

I was surprised Brody remembered me from kindergarten. I remembered *him*. He'd fallen from the top of the monkey bars and split open his chin. (Or he'd jumped. Two versions of the event circulated in the class. Now that I knew him better, I was more inclined to believe he'd jumped.) For the week he was out of school recovering, Chelsea and I had kept vigil for him over a big rock with his blood on it, even though the teacher pointed out that the rock was on the opposite end of the playground from the monkey bars. She assured us the blood was red paint from an art project the year before. That story wasn't as romantic.

I said, "We were in Alaska for a year right before I started kindergarten."

Brody's face lit up. "Did you love it?"

I wished I could tell him I had. "It was cold, and so big I got scared. I think I clung to Mom's skirts the whole time we were there."

Brody nodded. "I want to see it, but if I had to stay there, I'm sure I'd freeze to death." He leaned closer and lowered his voice conspiratorially. "I usually don't admit this, but you're good at keeping secrets, right?"

I grinned as he repeated what I'd said in the pavilion yesterday. He might not take a relationship with me seriously, but at least I knew he'd been listening.

"I've always been terrified of being voted Least Likely to Leave the Tampa/St. Petersburg Metropolitan Area," he said. "The class is passing judgment on the girl and the guy who win that election. But I really like it here."

"Me too," I said.

Brody took a sip of his iced tea, then said, "My dad is a smoke jumper."

"I'd heard that." And it hadn't surprised me at all. Brody Larson's dad went around the country, parachuting out of airplanes to fight forest fires? Knowing Brody, it made sense.

"He's not going to be able to do it much longer. He's pretty old already to make a living that way. His back bothers him. He'll have to retrain for a different job—a boring job. He says I need to find an exciting profession that I can still do when I'm older. I was thinking about law enforcement of one kind or another."

"Perfect!" I exclaimed, and I meant it. "I can see you kicking in doors for fun and profit."

"Yeah." He grinned at the thought. "Well, speaking of high drama and nonstop action, why don't we take this Superlatives photo?"

I set my camera bag on the table. "I guess . . . should I come over there?" The restaurant was behind me, including the windows onto the street, which would glow in the picture and likely ruin the light. Brody's back was to the wall hung with tangled lights and a carved wooden mermaid. Everyone seeing this photo in the yearbook would know exactly where Brody and I had taken it.

"Be my guest," he said, scooting toward the corner. But the seat had room for only one person.

Which was okay with me.

I slid close to him on the bench. My thigh pressed his. "Sorry," I said.

"I'll manage." He freed his arm from where my body was pinning it to his side. He accidentally, maybe, brushed my breast, then laid his arm along the back of the booth.

Around me, sort of.

He smelled like cologne.

My body vibrated with excitement at having him so near. I couldn't take a deep breath to calm myself, because he would notice—and I would likely faint in a cologne-induced swoon. I had to concentrate to keep my hands from shaking as I moved aside the plates, then turned the napkin holder on its side as a platform for the camera. "I may have to do several trial runs to get us centered," I apologized.

"It's not torture, Harper."

"Ha ha, okay." I had never felt so nervous. I set the camera to take five frames in rapid succession on a time delay, then placed it on top of the napkin holder. "Smile when you see the red light, and keep smiling," I told him.

We watched the camera, but my eyes naturally focused on the bright windows beyond it. I wondered if anybody we knew was eating here and watching us. Maybe they'd tell Kennedy that Brody and I had been up to something suspicious. He would break up with me. It would all be for nothing, because Brody would stay with Grace. But as long as the windows filled my vision, I couldn't see the other restaurant patrons. If I couldn't see them, they weren't there.

Only Brody was in my world right now.

The red light blinked on. The camera flashed five times.

I retrieved the camera and showed Brody the view screen. With our heads close together, we looked down at our heads close together in the photos, too.

I had a dumb moment when I thought I'd opened the wrong file. I hadn't recognized myself with my glasses off and my hair down, cuddling with Brody. He looked perfect with a genuine smile, as usual, but half my head was cut off. I put the camera back to try again.

This time Brody moved his arm down from the back of the booth to my shoulder, with his hand holding my upper arm.

The camera flashed.

We peered at the screen. I was grinning at the camera. Brody was looking at me.

"Oh, God," he said. "I look so lovelorn." He sounded amused, not mortified like I would have been if I'd gotten caught gazing moonily at *him*.

"Or like you're in pain from a possibly, probably not, broken finger."

He laughed. "Or a concussion. Or indigestion. Sure."

Sawyer arrived at our table. He did not have good timing. Brody and I both saw him in the same instant and tried to move away from each other. In such a small booth, there was nowhere to go. Brody removed his hand from my arm.

Sawyer laid our bill on the table very slowly, as if he was trying not to startle us again. "Whatcha doing?" he asked innocently. Sawyer was anything but.

I glanced at Brody. His lips were pressed into a thin line. He gave me a small shake of the head: *Don't tell him.* But I was the world's worst at coming up with lies, and I couldn't think of another way out of this. The truth seemed like the best policy.

"We're taking our Superlatives picture for the yearbook," I admitted. "Want to see?" I slid the camera across the table.

Sawyer peered at the view screen. "Wow," he said. "You're trying to break up with your girlfriend and your boyfriend?"

I was sure my face flushed beet red. I didn't dare look at Brody. I only told Sawyer, "The yearbook won't come out until May."

Sawyer put his tray down on the table and his hands on his hips. "Harper Davis, are you telling me that you're dating a guy you assume you won't still be with in eight months? Why are you with him at all, then? Girl, life is too short."

The truth was, I *did* assume I wouldn't still be with Kennedy in eight months. I'd been cured of any expectation for the future yesterday, when I pictured us sitting together on a college quad. No, thanks. I didn't want to admit this in front of Brody, though, when his long-term relationship with Grace wasn't at issue.

I nodded to the camera and asked Sawyer, "You're saying Kennedy would be mad if he saw this photo of Brody and me? We're not doing anything wrong."

"Oh, sure," Sawyer said. "You can tell the picture is taken here at the Crab Lab. You've shot all the others in the courtyard at the school. You're making *me* take *mine* in the courtyard tomorrow. The only reason you're taking this one here is so you two have an excuse to see each other alone."

I opened my mouth to defend us, but nothing came out, because there was no defense. I hoped Brody could think of something.

He didn't say anything either. He just slid his hand onto my thigh—not high enough toward my crotch to be dirty, but much more familiar than two people taking an innocent photograph for school. Kind of like patting my hand in reassurance as Sawyer gave me the third degree, except *on my thigh*.

Sawyer couldn't see under the table. "To answer your question, Harper," he said, "I don't give fuck one what Kennedy thinks." He turned to Brody. "I've had the pleasure of spending a lot of time with Grace lately during PE. She's going to shit a brick when she sees this picture." He picked up his tray. "There's no charge." He headed for the kitchen.

We watched him go, speechless.

"I think he meant no charge for the advice," I finally said. "There's no way he's eating the cost of the food." Reluctantly I slid off Brody's seat and returned to mine, taking the camera with me. I pulled a few bills out of my purse.

"I've got it," Brody said, opening his wallet.

"Let's split it," I suggested, "since it's a fake date anyway." I sounded bitter.

Closing my purse, I picked up the camera and glanced again at my favorite of the photos on the view screen, the one with Brody looking truly enraptured with me, or in great pain. "I don't know. Maybe Sawyer's right. Should we try taking this photo again somewhere else?"

"You tell me," Brody said. "You're the one who's so concerned about what Kennedy thinks."

I looked Brody in the eye. He held my gaze. A chill washed over me. Electricity zinged between us just as it had in the pavilion, even though now we weren't touching. It sounded like he was asking me to cheat on Kennedy with him, as if whether he cheated on Grace made no difference to him whatsoever.

But if that's all he wanted, I couldn't play along. I felt such a strong connection with him, way stronger than I'd ever felt with Kennedy. If he didn't feel the same way about me—and he obviously didn't, if he wanted to stay with Grace—we needed to take this relationship back to a friendly flirtation, where it belonged.

"I don't have an idea for another photo right now." I scooted out of the booth and stood.

"If you do," he said, standing too, "let me know."

I was left with the feeling that Brody and I were in a fight. But Brody didn't do the silent treatment. The day after our non-date at the Crab Lab, he chatted with me in all the classes we had together, same as always. In fact, we talked more than I talked with Kennedy. Brody showed me his purple finger without the splint and told me it wasn't broken. Kennedy only bugged me about my deadline.

The only way I could tell there was tension between Brody and me was that in study hall, he offered me a fist-bump but didn't call me his girlfriend, even though Kennedy had stayed behind in journalism class again. Brody said "Hey," not "Hey, girlfriend," and that was it.

I wasn't in study hall very long. As soon as Ms. Patel came in, I asked her to excuse me so I could mark some Superlative photos off my to-do list. I'd called several people who had stood me up for previous photo sessions and told them to meet me in the courtyard—or else. And then, wonder of wonders . . . they showed up! Being stressed out to the point of rudeness might wreak havoc on my nerves, but it was great for locking down these photos.

Halfway through my study hall period, I hurried into Principal Chen's office. After Sawyer's comment last night about all the Superlatives photos being taken in the courtyard except mine with Brody, I'd decided I'd better switch things up for some of the others. We had Ms. Chen's permission to use her office while she was at lunch. I could take an adorable picture of Kaye and Aidan, Most Likely to Succeed, behind Ms. Chen's desk. I'd asked Sawyer to meet me there too. I wasn't sure what we would do for his Most Likely to Go to Jail photo, but surely there was something in Ms. Chen's office he could steal or tag with graffiti. Sawyer would think of something.

When I arrived, Aidan already sat in Ms. Chen's chair. Kaye stood nearby with her arms folded. "Harper," she called sharply when she saw me, "you didn't say *Aidan* should sit behind the desk while *I* stand by, ready to assist him, right? That's not the message *I* got."

"No," I said impatiently. I had only fifteen minutes to snap this photo and Sawyer's, or I would have to reschedule them for tomorrow. And I couldn't do that, because I was photographing other people then. "Look, just—"

They both shifted their gaze over my shoulder. A six-foot pelican sauntered in behind me. Sawyer was dressed in his mascot costume. His backpack was slung over a feathered shoulder, and in one bird hand he held a tattered copy of the book we were reading for Mr. Frank's class, *Crime and Punishment*.

"Sawyer," I complained. "Is that what you're wearing?"

He bobbed his big head.

The purpose of the photos was to capture the Super-latives as people, not hiding in a costume, especially when the costume included a foam bird head. But I was desperate to complete this mission, and I wasn't going to let any of these three go while I had them. I didn't dare send Sawyer to change. And I didn't want him to strip, because underneath he probably had on nothing but underwear. Maybe not even that, knowing him.

I opened the blinds over the windows onto the courtyard. Sunlight flooded the office and glinted on the four-foot-tall sports trophies too big to be stuffed into cases in the lobby. Then I turned back to Kaye and Aidan. They were arguing again. "I'm the president of the student council," Aidan told Kaye haughtily. "You're the *vice* president."

"We're *both* Most Likely to Succeed," Kaye said. "We're equal."

"Not true," Aidan said. "The class selected us for that title because we're in charge of the student council. And in student council, I'm above you."

"I hope to God that's the *only* place he's above you," came Sawyer's muffled voice from the depths of the foam head.

We all looked at him. I'd thought it was his rule to stay silent while in costume.

I couldn't let this session devolve into a three-way fight. The two-way fight was already bad enough. I told Aidan and Kaye, "Let's take some shots with Aidan behind the desk, then with Kaye behind the desk, then—You know what? Let's kill two birds with one stone—"

"Hey," said Sawyer.

"—and have both of you sit behind the desk at the same time. Kaye, sit in Aidan's lap."

"I don't like Aidan enough right now to sit in his lap," Kaye said. "Anyway, we would just be reinscribing the traditional patriarchal hierarchy of a man being in charge and a woman infantilized in his lap."

"Yeah!" came Sawyer's voice.

"Shut up," she told him.

"Scoot over, Aidan," I said. "Both of you sit on the edge of the chair and share it." I would have given anything to be told to pose like this with Brody. It was sad that Aidan and Kaye were still dating but didn't care anymore about the golden opportunity of sitting together in a chair. "Parliamentary procedure. All in favor?" I asked. "Aye—and my opinion is the only one that counts. I am on deadline with this shit."

"Cussing in the principal's office!" Sawyer managed to make his voice sound horrified even through the padding of his costume.

"I liked you better when you wore glasses and took orders," Aidan told me.

Without adjusting the settings, I brought my camera up from its strap and snapped a quick photo in Aidan's general direction. "There," I said. "I've got a shot of you with your eyes bugged out and your mouth wide open. That's probably all I need." I turned to leave the office.

"You look great without your glasses," Aidan said promptly, "and this newfound assertiveness becomes you." Kaye was laughing.

I waited for them to get into position, then started taking pictures. I was focusing on their faces and snapping photos so fast that I almost didn't notice the light had changed and a sunbeam streamed white through the window. It took me a few frames to realize the light was actually Sawyer's white costume. He'd walked behind Kaye and Aidan. All the shots had a giant pelican in the background.

A picture in the yearbook of Sawyer photobombing Kaye and Aidan would have said volumes about our senior class. But Aidan would resent it. Kaye would be hopping mad. And Kennedy had a sense of humor about his own projects, not mine.

"Sawyer!" I barked. "The white pelican is about to become an endangered species."

He put his hands on his padded hips. "That is insulting," he said, his voice thin behind the foam head. "All our large waterfowl are in danger because we're destroying their wetlands. It's not something to joke about."

No topics were off limits for *him* to joke about. I suspected I'd found, for the first time, Sawyer's sensitive spot. He was an animal rights supporter. Sawyer, *sensitive*!

That was okay. I was sensitive too. Kennedy had called me disorganized last Friday, and I was determined to prove him wrong. I pointed to a chair in front of Ms. Chen's desk, where I assumed Brody sat when he got lectured for playing practical jokes and sentenced to on-campus suspension. I told Sawyer, "Sit down and shut up."

He commanded everyone's attention as he sat, wiggling his bird butt to fit it into the chair's confines. He casually crossed one big webbed bird foot on the opposite knee and opened his copy of *Crime and Punishment*. I wasn't sure which part of the bird head he saw from, but he appeared to be actually reading.

I snapped ten pictures of him. One of these would be perfect.

11

WHEN I FIRST GOT HOME FROM SCHOOL,
Mom was wearing paint-stained clothes and carrying a ladder, but then I lost track of her. I closed myself in my bedroom, sat down at my desk, and went right to work on the race photos for my website. I'd made a lot of progress on them the last two nights. I wanted to finish that night and send out an e-mail to the 5K racers saying that their photos were available for purchase.

Then I could get back to processing the Superlatives photos. I'd scheduled my last few photo sessions for tomorrow during school. I could continue fixing the photos over the weekend. I assumed I would meet Kennedy and our friends at the Crab Lab after the game Friday night. He'd also invited me to a jazz concert in the park on Saturday, which sounded suspiciously like we would be the youngest ones there. That happened on a lot of dates with Kennedy. But if Tia was right about Kennedy's pattern of picking a fight with me before our dates, we wouldn't go anyway.

I suspected I knew what the subject of the fight would be too. My photo of Brody, Will, and Noah took up half the front page of the day's local paper. PHOTO BY HARPER DAVIS was printed in the bottom corner. I was so proud. And I was afraid my admiration for Brody shone through in that shot. Even if it didn't, I'd gone out on my own and sold my work to a publication outside school, something Kennedy had never been able to do, despite all his attempts to submit movie reviews and peevish columns about tourists. Either way, he was likely to be pissed with me.

So be it. Frankly, I was getting pretty disillusioned with dating. My boyfriend annoyed the crap out of me, and the guy who made me feel like heaven didn't want to be my boyfriend. Anyway, if Kennedy decided to give me the silent treatment again, that would free up plenty of time for me to perfect the yearbook photos and turn them in to him by Monday. I would get the rest to him on a rolling basis, as he'd requested, so he could complete his (awful) layouts. At the end of the week, he would have them all, and he could put the section to bed by the deadline.

That was my plan.

My dad was shouting. I blinked at my computer screen and glanced at my bedroom window. Night had fallen. My heart sped as fast as it had when he'd reprimanded me on the phone. He was yelling at Mom. He said she wasn't giving them a chance. She was going through with this ridiculous divorce to punish him. No, he would not shut up just because he was disturbing the guests at her Goddamned bed and breakfast.

He'd come over and shouted like this every time my parents got close to finalizing the divorce. Mom said he did it because the best way to hurt her was to make her B & B look bad. He wasn't just shouting at *her*. He was alienating the guests at the B & B, leading them to think the house wasn't safe, and ruining their peaceful vacation. He was trying, in this small way, to destroy her business, which she saw as the one good thing that had come out of their separation.

I did what I always did in this situation. After a few deep breaths so I no longer felt like I was about to faint, I opened my door and walked into our tiny living room. My dad was standing and pointing and shouting at Mom, who sat on the couch with her head turned away, as if he was about to hit her. He wasn't, but that's what it looked like.

I had defused this sort of argument between my parents

plenty of times before. Throughout childhood, I'd convinced my dad to stand down by crawling into his lap. Recently when he'd loomed here in the living room and shouted, I'd given him a hug and told him I'd missed him.

This time was harder to stomach. I wasn't sure what the difference was—that I was tired of my own boyfriend dismissing my projects as worthless, or that I knew now how good it felt to start a business independent of everyone—but I had to stop this. He was still yelling at Mom. But I was immune because he never yelled at me. I walked toward him with my arms open for a hug. "Hey, Dad! I—"

He whirled to face me. His eyebrows shot up, and he gave me a quick look from head to toe. I took people aback now that I'd removed my glasses.

Then he said, "That shit doesn't work on me anymore, young lady. I know exactly what you're doing, and so do you. If you want to act like an adult now, you can do that by staying out of your parents' business. If you want to keep acting like a child, you can *go to your room!*" He was yelling louder than I'd ever heard him, and the finger that had been pointed in Mom's face was now pointed in mine.

I turned, hurried for my room, and closed the door.

The shouting continued.

Panting, I lay down on my bed, pulled the phone and

earbuds from my nightstand, and turned on one of my deep-breathing relaxation recordings. *Try to clear your mind*, the lady said. *If you have an intrusive thought, that's fine. Just let it go.* But I couldn't let it go. Now that the initial wave of panic had passed, I couldn't believe I'd done exactly what my dad had told me to do. Just like Granddad, I'd abandoned my mom.

One deep breath. I could call 911. But my dad wasn't breaking any laws, except disturbing the peace. If Mom's guests in the B & B were listening to the commotion, the one thing worse for business than my dad yelling would be for the police to come.

Two deep breaths. I could call some friends to hang out. They could knock on the front door and interlope, making my dad see he was affecting real people when he flew off the handle like this. But Kaye and Tia had been popping in since we were in third grade. They might be so familiar that he wouldn't stop yelling. He might shout at *them*.

Three deep breaths. I took out my earbuds, thumbed through the school's student directory on my phone, and called Brody.

He answered right away. I said breathlessly, "It's Harper. Can you come over?"

"So, you finally got another idea for a Superlatives

photo?" My dad's shouting grew louder, and Brody must have heard it through the phone. "What's going on?"

"Nothing."

Brody knew exactly what kind of nothing I meant. "I'll be right there."

I clicked my phone off and lay on my bed, waiting. I wanted to put my earbuds back in and play the relaxation program to block out my dad's voice, but I didn't dare. My dad had already shouted at me, personally. That *never* happened. I listened to make sure my parents' fight didn't escalate. If it did, I would call the police after all. And I listened for Brody ringing the doorbell.

In the meantime, I stared across my tiny bedroom wallpapered with photographs and art I'd cut from magazines. It had seemed cozy in the past, a great place to hide from the world and work on my photos. Now it seemed claustrophobic. I was trapped here, suffocating on what my dad hollered at Mom, and her silence in response.

The doorbell rang.

I opened my bedroom door too quickly. I needed to cool it or my dad would know I'd called Brody to intervene. I waited in the short hallway until I heard Brody's voice. Then I walked into the living room.

"—Larson. I'm here to see Harper," he was telling my

dad, who had answered the door as if he lived here. Mom stood behind him, looking lost rather than pissed.

"Brody!" I said in my best impression of pleased astonishment. "Dad, this is my boyfriend, Brody Larson. He's the quarterback on my high school's football team."

"Pleased to meet you, sir," Brody said. He stepped forward and extended his hand, grinning like he wanted to impress, even though he was wearing his usual athletic shirt and gym shorts. A drop of sweat slid down his temple.

The interruption had the desired effect. My dad changed from a monster back into a reasonably friendly guy with a toned, muscular body and a military haircut. "Brody," he said quietly, shaking Brody's hand.

"Not sure you remember my mom," I said.

"Nice to see you, ma'am," Brody said, shaking her hand too.

"Pleasure," she said. I half expected her to widen her eyes at me, wondering why I hadn't told her about my new boyfriend, and what had happened to Kennedy. But my dad had been shouting at her for quite a while. I suspected all she could hear was the ringing in her ears.

Taking Brody's hand and pulling him toward my bedroom, I made small talk so his appearance would seem casual. "Did you get all your homework done?"

"Not quite," he said. "I still have maybe eight calculus

problems left." He stepped into my room and closed the door behind him.

I hugged him.

He wrapped his arms around me and squeezed me gently.

I'd only meant to thank him. But now that I was in his arms, I didn't want to leave. I settled my ear against his chest and listened to his heartbeat: slow, steady.

Finally I let him out of my death grip and stepped back. "Thank you so much," I whispered.

"No problem," he said solemnly.

"I'm sorry about the boyfriend thing," I said. "I was trying to make it seem normal that you'd pop in." Belatedly I was realizing that Kennedy did not pop in. Not once had he crossed my mind when I was considering which friend to call.

"Can you stay for a few minutes?" I meant until my dad left. I swept my hand around the small room, offering him a beanbag chair or my desk chair or . . . the bed seemed a little forward.

"Sure." He kicked off his flip-flops and scooted back on the bed until he sat propped up against my pillows. He seemed comfortable.

I crawled onto the bed and settled beside him. Our arms touched from our shoulders to our elbows. I racked my brain for something to say to the guy I'd fallen for, who was someone else's boyfriend but was pretending to be mine. I glanced at him and was shocked all over again at how green his eyes were.

He watched me intently and opened his mouth to say something. Then he grimaced, shifted on the bed, knocked me with his elbow, and pulled my phone out from under him.

"Sorry," I said. "Remember you asked me how I could just take a deep breath and relax? I was listening to a relaxation program. It's a directed meditation."

"On a recording? I can think of a better way to relax."

"If you can think of a better way, why don't you do it before games, instead of worrying?" Then it hit me. "Oh, you're making a sex joke."

He gaped at me.

"A blow-job joke?" I suggested meekly.

"Harper Davis!" he exclaimed. "Would I make a joke like that while I'm sitting on your bed? I had no idea your mind was so dirty."

"Uh." In my mind I backpedaled through what he'd said, trying to remember what had sent my thoughts in that direction. "Sorry, I—"

"It was a hand-job joke," he said. "I mean, my gosh, a blow-job joke? You have a *boyfriend*."

I burst into laughter—because what he'd said was funny,

and because he excited me to the point of giddiness. I swallowed the last remnants of my giggle and said, "You're so different from the guys I usually hang out with. I can't tell when you're kidding."

"I'm always kidding," he said. "And it's always dirty."

"Ha ha, okay," I said.

"Harper!" he said, astonished all over again. "You didn't believe that, did you? I was not making a hand-job joke. It might have been a kissing joke." He was blushing.

I took one of the deep, calming breaths I was famous for. "Sorry. I feel kind of"—I was talking with my hands, but my hands were not forming any shape that was remotely related to what I was trying to say—"deprived sometimes. I haven't done a lot of kissing or . . . anything. And then I talk about it and go overboard, sounding like I'm starving to death."

"You don't," he said firmly, turning on my phone and thumbing through the list of recordings.

"You could download some of these programs and listen to them in the locker room before a game," I suggested. "Or is that not allowed?"

"It's allowed," he said, "but only kickers do superstitious shit like that."

"Well, if you're still feeling anxious, maybe you should start hedging your bets like a kicker." I put my head close to his, peering at the phone, and cued up one of the programs. "Want to try?"

He gave a shrug, meaning he would try anything once. He put the earbuds in. I started the recording.

He laughed. The meditation lady had a British accent. I smiled at him.

He sank down on one forearm on the bed, watching me. I remembered that the program's first instruction was to lie down. I patted my thigh.

He rolled over with his head in my lap. His hair was a lot softer than I'd imagined. Half the time I saw him, his locks hung in clumps, wet from sweat or a shower or the ocean. His hair was clean and dry now, and baby fine, only a whisper against my skin.

Brody Larson's head was in my lap.

Something told me we were not just friends anymore.

But even as I thought this and felt my face flush hot, Brody seemed oblivious. *Relaxed*, even. He crossed his ankles—the meditation lady was telling him to make sure all parts of his body were comfortable. He rotated his throwing shoulder—the lady said he should work out kinks in any joint that hurt.

I lowered my hand to his shoulder and circled my fingers on his shirt, rubbing gently. This was not part of the relaxation technique, having his not-just-friend-anymore rub his kink. I was probably unrelaxing him.

Maybe I didn't care.

He lifted his opposite hand and put it over mine, as if to tell me he approved.

His breathing deepened. He'd moved on to the part of the program in which he inhaled slowly and visualized his body growing heavy and sinking into the mattress. So I wouldn't distract him, I stopped rubbing his shoulder. He kept his hand on mine.

I gazed down his long body stretched to the end of my bed in the dim lamplight. When I looked at him from this angle, free to let my eyes roam across the whole of him, he seemed taller, but thinner, as he had when I photographed him at the 5K without his football shoulder pads. His crossed ankles were slender, and his feet were long, not wide, almost elegant.

After listening to a few more of his slow breaths, I started to feel ridiculous that I was still so tense, hovering over him like a buzzard about to swoop down on dead meat. I eased my shoulders back against the pillows, careful not to disturb him, and tried to practice what I'd been preaching, letting myself relax.

Without warning, the door opened. Mom was silhouetted in the bright light from the hallway.

It was like her to walk into my room without knocking. She wasn't trying to catch me doing something wrong—she just thought of herself rather than me. It didn't occur to her that she might startle me. I went out of my way not to startle her, but she didn't do the same.

Now, though, her unannounced entrance felt like an intrusion. I wanted to snatch my hand off Brody's, but that would alarm him and ruin everything. I left my hand where it was and lifted my chin.

Taking just enough steps into the room for her face to appear in the lamplight, Mom mouthed, "Thank you." She knew why I'd called Brody, and she wasn't mad. She was grateful.

I gave her the smallest nod.

She walked her fingers in the air and pointed behind her. She meant my dad had left and she was going over to the B & B for a while. She backed out of the room and closed the door as silently as she'd come in.

Brody moved anyway. We'd disturbed him. But no, he was rolling on his side, as the meditation lady told him. Sitting up was next, and a stretch and a yawn.

Then he pulled out the earbuds and scooted up to sit beside me against the pillows again.

I raised my eyebrows. "Well? Do you feel calmer?"

"I did," he said softly, looking at my lips. "But not now."

Our eyes locked. He moved toward me. We'd shared a moment like this before, with my face on fire and my heart speeding, but it had ended in disappointment. This one would likely end the same way. I waited for Mom to burst back in or for Brody to tell me he'd been kidding.

He reached up to cradle my cheek. His thumb traced my lower lip, sending chills shooting up my arms.

His lips met mine.

He kissed me hard for a second, then opened his mouth. This was a kiss. Quinn and then Noah had faked it pretty well with me in crowded movie theaters when lots of our classmates were around to see. But Kennedy, despite all his sarcasm directed at people who were less worldly than him, had zero idea how to kiss. I kept trying to show him. He obstinately refused to learn.

I didn't need to teach Brody anything. As we kissed, his hand crept across my waist and circled my hip like he wanted to hold me steady forever. When I took a turn at kissing along his jawline, he lifted his head to give me better access to his neck, then gasped as if he'd never felt so good. This couldn't be true, but he made me feel like I was giving him the sexy experience of a lifetime.

I kept expecting him to touch my breast, which made

me nervous with my mom around. But he didn't try—maybe for the same reason. After we'd made out for a good half hour, though, I wanted something more. I slipped my hands underneath his shirt. That's when he slid his hands under my shirt and fingered the hook of my bra.

But in the end, he decided against unhooking it. He broke our kiss and backed a few inches away from me, panting. Between breaths, he grinned at me and said, "You have to know what you can get away with."

"Yeah." I smiled, showing him I understood. But I had something more I needed to say to him, something I was afraid I would regret. "I . . . ," I said, and sighed. I couldn't catch my breath. "Um . . ."

Kennedy would have interrupted by now, asking me if I spoke English. Brody only raised his eyebrows and watched my mouth like I was beautiful.

"I . . . don't want to do this anymore," I said in a rush. "I don't like sneaking around, cheating."

He chuckled. "Yes you do."

He must have been referring to the head rush I got every time he came anywhere near me. Was I that obvious? I clarified, "It's not right."

"Well, why don't you break up with Kennedy, then?" he asked. "I've been waiting for you to do that."

"Me!" I exclaimed. "Why don't you break up with Grace?"

"I'm not *with* Grace," he said. "I told you, she spent half of Monday with that jerk from Florida State."

"But when she came back," I pointed out, "you sandwiched her between your legs and massaged her shoulders."

He pursed his lips and shook his head. This was the first time since Ms. Patel's homeroom that I'd seen his green eyes look angry. "I did it because *you* were in the ocean with Kennedy—*right* after we made out in the pavilion. Like that meant nothing to you. Like you didn't care."

"Brody!" I said, exasperated. "I stayed out there with Kennedy because the second Grace came back from getting drunk with those college dudes, you had your hand on her ass."

He tilted his head to one side, looking genuinely perplexed. "I had my hand on her ass?"

"Yes!"

"I don't even remember that, Harper. I was probably just holding her up because she was falling-down drunk."

"How can you not remember putting your hand on a girl's ass?" I insisted.

"I dated her on and off all summer. I'm sure I've put my hand on her ass plenty of times. This one instance doesn't stand out."

"I've dated Kennedy for six weeks and he's *never* put his hand on my ass."

"Kennedy is from another planet. That's my only explanation for why he doesn't see you're hot."

I frowned hard. When Mom caught me making that face, she warned me, only half-jokingly, that I'd better lighten up or I'd get wrinkles. I smoothed my brow and relaxed my jaw, then sighed. "You know I don't have a lot of experience with this, Brody. If you're lying to me, I wouldn't get it."

"You think I'd mislead you for fun?"

"For a little thrill, yeah."

He gave me a slow, clear-eyed, disappointed look.

Then he picked up my hand and placed it on his shirt. His heart raced under my fingertips.

"That could be excitement from misleading you," he acknowledged. "Or, just possibly, you turn me on." He held my gaze as he leaned toward me.

I met him more than halfway. I kissed him. He uttered a soft groan and put his hands in my hair. His mouth was soft and warm and sweet. My whole body glowed so brightly that I decided Kaye and Tia had sold this making-out business a little short. It wasn't just the addictive physical sensations, but also something that shifted inside me, in my heart.

He let me go, panting again. He rubbed his rough thumb back and forth across my bottom lip. "My God, Harper."

"I'll break up with Kennedy at school tomorrow," I said hoarsely.

"Do you want me to be there?" Brody asked.

"Oh, no," I said. "Kennedy's never been into me. I doubt he'll mind. He'll probably feel relieved."

"I seriously doubt that." With a final sigh, Brody said, "I'd better go. Calculus calls, and if I'm out too late, my mom will call too."

I scooted off the bed, then held out both hands to help him off—which was a joke. He probably weighed almost twice as much as me. I led him by the hand through the house and out to his truck behind the B & B.

"Now that I think about it," I said, "how'd you know I live in the house out back instead of the big Victorian?"

"I didn't," he said. "I knocked at the B & B first. One of your guests came down in a bathrobe and told me where you live."

"Great," I said. "I'll hear about how cute you are at the guests' breakfast tomorrow."

"Aw, shucks." He laughed. "Speaking of tomorrow, will you come with me to Quarterback Club for dinner? It's a bunch of old people who raise money for the team and invite someone from the community to speak about how violent sports enrich our lives."

"Fun!"

"Yeah. The football players go, and their girlfriends, and the cheerleaders, so Kaye will be there."

"And Grace," I guessed.

"And Grace," he agreed, "but I'm not with Grace."

He didn't add, *I'm with you*. But he didn't have to. It was finally sinking in that I was the star quarterback's girlfriend.

"By the way," he said, opening the door of his truck, "do we still need to take a new Superlatives picture, or was that just a ploy to go out with me?"

"Both," I admitted. "I wanted an excuse to see you again. But we do need to take another picture. The one from the Crab Lab doesn't go with the others I've taken. We don't have to do it tonight, though. We have time."

And when I said this, I believed it was true.

12

THE NEXT MORNING, THE LOCAL TV NEWS
was tracking a hurricane headed for central Florida. Two
rooms of guests in the B & B announced at breakfast
that they were leaving. Mom explained that the hurricane
wouldn't hit us just because it was moving in our general
direction. The storm was still five days away. Anything
could happen before it made landfall. It could peter out, or
stay strong but veer toward Alabama. If Floridians packed
up and left every time a hurricane headed our way, we'd be
gone from August to October.

The tourists weren't convinced. The TV news had really
done a number on them, pointing out that the Tampa Bay
area was way overdue for a direct hit from some kind of
Hurrigeddon. They packed their cars and hit the road right

after breakfast, determined to make it out of town before everyone else got the same idea and the hurricane escape routes were immobilized with gridlock. Whatever.

The terror was infectious, though. At school, people were tense, talking about the coming storm and the Yankee transplants in town who'd decided to drive inland for a long weekend, just to play it safe. Maybe the charged atmosphere affected me, too, and that's why I sounded so on edge when I told Kennedy during journalism class that I didn't want to see him anymore. He sensed my weakness, and that's why he said what he said next.

He crossed his arms and demanded, "Is it because of Brody?"

I glanced around the room. Mr. Oakley was out of town. His son played for the Gators, and he and his wife had driven to an away game up in Georgia. We had a sub who babysat for the school a lot. Her agenda was to spend the whole period texting on her phone unless someone actually started shouting, in which case she sent the offenders to Ms. Chen's office.

Therefore, the class was even more disorganized than usual. Instead of working on our projects for the newspaper or the yearbook or journalism independent study, everyone was goofing off like it was study hall—except Kennedy and me, of course. They weren't paying attention to us. The room was so loud with conversations and laughter that nobody could hear us when we talked in a normal tone. I'd thought it was safe to sit with Kennedy and break up with him between assembling the layouts for two Superlatives pages. It never occurred to me that he would care enough to get mad—much less raise his voice.

Quinn and a few other guys eyed us, then turned back to their own computers. I kept my voice quiet, hoping Kennedy would follow my lead and calm down. "You and I have dated for six weeks," I said, "and we've argued for probably five of them. We got along better when we were just friends, remember? Some couples don't work out."

Kennedy nodded. "Some couples aren't *perfect* like you and Brody. You know he only wants down your pants, right?"

At least somebody does, I thought. "If he did," I said carefully, "it's none of your b—"

"He never would have noticed you if you hadn't started following him around like some rock-star groupie after that stupid vote. And dressing like you wanted it." Kennedy waved at my fitted V-neck T-shirt (no cleavage), chunky necklace, Bermuda shorts, and high-heeled wedges.

What?

"Everybody says you're trying to get Brody by dressing and acting like Grace," Kennedy sneered.

"Oh, really?" I tried to sound scathing, but I didn't feel very scathing. What Kennedy was saying hit too close to home.

Until he said this: "I thought you were a nice girl."

"You thought I was a nice girl," I repeated. "You thought I was a *nice girl?* What the fuck does that mean?" Now everybody from the surrounding computers was staring at us. I lowered my voice. "I can't be a nice girl anymore because I don't wear glasses, or I don't wear high-necked dresses? Or is it because I don't do what you tell me?"

"You know what it means," Kennedy said darkly.

"No, I honestly don't," I said. "But I know it's sexist. Like girls are supposed to be vessels of purity, and I've sprung a leak. Boys, meanwhile, can do whatever they want.

"You know what?" My voice was rising again. I'd stopped caring. "You've never treated me like you genuinely wanted to be with me. You wanted the *appearance* of dating without caring about me or my feelings. I deserve better. I should have broken up with you the first time you gave me the silent treatment."

I got up then, taking my bag and moving toward the back of the room. When I'd brought up the subject, I'd intended to break up with him gently and then listen carefully to his response. But I didn't care what he had to say anymore.

I didn't look forward to sitting at the back of the room for the rest of the period either. Everyone who'd been in earshot of our breakup was still staring at me. But before I'd even sat down, Kennedy was standing close, towering over me.

"I need all of the Superlatives photos tomorrow," he said smugly.

"Tomorrow!" I exclaimed. "My deadline is a *week* from tomorrow."

"No, *my* deadline is a week from tomorrow," he corrected me. "For the whole section. *Your* deadline is whenever I say it is. I've given you as many breaks as I could, but I've told you I need those photos on a rolling basis so I have time to lay out everything. You haven't been turning many in. So I want them all tomorrow."

I looked slowly around the room. All conversations had hushed when Kennedy followed me to the back. Now everyone—not just the people who'd overheard us before, but *everyone*—stared at us like we were a reality show. Only the sub wasn't paying attention. She had her earphones plugged into her phone.

"Kennedy," I whispered hoarsely, "I know you're mad at me, but I can't do that. There's no way. I haven't even taken all the photos yet. And once I did, I'd have to stay up all night to format them."

He shrugged, as if to say, *Serves you right.* "You'd have the section photographed and turned in by now if you hadn't spent the last week creating an after-school job for yourself with that 5K. Maybe we need a different yearbook photographer."

I'd felt myself blushing under everyone's attention before. Now I felt the blood drain out of my face, and my fingers tingled. Photography was what I loved most in the world. I'd busted my ass to get this position. Kennedy couldn't do this to me.

Yes he could. Mr. Oakley had told us to handle our problems like the yearbook was a business and we were employees. That meant Kennedy could fire me.

I gaped at him, wishing away the tears in my eyes. "That makes zero sense! I'm busy, but I'm turning everything in on time. If you'd set my deadline for tomorrow in the first place, instead of a week from tomorrow, I wouldn't have asked for the 5K job."

He smiled. "If you turn all the Superlatives photos in tomorrow during class, I'll consider letting you keep your position."

I wasn't sure whether it was his patronizing tone, or the fact that he'd chosen to make a scene in front of the whole class, or the entire six weeks of him acting like I wasn't good enough for him. But something made me snap. I shouted, "You know what? Don't bother. I quit."

His face fell. His eyes were wide, looking around at the staring class for the first time. "You can't quit! This section is due. Nobody in our class will get a yearbook on time!"

"Oh, I'll make your stupid deadline tomorrow," I said. "The section and the yearbooks won't be late because of me. After that, as long as I can get into journalism independent study and Mr. Oakley promises not to flunk me, I'm quitting. I'm not going to work for a boss like you."

The bell rang. Kennedy and I faced off, with the rest of the class circling us. I wasn't backing down, but the bell seemed to go on forever.

Finally it ended. I grabbed my bag and hurried for the door.

"Harper!" Quinn called, but I made my way to Ms. Patel's room without him. He was the one who'd told me to stop worrying about appearances. And now that I'd stopped—boy, had I stopped. I was already going over and over my public screaming match with Kennedy in my mind, wishing I could take it back.

At least, the part where I quit.

Brody looked more than ready for his daily catnap, arms folded on his desk, chin propped there. He looked so sleepy that the dark circles under his eyes made sense for once. He was watching the door for me, though. When he saw me, he grinned and sat up. "Did you do the deed? Uh-oh, what's wrong?"

"I'll tell you in a minute," I said, unpacking my camera. "We're out of time to take our Superlatives picture. Spend study hall in the courtyard with me."

After the bell rang, we stepped into the empty hallway. As we walked together, I said quietly, "I can't go to Quarterback Club with you tonight. I'm really sorry." I explained that Kennedy had changed my deadline and threatened to fire me.

"Kennedy can't fire you," Brody protested. "Students can't fire each other."

"We can in Mr. Oakley's class."

"But did you complain to Mr. Oakley?"

"He's driving to the Georgia game to see his son play. He won't be back until Monday."

"Oh, right." Brody nodded. I didn't think he'd ever had Mr. Oakley as a teacher, but he must have played on the team with Mr. Oakley's son before he graduated.

"And even when he gets back, I can't complain. He's told us we're supposed to settle our differences ourselves."

"This isn't what he meant," Brody said firmly. Then his face softened, and he touched my elbow. "You should have let me come with you when you broke up with Kennedy. If I'd been there, he wouldn't have gone ballistic on you."

"The next time you offer to strong-arm somebody for me, I will totally let you," I said. "Anyway, Kennedy won't be able to jerk me around like that again, because I told him I'm quitting after I turn in the Superlatives photos."

"Quitting as yearbook photographer?" Brody sounded astonished.

"I mean, it's *high school yearbook photographer*," I defended myself, gesturing with my camera. "I've already made a couple hundred bucks for college from the photo in the paper and my pictures from the 5K finish line. I don't *need* to be yearbook photographer."

Brody nodded. "You'll regret it, though. Didn't you *apply* to be yearbook photographer? You submitted a portfolio, the same way Kennedy had to be chosen for editor, right? You earned that position, just as much as Kennedy earned his."

"Yeah." Unfortunately, I saw his point.

He pushed open the door for me and followed me into the courtyard. "It's not the end of the world, sure, and it's not making you any money, but I'd think about the decision to quit if I were you. It's part of your life. You're throwing away the position because you're mad at Kennedy, which means he's still got control over you. Is that what you want? You're only in high school once."

We were alone in the concrete space dotted with palm trees

in planters. I sure hoped the last few Superlatives showed up for their photo sessions, or I was going to miss my new deadline tomorrow. After twelve years of school with Xavier Pilkington, Most Academic, I'd never been so anxious to see him.

"Stand over here, please." I pulled Brody under a palm tree and snapped a few shots of him, then looked around and moved him to a spot where the light was more muted and his green eyes stood out in the photos. He was smiling self-consciously, though, like he was posing for the football program that the student council sold at games. To distract him, I asked, "Are people talking about me behind my back because I got contacts and I'm dressing differently?"

"No," he said. "Well, no more than they talked about you before. You've been a favorite subject of the football team since school started this year. Though, come to think of it, maybe that's my influence."

"That would be very sweet," I said, "except that discussion is about my fine ass."

"Not *just* your fine ass," he corrected me. "You have many quality features. I used to look up from the table in the lunchroom and see you and say, 'Harper looks hot.' Lately I look at you and say, 'Hey, a new hot girl. Oh, wait, it's Harper!'"

"Okay," I said, laughing. I was capturing handsome photos of him laughing too.

"I like surprises." He tilted his head and considered me. "You should wear your glasses sometimes."

"Really?" I could not have been more astonished that he'd said this.

"Yes, really. You look sexy in those glasses. Wear them and surprise me when you're gunning for a little something extra."

"Noted. Okay, you're done." I attached my camera to my tripod and set it to take five photos. Then I took my smaller camera out of my pocket and posed where Brody had been standing. Now I had a picture of me taking a picture.

I scrolled through the view screen, then showed Brody. "Here's what I was thinking of for the yearbook. We'll use this one of me, side by side with this one of you." I flipped back to the best photo of him grinning, on the verge of cracking up. "Before, we weren't a couple. The joke in the picture was going to be that we looked like one. Now we *are* a couple. The joke in the picture is that we're separate."

"I don't get it," he said.

Xavier Pilkington arrived in the courtyard. We gave him a lukewarm welcome, then eyed each other again.

"I know this is your last day to take these," Brody said. "And Lord knows you don't need another guy making trouble for you."

"Thanks for recognizing that."

"I'm just saying, if I had my choice for this picture, we would be together."

I stayed up the entire night perfecting the Superlatives photos. Mom knocked on my door around midnight and told me with a yawn to go to bed. I lied and said that I would. Six hours later, I showered and schlumped over to the B & B to help her with breakfast. By the time I got to school, I was completely brain dead. This must have been what it felt like to be our classmate Jason Price, who came to school stoned.

Lucky for me, the beginning-of-school testing frenzy had died down. I was able to stare into space through my first three classes and avoid Kennedy by sleeping through journalism, since my work there, at least for the yearbook, was done.

I woke, slowly realizing that people were shifting their chairs and talking more loudly in anticipation of the ending bell. As I sat up, blinking, Quinn turned around in his seat, watching me.

"You finally stood up to Kennedy, like I told you," he whispered. "Congratulations!"

"And this is what I have to show for it," I said, yawning.

"Plus Brody," Quinn pointed out.

"Plus I quit the yearbook."

"That's where you went wrong," Quinn said. "I told you to stop worrying about how things looked. You only quit to save face."

Had I? My brain wasn't working well enough for me to remember clearly what I'd been thinking.

"Come on." He put his arm around me and half dragged me to study hall. I muttered a hello to Brody in the desk across the aisle from mine and folded myself onto my desktop, Brody style.

"Are you going to make it?" he asked. I felt him fingering strands of my hair away from my face.

"Mmmm," I said. "And I'll be at the game to watch you play, but I'm afraid I can't go out with you after. Bedtime. Catch up with you Saturday."

He chuckled. "That's fine."

When I woke, the bell was ringing. It wasn't the end of study hall, though. I'd slept right through lunch. Ms. Patel's classroom was dark and empty. A salad, a container of yogurt, and a drink sat waiting for me on Brody's desk.

13

I RODE WITH TIA AND WILL TO THE GAME
that night. Brody couldn't take me because football players
didn't go home on game days. They stayed at school until the
game was over. And after Will heard why I wasn't at lunch,
he told Tia not to let me drive myself. He insisted that driving while sleep-deprived was like driving drunk. The way I
felt, I believed him.

Much as I longed for bed, I tried to enjoy my last game
on the sidelines. Since I'd quit the yearbook, Mr. Oakley
would revoke my press pass when he returned on Monday.
For now, I snapped the best photos I could and kept my eyes
on the game.

In the first quarter, the visiting team ran some trick plays
and got down to our ten-yard line. Alarming! Mr. Oakley

had taught me that the first team to score had the advantage, because morale was on their side after that. To stop the other team from getting on the scoreboard first, our defense had to prevent them from making a touchdown for three more downs.

But after the next play, I couldn't focus on the excitement. My attention was drawn to Brody *not* acting excited, not even watching.

He sat alone on the bench, feet spread in front of him, arms slack by his sides with his palms up, eyes closed. Underneath his jersey and pads, his chest expanded in long, deep breaths. Another player walked by and socked him on the padded shoulder. He didn't move or even open his eyes.

He was relaxing like I'd taught him. I only hoped this was the answer he'd been searching for.

When the screams of the crowd let him know our defense had held and the visiting team's chances had run out, Brody jumped up. He pulled on his helmet as he ran for the field.

By the end of his first play, I could tell something was different from the last game. Relaxed and in the zone, he managed to complete pass after last-second pass. He waited until he was about to get sacked to toss the ball to our star running back or bullet it to a fullback. With every play, he proved why the local newspaper had fawned over him during the summer.

Brody Larson was back.

And I had helped.

"Harper," called a young woman's voice. I turned around. Brody's sister stood on the other side of the fence, holding one of the chain links. I remembered her vaguely because she'd been a senior when we were sophomores, but I would have known who she was anyway because she looked so much like Brody, with light brown hair and clear green eyes.

She grinned. "I'm Sabrina, Brody's sister."

"I can tell!" While she was still laughing, I asked, "Does he know you're here?"

"Yeah. It was a last-minute thing. I'm driving back to Gainesville tonight. I have to be at work on campus tomorrow morning. I just wanted to see him play."

"So far, so good."

"Yeah! And I wanted to meet you." She put her hand over the fence. I detangled one arm from my camera to shake hands with her. "He's been texting me about you ever since yearbook elections. I can't believe you've started dating. That's so romantic!"

I shrugged and smiled, because I wasn't sure what to say. Honestly, I was flattered that he'd told her about me at all, and floored that he'd been talking about me since the election, weeks before we got together. My hopeful daydreams about him hadn't been one-sided after all.

"When I was a senior," Sabrina said, "a guy and a girl on the track team were our Perfect Couple That Never Was, and they *hated* each other. You can see them in the yearbook turning up their noses at each other. What are the chances that you'll actually get along with the person your senior class picks out for you?"

I grinned at her for a moment, letting her words and the warm fuzzies that came with them wash over me. Then I asked, "Can I get a few shots of you cheering Brody on? He would love to see that."

We didn't have to stage anything. I caught the cutest images of her holding the fence with both hands and screaming at the top of her lungs for her little brother.

Then she returned to the stands. I still snapped photos, but the end of the game had taken on a dreamlike quality. Every time I blinked, I felt like my eyes had been closed for two minutes. And when our team finally won, I didn't realize what had happened at first. I wondered why all the players and cheerleaders had suddenly rushed onto the field. I should have been taking pictures of the melee, but I needed to lie down.

Brody burst out of the crowd, looking huge in his uniform and pads, carrying his helmet. He glanced around at the sidelines and spotted me. Grinning, he dashed straight for me. Recalling how I'd been afraid he would make me drop my camera if he ran into me at the 5K, I removed the strap and packed everything away just before he reached me.

He dropped his helmet on the grass, grabbed me, tilted my body backward, and captured my mouth with his.

I was vaguely aware that some football players and a few kids in the stands were hooting at us. Maybe this kiss looked wildly inappropriate to some people in the crowd. To others, I imagined it looked a lot like a certain sailor grabbing and kissing a certain nurse in Times Square. If two of my friends had kissed like this instead of Brody and me, I would have made sure I got the shot.

But if the purpose of a picture was to capture the memory of a moment, I didn't need one. I would carry this feeling in my heart forever. For once, I honestly didn't care how this looked. I put my hand in his wet hair and kissed him back.

He broke the kiss, then thought better of ending it and kissed me again. He rubbed the tip of his nose against mine and said, "Harper. Thank you."

I giggled. "No, thank *you*."

He kissed me one more time, then set me on my feet. "See you tomorrow."

"See you then."

I watched him jog back to the players on the field and slowly ascend the stadium steps with Noah. Unlike last game, this time they were laughing.

A few minutes later, I sat in the back of Will's ancient Mustang in the school parking lot, transferring the night's pictures from my camera to my laptop. I was so sleepy I could hardly remember my own password. I'd be gone to dreamland as soon as he and Tia took me home and I caught sight of my fluffy bed. But I wanted to get these pictures uploaded. Then I could e-mail Brody the cutest one of Sabrina, my way of saying *Great job* and *Have a good night* and *Thank you for that kiss, which made my senior year.*

Tia and Will were busy clunking their snare drums into the trunk, then peeling off their band uniforms to reveal their shorts and T-shirts underneath, then tickling each other, it sounded like. I was concentrating on sending an e-mail to Brody that didn't seem high. Tia and Will's voices suddenly became hushed and concerned. The change hardly registered with me until Tia appeared in the open door.

"Did you see Brody?" she asked.

I didn't understand what she meant. "Did I see Brody? You mean right after the game? Oh, boy, did I. We were *making out*, I tell you, and not just a little."

She tried again. "Did you see Brody leave?"

"Did I see Brody leave?" I hadn't, and I wasn't sure what she was getting at.

"Is there an echo?" Tia asked, exasperated. "Brody just drove off with Grace."

Brody just drove off with Grace. Brody just drove off with Grace. I'd heard Tia, but what she'd said did not compute.

She called to Will, "Did you know Brody was going out with Grace again?"

"No." Will rounded the car to stand with her and peer inside at me. "That's shocking. I don't understand why he would do that."

"You warned me about him," I said quietly.

"Yeah," Will admitted, "but . . ." He stared up at the sky. He couldn't think of a *but*. "Yeah," he repeated.

Tia could think of plenty to say. She was asking me questions about Brody, bad-mouthing him, and grilling Will about how he and Brody could possibly be friends. I didn't really hear her. I was remembering the first time Mom had found out about my dad cheating on her. I was very little. She had told me, "I don't know why that girl thinks he's going to stay with her. If he cheated on me with her, he's just going to cheat on her with the next girl." And he did.

Once a cheater, always a cheater.

Tia clapped her hands, looking irate. Apparently she'd

been trying to snap me out of my daze for a while. "Here's what you're going to do. See that truck over there?" She pointed across the rapidly emptying parking lot.

"Sawyer's truck?" I asked.

"Exactly. You're going to march right over there and get in the truck with Sawyer. You're going to drive around town until you find Brody and Grace, and you're going to make out with Sawyer right in front of them."

I squinted at her. "Is that going to help somehow?"

"No," said Will.

"Well, it's sure as fuck going to make *me* feel better," Tia said. "How could he do this to you?"

I was having trouble holding my eyes open, and I felt dead. But somewhere deep down, I was almost as angry as Tia sounded. I'd attracted Brody in the first place by wearing a bikini like Grace. Now, acting like Grace to get revenge on him made a perverted kind of sense. "Okay." I started to tumble out of the car, then paused. "Should I take my laptop and shit or leave it here?"

"Leave everything in Will's car. People are in and out of Sawyer's truck and it can get sticky."

"You don't have to do this, Harper," Will told me. "I vote no." He said to Tia, "I don't see what this is going to solve."

"We're not *solving* at this point," she said. "There's nothing to *solve*. We're getting even. Maybe you don't have revenge in Minnesota, but this is how we roll in Florida." She turned to me again. "Let's go, girl. *Vámonos*. We'll be right behind you."

I stumbled off the seat and staggered toward Sawyer's truck. The floodlights far above me seemed brighter than they should have been, and the night was blacker. A sudden stiff breeze rattled the fronds of the palm trees scattered around the parking lot, reminding me that a hurricane still barreled toward us.

As I approached the truck, Sawyer, blond hair dark from a shower, looked up from talking with Noah, also freshly showered after the game, and Quinn, dressed completely in black. "What's up?" Sawyer asked me.

"Brody just left in his truck with Grace. They are probably having sex or whatever. Tia says you and I should find them and make out in front of them. Revenge kissing." I laughed like I'd gone insane.

"I think you should go home and go to bed," Quinn said.

"I think you should do the revenge kissing," Noah said.

"Wait a minute," Sawyer said. "If they're having sex, why can't we have sex too? Revenge sex."

"That would make me uncomfortable," I said.

"I guess I'll take what I can get." Sawyer opened the door of his truck for me. It screeched on its hinges. "Hop in."

As Sawyer started the engine, Will cruised up, stopping so that Tia could talk through the passenger-side window to Sawyer. They decided that we would swing by Brody's house and Grace's house near downtown before ending at the harbor. It was a common place for teenagers to park and cops to harass them. Irate old men wrote about the harbor's parking lot in their letters to the newspaper about the downfall of today's youth.

"You look nice," Sawyer said as he crossed the high school campus and pulled onto the road through downtown. "I'm not just telling you that because we're about to revenge-kiss."

"Are people saying I stopped wearing contacts and started dressing like Grace just to get Brody?"

"No," Sawyer said, "and I hear everything. Who told you that?"

"Kennedy."

"Kennedy," Sawyer repeated, low and husky, like Tia cursing in Spanish. "Why do you care what he says? Why don't you just wear what you want?"

"I guess I don't know what I want." I paused. "But everybody dresses the way they do for a reason, right? Even you." I gazed doubtfully at his beat-up flip-flops.

"Not really," he said. "I only have four shirts."

I blinked against the passing streetlights. "And you don't

eat anything you want. You're very strict about that."

"I'm a vegan because I don't want to cause the death of an animal," he said. "I mean, I'm not so strict about it that I'm going to insult other people for eating what I don't. I serve what I'm told to serve at work. But I'm not personally going to eat it."

"It's an anticruelty thing?"

He glanced over at me, seeming to consider this for the first time. "Yes."

"You didn't seem concerned with cruelty when you made fun of Kennedy's eyebrow piercing."

Sawyer's glance turned to a glare. "When I first moved to town two years ago, Kennedy ribbed me for one solid hour of PE because my dad had just gotten out of jail. You should have heard all the jail jokes. Oh, he was a fucking laugh riot, right up until I punched him."

I'd known Sawyer got suspended for fighting on his first day of school. I hadn't heard why.

"So fuck Kennedy and his eyebrow," Sawyer finished.

"I'm sorry," I said.

Sawyer heaved an exaggerated sigh. "It's crazy for you to apologize, Harper. You didn't do anything."

"I know. I just don't think Kennedy deserves to be made fun of. Like when you made that joke about him the day Noah and Quinn came out."

"I made the same joke about Brody," Sawyer pointed out, "and he didn't mind."

"Kennedy's dad puts a lot of pressure on him," I said carefully.

Sawyer rolled his eyes. "If you want to know what people are saying about you, they're saying you're hot."

"Really?" I asked skeptically.

"Yes."

"I felt like I needed to wear glasses so my face would have something in it. It just looks kind of blank to me, not pretty."

"We all have issues," Sawyer said, almost kindly.

I nodded.

"But that is the most fucked-up thing I've ever heard. You thought you weren't pretty, so you wore glasses? That's pathological."

"Sawyer!" I protested. "Why are you so mean?"

"I don't know," he said.

He slowed as we cruised past Brody's house. A car was there—probably his mom's. The outside lights were on, waiting to guide Brody safely into the house after his date with Grace.

"You should have gotten Most Original," Sawyer said. "You would have, if you hadn't been elected to that couples thing with Brody." Satisfied that Brody's truck wasn't parked anywhere around his house, Sawyer drove on down the dark, palm-lined street. Will was right behind us. The headlights of his Mustang shone through the back window of the truck cab.

"Who'd you vote for in the couples thing?" I asked Sawyer. "I still haven't found anyone who admits to voting for Brody and me."

"I voted for myself," Sawyer said.

"And who?"

"I can't tell you."

"Sawyer!" I exclaimed. *Sawyer* voted himself Perfect Couple That Never Was with a mystery woman? I was dying to know who.

"It's a secret ballot!" he protested.

I took a different tack. "Are you going to ask her out?"

"No," he said quickly. "It's just a fantasy."

"You never know until you try."

"This I know," he said ominously. He was after a girl he thought he couldn't have. And I was afraid he was right, if I'd guessed correctly which girl he had in mind.

"Is it Kaye?"

I watched blush creep into his cheeks. He asked evenly, "Why would you say that?"

"You wanted to be in the Superlatives photo with her

and Aidan, but only in costume. You bug her constantly and taunt her. You act like a seventeen-year-old with a crush, or a twelve-year-old with borderline personality disorder."

He winced, but that was the only indication he heard me, or that I was right about Kaye. The blush slowly drained away, leaving him looking pale.

"I keep secrets," I told him.

"Good." He slowed in front of a house that must have been Grace's. Several cars were parked in the driveway, but not Brody's truck. Sawyer turned the corner and headed for the harbor.

"Brody told me you've started working out with the football team instead of the cheerleaders," I said.

"Yeah," Sawyer said. "Not the plays, of course, just the drills. I want to be able to run a 5K without having to sit down."

"You'd just been in the hospital that week, Sawyer."

"I want to be able to wear a pelican costume without passing out from heat exhaustion."

"It was, like, ninety-five degrees that afternoon, wasn't it?"

"I guess I just want to feel . . . worthy."

"Worthy!" I laughed. "Sawyer, that doesn't make sense. Everybody loves you."

He eyed me skeptically across the cab.

"They do!" I protested. "In a love/hate sort of way."

"Thanks for not making me feel any better."

It surprised me that Sawyer felt bad in the first place.

He pulled his truck into the harbor's parking lot. No streetlights shone here this late at night, which made it perfect for teenagers parked in clusters, blasting music and sitting on tailgates. They squinted into Sawyer's headlights and shielded their eyes. We drove slowly until we saw Brody's truck.

Sawyer parked in front of Brody, about twenty yards away. Sawyer's headlights shone straight into the cab. Brody was behind the wheel. Grace was on the other side of the seat. They weren't touching, as far as I could tell, but who knew what they were doing behind the high dashboard? They blinked like deer.

Sawyer switched off his engine and the headlights. We could still see the dark forms of Brody and Grace. In a few moments, when their eyes adjusted, they would be able to see us, too, and everything we were about to do.

"No tongue," I said quietly.

"No tongue!" Sawyer exclaimed. "That's like saying we're going to have sex with no—"

I was already sliding toward him across the seat as he spoke these words. I slapped my hand over his mouth and gave him a stern look. "Did you just say that to me?"

"No, I did not," he said through my hand.

Cautiously, I took my hand away. And then, before I could think this through any further, we were kissing. The strange, sleep-deprived vibration I'd been feeling all day pushed me against his chest.

He whispered against my lips, "Just a little tongue."

I cracked up. I was so giddy and nervous that I couldn't stop laughing.

"Come on, just a little," he coaxed me. "You'll love it. You'll be saying, 'Sawyer, stud, I am sorry I ever doubted your tongue.'"

"O-*kay*, use it."

As the openmouthed kiss began, I hung on to his shirt with both fists, bracing myself until it was over. Quickly I found myself saying, "Mm," and kissing him back. Tia and other girls Sawyer had been with said he was worth the trouble. Now I knew why. I leaned forward.

We both jumped at a knocking on the driver's-side window. Brody, taller than the truck, glowered at us through the glass.

Sawyer reached toward the door.

"No," I said, putting a hand on Sawyer's arm. I could tell he was about to desert me.

"Sorry," he said. "My man is serious." He cranked the window down and asked Brody, "May I help you?"

"Yes, please," Brody said in the same polite tone with a threat underneath. "I would like to talk to Harper alone for a minute."

"Sure," Sawyer told him, "if I can 'talk' to Grace alone for a minute." He made finger quotes.

"If you can catch her," Brody said.

We all looked toward Brody's truck. It was empty. I could barely see Grace in the darkness, leaning through another truck's window. She opened the door and got inside. The truck roared off.

Brody looked back at us with his brows raised like Grace's departure vindicated him.

Sawyer rubbed my nape and told Brody, "Listen. This here's my girl."

He meant, I thought, that we were friends, and he was looking out for me. I'd never viewed Sawyer as anything more than an entertaining basket case, but he was standing up for me.

"Got it," Brody said.

"Seriously, Larson," Sawyer said. "Even Will thinks this business is shocking."

"O-*kay*," Brody said, ticked off now.

Sawyer turned to me. "Go," he said. "I'll wait here for you."

14

I GOT OUT AND FOLLOWED BRODY TO HIS truck. He started to open the door for me, but I shook my head. I wasn't going to sit where Grace had just been sitting, like I was her temporary replacement. I leaned against the hood. He leaned beside me.

He swallowed audibly. "I felt bad about leaving with her as soon as I did it."

"Congratulations," I said. "You know what would have been better? If you'd felt bad about it *before* you did it."

He nodded. His nearly dry curls moved against his neck. He said, "I really wasn't trying to get together with her again, because we really were never together in the first place."

Suddenly I was back at school, one week ago, lamenting my boring high school experience. *This* was my foray into the high school party lifestyle? Cross-eyed from lack of sleep, head over heels in lust, and resentful of my gorgeous boyfriend for cheating on me while he claimed he hadn't been cheating?

I stood back, closed my eyes, and put my hands in my hair—something I hadn't done for years, ever since I got on my careful-coif kick. I murmured, "This is some dumb shit."

"Harper," he said. "Are you okay? You're blinking like you can't keep your eyes open."

"I think . . . I've never worn my contacts this long."

"Do you have a case for them, and solution, like I told you?"

"Yes."

"Where?"

"In my purse."

"In Sawyer's truck?"

"No, in Will's car." I gestured vaguely to the Mustang, which had prowled to a position near both trucks so that Will and Tia could watch the show.

Brody hiked across the parking lot to the Mustang. The driver's door opened. I could hear them talking, but not what they were saying. Then came Brody's echoing shout. Everyone sitting on tailgates turned to look: ". . . shocking? What did you say that to her for, Will?" Will's voice was firm. Tia's rose above it: "This is Harper we're talking about, Brody. Harper Davis. You can't do this to Harper."

Brody returned across the asphalt, carrying my purse but not my laptop or camera bag. "Get in the truck, Harper. You're about to fall down."

I shook my head. "Only if I can sit in the driver's seat."

"Fine." He rounded the truck and opened the driver's door for me. It was my first time inside Brody's truck, where Grace and countless other girls had had all sorts of experiences I'd thought I wanted. I sniffed deeply, trying to detect perfume, but all I smelled was cleaner.

He got in the passenger side and closed the door, then offered me my purse. I dug out the contact solution. He held the case for me while I took out the lenses. Then he put everything back in my purse. My dad had made this sort of sweet gesture toward Mom, too, after he'd started a new affair and she'd caught him.

"I see where you're coming from now," I said. "On Wednesday night, you told me you didn't have to break up with Grace in order to go out with me, because you weren't *with* Grace."

"Right," he said warily.

"I assumed that, afterward, you would be *with* me." He opened his mouth, but I kept talking. "I was mistaken. What you meant was, you weren't *with* Grace, and you weren't *with* me either. You're not *with* anybody, and that gives you the freedom to be with everybody."

"Well," he said, clearly not liking where this was going, "not *everybody*."

"Sure, because you're not a slut. You're just a free spirit. You're an individual. Like you explained to me in the pavilion, everybody in your family's divorced. Couples aren't meant to be permanent. You get into a couple—a coup*ling*, like a train car—with one girl and then another."

"Exactly," he said. His shoulders relaxed, and he popped his neck, relieved that I understood where he was coming from.

I nodded. "That is fucking ridiculous, Brody. It's rifuckulous."

His brows knitted. "Are you drunk?"

"No," I yelled, "I am operating on almost zero sleep because my ex-boyfriend moved my deadline because I broke up with him so I could be *with* you!"

He huffed out a sigh. "I know, Harper. It's just that you said you were going home after the game, and Grace and I have been friends for a long time. She asked if I wanted to hang out. We came here and talked about that guy from Florida State, and I told her he's too old for her. I said guys from college trolling for girls from high school are usually up to no good. She got mad. That's when you drove up. She spotted some guys from the University of Miami and left with them. The end."

I wanted to believe him. I sort of *did* believe him, but I felt like I shouldn't. I felt like I was being taken advantage of, and that he'd been taking advantage of me the whole week, and everybody at school knew it but me.

"I shouldn't have done it," he said. "I'm just . . . friends with people. I'm not *with* girls. I figure we can go out, or sometimes make out, and later we can still be friends and *hang* out. It's the girls who don't agree to that plan."

I understood now why there always seemed to be a girl shouting at him in the hallway.

"I knew you were different," he said. "When Grace wanted to hang out, I said okay because that's what I'd normally do, but we hadn't even reached the edge of the school campus before I realized I'd done the wrong thing. I've worked on this—my mom made me go to counseling after my dad left—and I have this checklist in my mind and these things I'm supposed to say to myself, but they take a few minutes to kick in. I have an impulse-control problem."

"You sure as hell do," I grumbled.

"Harper," he pleaded.

"No," I said. "I came here with Sawyer because Tia was

mad at you and egging me on. I was trying to make you jealous, but not because I want you back. I don't. When you cheated on Grace with me and said you didn't owe her anything, I should have known you would treat me exactly the same way you'd treated her." I reached for the handle of the door.

He put his hand on my arm—gently, or I would have bashed the shit out of him. When I glared at him, he put up his hand in surrender.

"Harper," he said, "give me another chance. We haven't even been on a real date."

"What does it matter, when you say people aren't meant to be in exclusive couples? I don't want to be with a guy who thinks that way."

He opened his hands. "I thought that because of who I was with. Harper, I don't want this to be about Grace. I want it to be about you, and me. I don't want to lose you. You—" His voice broke. He cleared his throat. "You make me feel smart, and funny, like there's more to me than a good arm."

I drummed my fingers on my bare knee, halfway to a delirious decision. "You have to understand something. If we date, we're a couple. We're *not* the Perfect Couple That Never Was. We *are* a couple. There's no *never*. And it's *not* okay for you to go out with Grace." Hearing myself, I shook my head. "No, never mind. I shouldn't have to spell that out for you. I'm done." I reached for the door again.

"Hey," he said. Wisely he didn't touch me this time. His voice was quiet. I paused to listen.

"You said we would catch each other tomorrow," he said. "I'd really like to come over then. That can't hurt anything, right? We can talk again when you've had some sleep."

I gazed out the windshield. I couldn't see well enough to discern Sawyer, but I could see his truck, still waiting for me. Sawyer had my back. He'd acted like Brody and I had a claim on each other. Even Tia, in her warped way, had led me here to Brody. Somebody in our school—a lot of people, apparently, though I didn't know who—thought Brody and I were perfect for each other. And because my feelings for him were so strong, I wasn't ready to throw away that possibility just yet.

"You can come over tomorrow," I muttered. "But if you ever pull something like this again, you won't get another chance with me."

He said, "I won't need one. I promise."

My alarm went off at six a.m. I got up, showered, helped Mom serve breakfast, got quietly scolded for dropping a basket of orange rolls in a guest's lap, stomped back to my house, and crawled into bed. The talk at breakfast was that the hurricane had petered out into a tropical storm and was headed farther west into the Gulf, so we wouldn't get a lot of straight-line wind damage or flooding from the tidal surge—only a lot of rain, and possibly tornadoes on Tuesday, when my parents were scheduled to get divorced. I closed my eyes, listened to the light rain from a band of showers far in advance of the storm, and wished I could go back to sleep. I knew it would never happen with my mind spinning about Brody.

At eleven a.m. I woke again, smelling cinnamon. Something was very wrong. Mom seldom cooked for me, and she was never in the house on weekends. She spent all day every day cleaning and repairing the B & B. Taking the precaution of putting on a bra first in case criminals had broken into my house to fix me cinnamon toast, I wandered into the kitchen and saw it was Brody.

"Sorry," he said, looking around from the stove. "Your mom said it was okay. Have a seat." He slid a plate in front of me at the table: the best kind of cinnamon toast, with a buttery, sugary glaze baked to a crisp on top. Eggs. Bacon. Sliced banana. He put another plate with twice as much food down at Mom's place and dug in.

I tasted the toast. Heaven, but I didn't want to admit this. I asked coldly, "Is this a postgame phenomenon, or do you always eat this much for breakfast?"

He said between bites, "I already had breakfast."

"This is lunch, then?"

"No."

We ate in silence for a while. When his plate was clean and mine was still half-full, he said, "Tonight some of us are going to a movie and then the Crab Lab. Will and Tia, and Kaye and Aidan, and Noah and Quinn. Would you go with me?"

I took a bite of bacon.

"You're still mad at me." He sighed. "I don't know what else to do, Harper."

"Maybe there isn't anything else *to* do," I said. "Maybe, as you so eloquently put it last week, the school is on crack. They never should have paired us up."

He cocked his head to one side and considered me. "If you believe that, I'll leave you alone from now on. But I don't think you believe that. I sure don't."

I took a bite of egg. This boy could cook an egg, that was for sure.

"When we go back to school on Monday and everybody hears we've broken up," he said, "fourteen guys are going to ask you out, and probably two or three girls. But I'm thinking you don't have anything else on the horizon for tonight. And I'm better looking than Kennedy. I'm less weird than Quinn, and probably eighty percent less gay than Noah."

I laughed. "When you get all romantic on me, how can I refuse?"

"Good. What are you doing until then?"

I gazed toward the front windows. "Has it stopped raining?"

He nodded.

"I'll walk around town and take photos. The light's great and the colors are bright after a rain. When I had to stay up Thursday night, I thought I'd never want to take another photo again, but I've gotten over it."

"I'll come with," he said.

"No, that's okay."

"I want to," he insisted.

"I'm not just playing around, Brody. I had something specific in mind. Sites online post photos from freelance photographers for people to use in their newsletters and websites. I thought I might try to get in on that gig, but I need a bigger portfolio first."

"I can help you," he said.

"I don't want your help." When his face fell, I said quickly, "It's nothing against *you*. I prefer to work alone."

"How do you know?"

He had me there.

"Ah-ha," he said. "See? You *don't* know. You *think* you

prefer to work alone because you've never had a good-looking guy to carry your camera equipment."

"It's a tripod and one small bag," I said. "You just want to grovel to me all afternoon and talk me out of being mad."

He lifted his chin. "I want to spend time with you," he said self-righteously. "And I could help you. I could model for you."

"Now *there's* an idea," I admitted, mind suddenly racing. "I would pay you if I sold any of those shots, of course. But you wouldn't have any control over who bought your picture and what it was used for. Your face could end up as an advertisement for a porn site."

"That could make me *very* popular next year, in college." When I just blinked at him, he hurried on, "No, I'm kidding. You're right. You can't use shots that show my face. My mom makes me keep my online accounts super private, even though my picture has been in all the newspapers. She thinks I'm going to get kidnapped."

"If people tried to kidnap you, wouldn't you just break their heads?"

"My mom still thinks I'm twelve," he said, "but I try not to argue with her. My dad wasn't very nice to her. My step-dad wasn't either. Her new boyfriend is okay so far, but I don't know. I feel bad for her. If I can, I do what she wants."

I was taken aback. I hadn't realized Brody was this mature.

"I mean," he went on, "for a case like this, where she'd find out."

Never mind about the maturity.

"So we can't use my face," he said, "but that doesn't mean you couldn't use the rest of me. Have you seen this?"

Afraid of what he was about to show me, I glanced toward the door, sure Mom would choose that moment to appear. But he only pulled back the sleeve of his T-shirt to show me his biceps.

"That's a great idea," I said. "You can flex your arm with the ocean in the background. I'll type 'The View from Florida' across the photo and have it printed as a postcard to sell in the gift shops around town. Every lady over sixty will want to mail one to her friends back home."

"Only ladies over sixty?"

"Well . . ." Jumping up from the table, I slid the TV remote to him. "Here, you can watch whatever game is on. I'll be ready in a sec."

I dashed back to my room to change clothes and brush my hair, excited about this new project. Afterward, I would need to update my website to read HARPER DAVIS, PORTRAITS, EVENT PHOTOGRAPHY, GRATUITOUS BICEPS.

*   *   *

I was all too familiar with going out with a group of friends and being one half of the Couple That Wasn't Getting Along. I'd spent the last six weeks that way with Kennedy. It was strange to arrive at the movie theater with Brody as half of a brand-new couple who'd spent the entire afternoon together having so much fun that we couldn't stop grinning. Tonight the Couple That Wasn't Getting Along was the one that had been dating for three years, Kaye and Aidan. Kaye made Tia trade places with her so she could sit by me, with Tia and Will between her and Aidan.

"Oooh, I love your hair!" I exclaimed as she sat down.

"Thanks," she said flatly. "Aidan said it looks like I have an afro."

Not the thing to say to Kaye. "An afro would be cute on you, but that's more fashion forward than you usually go."

She glowered at me. I wasn't making her feel better.

"It's not really an afro, the way you have it styled in front. I think of a real 1970s afro as being round all over. Anyway, calling it an afro is not an insult."

"He meant it as an insult," she said.

"If he did, he must have meant you looked retro. He wasn't being racist. Aidan isn't like that." He had many qualities I didn't like, but that wasn't one of them. "I'll bet he was just surprised. You've worn it in twists for a long time."

Her mouth flattened into a line, and flattened again whenever Aidan leaned around Tia and Will, whispering her name to get her attention. She wouldn't turn in his direction.

They were still fighting when we filed around a big table in the center of the room at the Crab Lab.

"Sorry," I heard Tia tell Sawyer in his Crab Lab T-shirt and waiter's apron as we sat down. "I didn't think you'd be working this late tonight, or I would have convinced everybody to go somewhere else."

"I took a longer shift. I have nothing better to do since I quit drinking." He smiled wryly. "It's okay." He moved toward the kitchen.

"What was that about?" I asked Tia across the table.

"He has a little problem with one of us," she said quietly.

"Oh. With Brody or me, because of last night?"

"Gosh, no," she said. "Believe it or not, it's more fucked up than that."

I figured he must dread having to serve Kaye and her boyfriend. Lucky for Sawyer, Kaye and Aidan were still three seats from each other. Anyway, I'd hardly had time to ponder this before Sawyer marched back with a tray full of drinks balanced precariously high on one hand. He set a soda in front of me and an iced tea in front of Brody.

"Wait," Brody said. "Did we order drinks?"

Ten minutes later, it was the same thing: "Wait. Sawyer. Did we order food?"

"Y'all, save it," Tia warned. "He's in a bad mood."

"When was he ever in a *good* mood?" Kaye asked.

Tia glared at her.

Kaye spread her hands. "If you know he's in a bad mood, don't you need a good mood for comparison? I've never seen it."

"You're picking on him."

"We're not picking on him," Will clarified. "At least, I'm not. *I'm* eating grouper when I wanted shrimp."

Sawyer came back from the kitchen again and bent over the table between Noah and Quinn. "I didn't put in an order yet for you two. Sometimes you want one thing, and sometimes you want another."

A spontaneous snicker burst from two or three people, then instantly hushed. After a moment of silence, Quinn said, "You know what's consistent? You're a complete jerk-off," at the same time Noah stood.

Before I even registered what I was doing, I jumped up and put a hand between Noah and Sawyer. Just as quickly, I was pulled backward. Brody had his arm around my waist, wrestling me back down into my chair. He said in my ear, "Don't."

Sawyer stared defiantly up into Noah's dark eyes, pen to his pad. "Cheeseburger or patty melt?" he asked.

"Cheeseburger," Noah said grudgingly.

Sawyer leaned around him to ask Quinn, "Fried or broiled shrimp?"

"Broiled," Quinn said.

Sawyer made a show of jotting the orders on his pad with a flourish. "Mm-hm," he said as he turned for the kitchen. The way he intoned it made it sound like a "So there."

Noah sank back down into his seat and told Quinn, "I won't miss him when he goes to jail."

Sawyer came back out with another laden tray. Working his way around the table, he set a plate of shrimp and fries in front of Kaye. The food had been arranged in a smiley face. The fries were the mouth, and two cherry tomatoes were the eyes. The shrimp had been spaced in a semicircle across the arc of the head, like Kaye's beautiful new pouf of hair.

"Sawyer, dammit," she said. "What is this supposed to be?"

"It doesn't look quite right, does it? Here." He took one of her shrimp from the picture and tossed it onto Tia's plate.

"We didn't even order," Aidan complained from down the table.

"Kids' grilled cheese?" Sawyer asked. "That's what you

always order when you come here with your mommy and daddy, Aidan."

Kaye burst into laughter.

"Kaye," Aidan barked around Tia and Will. When he got her attention, he pointed at her, then firmly pointed to the empty seat beside him.

She set her jaw and shook her head.

He raked back his chair. Everyone in the restaurant turned to stare. He blustered out of the restaurant, hitting the swinging front door so hard that it took several moments to close behind him. Kaye looked sick.

Without missing a beat, Sawyer swept up Aidan's untouched plate and set it in front of Brody, above his usual dish of fish sandwich and vegetables.

"Thanks, buddy," Brody said.

"You're welcome, buddy." Sawyer rounded the table and bent close to Kaye's ear. He said, so quietly I could hardly hear him, "I love your hair like that. You look very pretty."

She blinked in surprise, then stared across the restaurant at him as he headed toward the kitchen. After the kitchen door had already closed behind him, she mouthed the words "Thank you."

Even though I didn't believe Aidan had meant to hurt Kaye's feelings so deeply, I did think he was being insensitive to her. He should have known better after dating her so long. Or cared more. And I wasn't too surprised when Tia leaned over and whispered to me that we should both spend the night at Kaye's house. When Kaye and Tia and I needed each other, boys came second. Whatever adventure Brody and I might have had after dinner, it would need to wait.

Brody drove me home to pack. As we got back on the road again, headed across town to Kaye's house, I asked, "Did it freak you out when Noah and Quinn were holding hands in the movie?"

He was silent for a few seconds. "Was I acting weird?"

"You kept looking over at them."

He laughed uncomfortably. "A little. But Noah is so happy. I mean, if the guys on the team would leave him alone about it, he'd be happy. This town is full of people who are out, but they're not seventeen, you know? It took cojones to do what he and Quinn did. They stood up for themselves. If they can do that, they can get through anything."

As we drove on in silence, I thought about the couples who'd sat at the table. Other than Will and Tia, Quinn and Noah seemed the most stable. Kaye and Aidan were starting to act like Kennedy and me. I could only imagine Kaye must feel lost, especially after spending all of high school together with Aidan.

"Are you mad I'm going over to Kaye's?" I asked Brody.

"No." Pulling to a stop at a traffic light in a quiet intersection, he glanced over at me and smiled. "Disappointed." He accelerated as the light changed. "How about we meet up tomorrow? Would you like to go surfing? Can you surf?"

"Yes. Badly." Surfing was something most of my friends knew how to do. We'd learned when we were too young to know that the small waves on the Gulf Coast weren't worth the trouble. Canadians probably felt this way about swimming in frigid water. But the downgraded hurricane way offshore might produce good waves tomorrow.

I snapped my fingers. "I don't have a surfboard."

"I'll bring Sabrina's for you."

"Will surfing still be safe as the storm gets closer?"

"Define *safe*."

Right. To take advantage of the thrill, we'd have to swim in waters that were far from calm. Kind of like dating Brody. But some thrills were worth the trouble. I'd enjoyed my day with him enough that I was willing to take on the next challenge.

15

KAYE LAY TUMMY DOWN ON HER BED, HER bare feet swinging behind her in the air, while Tia slipped on one of my A-line dresses and I pinned the side seam to fit her slender body. There wasn't enough material in the bottom to let the hem out. What had been a minidress on me would be a micromini on Tia. She didn't mind.

I'd brought a few other dresses I would tailor for Kaye. She and Tia kept trying to talk me out of it. "I worked hard on all my clothes," I said, "and I don't want them to go to waste. I'm really attached to some of the dresses, but they do seem kind of stuffy now. I might keep a few for myself and alter them with a shorter hem or a lower neckline. But if I wear them again, do you think people will say I'm not being consistent? They can't figure out anymore whether I'm supposed to be Old Harper or

New Harper?" I'd told them what Kennedy had said about me trying to dress like Grace, which still bothered me.

"Consistency is overrated," Tia said over her shoulder as I pinned her other side. "Some days I look cute, if I do say so myself. Some days I oversleep and don't bathe. I like to keep people guessing."

Straightening, I sniffed her hair and didn't smell anything. Mostly she bathed.

"Brody told me he wants me to wear my glasses sometimes because they're sexy and he likes surprises."

"I would be wearing my glasses, then," Tia said at the same time Kaye said, "Oooh, that sounds like an invitation. So, you guys made up? You seemed really happy tonight."

I nodded, smiling as I thought about our day together, and my new collection of gratuitous biceps photos. "I have fun with him. He's hard for me to get used to, though."

"Because he's talking about football the whole time," Kaye asked, "and you don't understand?"

"No, he doesn't talk much about football. I guess I've always dated guys who constantly make fun of stuff and show off how smart they are. Brody doesn't do that. Sometimes he says things that aren't even sarcastic."

"It sounds to me like you've never dated a guy who wasn't an asshole," Tia said.

"Ha," I said. "Tia, take that off. Switch." Carefully we pulled the dress over her head without dislodging the pins. I would have plenty of free time to sew it for her at home now that I wasn't the yearbook photographer, I thought ruefully. Kaye slipped on the next dress, which only needed to be altered to fit her athletic A-cup.

"I don't know," I said, carefully pinning the bust seam. "I had so much fun with Brody today, but I still have misgivings about what happened last night."

"Why does it have to be perfect?" Tia asked. "Why can't you just enjoy him while he lasts? It's not like you're going to marry him."

Marrying Brody had never entered my mind. But now that Tia had brought it up, the idea didn't sound too bad. I asked, "Do you know you're not going to marry Will?"

"I could marry Will," she acknowledged. "He's endlessly entertaining. Except I'm never getting married."

"Oh," I said in protest at the same time as Kaye voiced my thoughts: "Will is more traditional than you. He'll get married to *somebody*, if not you."

Tia said, "I will cut a bitch," and she sounded upset, like she was actually picturing Will dumping her because she wouldn't commit.

"Calm down," I said. "Who knows? You might change

your mind. Anyway, you have years of dating before it's an issue."

"God knows you don't have to hurry things along because you're saving yourselves for each other," Kaye said. "I don't know about Will, but you took care of your end of that a couple of years ago with Sawyer."

"Excuse me, but *you* took care of *your* end a couple of years ago with Aidan," Tia pointed out.

"But I'm *with* Aidan," Kaye said. "You were never *with* Sawyer."

I interjected, "I just had this huge argument with Brody last night about who he was *with*. You two are giving me flashbacks."

Tia talked right over me. She asked Kaye, "What is this obsession you have with Sawyer?"

I figured Kaye would explode, but she didn't. She asked softly, "What do you mean?"

"I mean, lately you're always bringing up what I used to do with Sawyer and being judgmental about it. Do you have a crush on him?"

Now Kaye sounded outraged. "*No!* I'm going to marry Aidan!"

"We know," Tia and I chorused. Kaye had shown us a picture of her wedding dress in a magazine. In tenth grade.

"But that means you'll be with one guy your whole life," Tia said. "Before that happens, maybe you need a little sample of someone else. Like Sawyer."

Kaye muttered, "No, thanks."

"It's good stuff," Tia said. "Right, Harper?"

"We didn't kiss much, but it wasn't bad," I said appreciatively. "I mean, yeah, I enjoyed my sample."

"I'll bet," Kaye said, with surprisingly little scorn in her voice. She cleared her throat. "Anyway, Harper, the one thing I worry about with you and Brody is that he's so much more experienced than you. You hardly dated before this year. You never even had a date for homecoming."

"True," I said, not quite able to edit the glee from my voice. This year I *would* have a date for homecoming. My date would be the star football player. He would give me the traditional corsage, which would be too bulky for me to wear while I was photographing the game, so I would pin it to my camera bag. After he won the game, we would go together to the homecoming dance, and it would be the best night of my life.

So far.

"He doesn't make me feel inexperienced when I'm with him," I said. "It's not like I've *tried* to stay alone and inno-cent all this time. I've just been searching for the wrong kind of guy. I *thought* I wanted a funny, artistic guy. A successful guy."

I'd meant to describe Kennedy. But when Tia furrowed her brow, perplexed, and Kaye sat back, I realized they seemed to think I was talking about Will and Aidan.

I shook my head and went on, "It took the senior class electing us Perfect Couple to show me what I really wanted, and that's Brody. An athlete with a sense of humor I don't quite understand, who plays dumb sometimes but who's book smart and sensitive when he tries, with impulse-control issues that get him in trouble."

"Yeah!" Tia cheered. "I told you the day of the elections that he would be better for you than Kennedy."

Kaye shook her head. "Just be careful that it's the good kind of trouble."

Brody parked his truck at the edge of Granddad's private beach. Several hundred yards away, on the public section of the beach, we could see the yellow flag flying. That meant medium risk in the high surf. We waded into the ocean with our surfboards under our arms.

Hours later, completely exhausted and tingling from exertion, I floated on my board and watched a lifeguard haul down the yellow flag and hoist a red one. Two red flags would have meant the surf had gotten so rough that the beach was closed to swimmers. One red flag meant the lifeguard eyed us resentfully and only *wished* we would get out of the water so she didn't have to save our asses later.

"Do you think we should go to shore?" I asked Brody, who was floating on his board beside me. The sunset was beautiful and violent behind him, with strange clouds stirred up by the approaching storm. The bright pink light smoothed the ugly purple bruise on his side, courtesy of Friday night's game.

"Brody?" I called over the noise of the tide.

"I heard you," he said. "I'm thinking. I have trouble giving a shit about my own safety. I'm trying to consider this as a normal person would, for the sake of *your* safety."

"That's sweet of you."

He laughed. "You're welcome. Yeah—"

His voice was drowned out by an approaching roar. Before I could turn, a huge wave crashed over my head, forcing me under the water. The surfboard squirted out of my arms, and the tie tugged my ankle. I did a flip and grabbed for the board before it escaped out to sea, dragging me with it.

I surfaced spluttering. Brody was laughing and trying to shake the water out of his ears. "You okay?"

"Fine."

"As I was saying," he said, "yeah, I think we should go to shore."

An hour later, we were still lying on towels on Granddad's deserted beach, kissing in the darkness. Though he'd been exploring my breasts with his hands and then his mouth, I'd wanted to keep on my bathing suit top for a while, in case someone strolling on the beach wandered by. But when Brody fitted himself between my legs and lay on top of me, with only his bathing suit and my bikini bottoms between us, I forgot my modesty. He slowly circled each of my breasts with his tongue.

He held himself above me in mid push-up, his forearms trembling. He said softly, barely audible above the wind in the palms above us, "I have a condom."

I swallowed. "Okay."

"Do you want to?"

My whole body said yes, rising along the length of him, desiring him. And he felt it. He sucked in a small gasp.

"I want to," I breathed. "But I'm not on anything, and I would be terrified of getting pregnant, even with a condom."

He smiled with his mouth only. His eyes were worried.

"But I'll get on something," I said, "and then I want to."

He nodded. "Okay." He lowered himself over me and kissed my lips once more, deliciously, slowly. Then he rolled off me. "Sit up. Let me tie you."

I found my bathing suit beside me and clutched it to my chest as he tied two bows in the back, his fingers sliding intimately across my skin. We both lay down on the sand again. His feet captured one of mine and massaged scratchy sand between my toes.

All the while, he was inhaling deeply like he couldn't quite catch his breath. "Wow," he murmured, "I feel like I've just run wind sprints in practice." His voice shook.

Down by our sides, I felt for his hand, grasped it, and squeezed.

He took one last long breath and seemed to relax. I couldn't hear him breathing anymore over the surf. The waves rolled in and slipped out. The planet was breathing. Overhead, the front edge of the tropical storm sped through the sky, dark purple clouds glowing on a periwinkle background.

"Are you thinking about how you'd compose a photo of this?" he asked.

"Not exactly. I was thinking I could never take this picture. It would be a huge disappointment, because the lens wouldn't quite capture the intense color of this sky."

"You're so artistic," he said. "It seems like you could just paint the world the way you wanted it, and then you wouldn't have to worry about catching it just right."

"The world is beautiful exactly like it is," I said. "You just have to know how to frame it, and bring it into focus."

I watched the clouds race overhead. Everything in my life seemed more in focus at that moment. My body still tingled where he'd touched me. I felt close to him. His transgressions of Friday night seemed a million miles away. I was beginning to understand how Mom could forgive my dad so many times, if this was how they kissed and made up.

"Do you think everything we feel for each other is physical?" I asked. "Like, we've done some things together and that makes our brains think we should be together?"

"You're dividing the mental and the physical," Brody said, "the head and the heart. I don't buy that division."

"What do you mean, you don't buy it?"

"I mean, sure, you see it in poems and songs, but it's a metaphor. It isn't real. Your brain is part of your body. It's one whole system that has to work together, or not. Nobody knows that better than me."

Right. He was still afraid of getting another concussion—as he should be, honestly. My relaxation programs had helped, but he was still working on staying in the game.

"What you're really asking me is whether what we have together fits into a box you've made." He held his fingers around an imaginary box in the dark in front of him. The box was small. And I was surprised, once again, that he understood what I was thinking a lot better than I understood it myself.

"I'm all for standards," he said. "But it seems to me that you built that box a long time ago, and it hasn't been working for you lately. Maybe it never did."

He turned to me and put one big, sandy hand up to cup my chin. "Here's what I know, Harper. I've never felt more comfortable than I do right now, right here, with you. If this was taken away from me, I would fight to get it back. I'm pretty easy to please, wouldn't you say? I'm more of a go-with-the-flow guy than a fighter. But I'm determined to keep football in my life. And I'll do the same to keep you in it too. Of course, now I've compared you to football, which is insulting, sorry." He took his hand off my chin, reclining on the beach again with the muscle control of many hours spent in the school's weight room, and closed his eyes.

"That's a huge compliment, coming from you," I said.

He opened one eye. "Right."

"I'm serious. You have a box too. You've wondered, 'Will any woman ever be as important to me as football? There is not such a woman. Despair!' Then you found me. I'm proud to sit in that box. Next to the box containing a football."

He rolled to face me. The smile had left his face. He wasn't kidding anymore. He said, "It's not just a game. I mean, it is, but it means more than that to me."

"I know." Admittedly, I didn't understand one hundred percent. But he seemed to love playing football like I loved taking pictures. At some point, an activity became a part of you.

"It could be a career for me," he said, "if not as a player, maybe as a coach."

"You would make an awesome coach," I said.

"But even if the game doesn't pan out for me," he said, "I've been good at it. I've worked hard for it. There aren't a lot of things in my life that I can say that about." He rolled on his back again and reached for my hand. We watched the clouds spin by above us.

After a long silence, filled with the roar of the excitable ocean, I said, "I want to talk about sex again."

He turned his head and gazed at me. "You only want to talk about it?"

"For now. Do you think we should wait for some special event, like graduation?"

"No," he said immediately.

"Prom?"

"No."

"Homecoming?"

He chuckled. "You're asking me if we *should* wait. My opinion is, no. But we *will*, if you want to." He pulled me closer. "I'll always be the one who wants to spend the summer after graduation touring Europe even though we don't have any money, who wants to cut class and go to the beach for the day, who drags you to Vegas the second we turn twenty-one. I'll say, 'Come on, it'll be fun.' You just have to tell me when to stop."

I laid my head on his chest, listening to his heartbeat. He wrapped his arm around me. Whatever my future was with Brody, it did sound like an awful lot of fun.

On Monday in journalism class, Mr. Oakley called me up to his desk. I hadn't planned to tattle on Kennedy. Quinn had done that for me.

Mr. Oakley asked me to tell him my side of the story, but Kennedy hardly let me get a word in edgewise. He followed me to Mr. Oakley's desk, stood right beside me, and denied everything I said. Mr. Oakley did not look happy. At first I thought he was furious with me. Then he barked at Kennedy to sit down—and Mr. Oakley was not a barker. He tried to convince me to stay on as yearbook photographer. I told him *I couldn't work like this* and resisted the urge to throw my hands in the air like a diva. He said we should table the discussion until he'd spoken to Kennedy, and he took Kennedy out into the hall.

Half an hour later, at lunch, Kaye told me, "I know some gossip about you! We're having some minor problems in student council, so I've been spending a lot of quality time in the teachers' workroom. I've overheard things."

"I'll bite," Tia said. We all moved closer together, knowing teachers' workroom gossip was the juiciest kind of gossip. "What are the minor problems in student council?"

Kaye's eyes cut to me, then to Tia. "Top-secret issues that probably will amount to nothing. Anyway," she said, splaying her fingers like this was going to be delicious, "Mr. Oakley was bitching nonstop about Kennedy. He wants to fire him as yearbook editor for moving up your deadline, Harper. He said you were reluctant to accuse Kennedy yourself, but several students told him Kennedy fired you just because you broke up with him."

"Really!" I exclaimed. "Mr. Oakley didn't say anything like that to me."

"He can't," Kaye said. "He doesn't think he can fire Kennedy, because the code of student conduct isn't clear enough. Principal Chen is afraid Kennedy's parents could sue the school. Mr. Oakley is mad. As. Hell. He keeps saying it's a fucking travesty that Kennedy gets away with murder and makes the yearbook's ace photographer feel like she has to quit."

"Did Mr. Oakley actually say 'fucking travesty'?" Tia asked.

"Listen," Kaye said, "I have learned some language in the teachers' workroom that would curl your hair. You should have heard them after Sawyer passed out from heat exhaustion. The principal and the cheerleading coach and the football coach all blamed each other. I cowered in the corner, waiting for them to shiv each other."

I felt like a million dollars for the rest of the school day. I had liked Mr. Oakley before, but it was great to be called an ace photographer. He appreciated me and was trying to come to my aid. Maybe Brody had been right and my decision to quit had been too rash. I would talk to Mr. Oakley about it again tomorrow. Paid or not, yearbook photographer was an important position I'd worked hard for, and I wasn't ready to give it up.

My good mood lasted until about five o'clock, when, as I was in the middle of altering one of my dresses for Kaye, she called my cell and asked me to come back to school. She had student council business to discuss with me and Brody as soon as he got out of football practice. She wouldn't tell me what the business was over the phone, but there was no way I could have missed this. I was afraid this was the reason Kaye had been spending so much quality time in the teachers' workroom: the minor problem, the top-secret issue that probably would amount to nothing. I hopped on my bike and pedaled back to school.

When I arrived, the football team was out of the showers and heading to their cars. Kaye, in her workout clothes and cheerleader shoes, sat on the tailgate of Brody's truck, talking to him. As I watched, Sawyer approached them. I couldn't hear what Kaye yelled at him from that distance, but I could tell she was shooing him. She pointed toward his truck. He retreated and sat on his own tailgate, waiting.

I leaned my bike against a palm tree. Kaye slid off Brody's tailgate and patted the place where she'd been. I hopped up next to Brody, looking in his eyes for some hint of what was about to come. He shook his head no. She hadn't told him yet.

"Sooooo," Kaye said. She'd started a million club meetings since we'd been in school together. She volunteered to give speeches in front of the class. I'd never seen her look this uncomfortable.

"Spill it," Brody said.

She pressed ahead. "The student council made a mistake. In ninth grade and tenth grade and eleventh grade, I was in charge of counting the votes for the Senior Superlatives. This year the student council advisor—you know,

Ms. Yates—wouldn't let me because I'm a senior myself and it wouldn't have looked good for me to count the votes for my close friends and for myself. She gave the job to some younger students. I should have found a way to do it, though. I *knew* they would mess it up."

Brody put his arm around my shoulders. "What happened?" His voice was loud.

"Most of the categories include a girl and a boy who don't necessarily have anything to do with each other. Like, Tia was the girl who got the most votes for Biggest Flirt, and Will was the guy. I was the girl who got the most votes for Most Likely to Succeed, and Aidan was the guy. That's how the student council tallied the votes for Perfect Couple That Never Was, too. But they shouldn't have. Because it's a *couple*."

She turned to me. "You won the girl's side of the vote because some people were pairing you with one boy, and some people paired you with another." She turned to Brody. "You won the guy's side because so many people paired you with two different girls. You and one of those girls should have come in second. Harper, you and another guy actually came in third. Two totally *different* people were paired together the most and should have won. But nobody paired Brody Larson and Harper Davis with each other."

16

BRODY AND I LOOKED AT EACH OTHER. HE must have seen something very dark in my expression, because he removed his arm from my shoulders.

"I didn't want to tell you." Kaye sounded almost pleading. "I explained to Ms. Yates that the two of you started dating because of the title. She said it was even more important that we tell you, then. It wasn't fair for you to base your relationship on false information. I see what she's saying about rules and honesty and what have you, but sometimes I think this school forgets we're human beings, just because we're not adults yet. They act like our relationships with each other aren't real.

"But!" She spread her hands and looked toward the sky for strength. "That's as far as their crusade for the truth extends.

Ms. Yates insisted I tell you this, but we're supposed to keep the mistake a secret. Otherwise there will be a chain reaction. Since each person can win only one title, they're all intertwined. If Harper wasn't part of Perfect Couple, she should have won Most Artistic, because she got the most votes for that. The girl who we thought won that gets booted to Most Original, and so forth. Brody should have won Most Athletic. The advisor doesn't want any of this to get out. It would take time to photograph the Superlatives again and the yearbooks would be late." She grinned wanly at me. "You're welcome."

"Well." I swallowed against the nausea. "Who'd the senior class pair me with as Perfect Couple, then?"

Kaye eyed Brody before she turned back to me and said, "Xavier Pilkington."

I took a deep breath and let out the longest sigh of resignation. The school had paired me with Mr. Most Academic. He might wind up the valedictorian. He might not. Kaye and some other folks were giving him a run for his money. But when the class had elected him Most Academic, what they were really calling him was Biggest Nerd. Most Repressed.

Just like me.

"And Evan Fielding," she added.

The old man's hat.

"Who'd they pair Brody with?" I asked. It was going to

hurt. But if I didn't ask, the curiosity would eat me alive.

Kaye glanced at Brody again, like she was asking permission, before she swallowed and said, "Cathy."

Grace's best friend and fellow cheerleader and beer-searcher-outer. Sure, that made sense.

"And Tia," Kaye said.

Of course. The free spirit. The sexy chick who didn't give a damn what anybody thought. My complete opposite. The girl Brody had a crush on in middle school.

I'd thought the senior class had gone insane when they put Brody and me together. Now that I knew they'd put Brody with Tia, I understood how smart the members of our class were, and how they'd seen through Brody's exterior to his deepest desires. We were never meant to be together. My admiration for him was real. I'd been talking myself into thinking we were compatible. But my week as his girlfriend had been a sham.

I turned to him. "I'm really sorry."

He frowned at me. "About what?"

About the fact that he was going to make this as hard as possible, but it had to be done. I soldiered on. "About last night. I should have known it was too good to be true."

"Oh, now, wait—" Kaye tried to interject.

"You sound like you're breaking up with me." Brody's voice was rising.

Yep, he was going to make this difficult, all right. I said, "I am."

"You are?" Kaye asked, sounding genuinely surprised.

I widened my eyes at her. Breaking up with Brody was hard enough without Kaye acting like I wasn't doing the right thing. I was sorry she felt guilty about the mistake. It truly wasn't her fault. But she must have guessed the news would break up Brody and me.

In a rush, Brody stood. The sudden shift of his weight bounced the truck and jolted me as he said, "I should have known."

"Known what?" I slung back at him. Sure, we'd been ridiculously mismatched from the beginning. I *had* sensed this, and he had too. But he didn't have to yell at me about it, as if I was beneath him because I wasn't more like him.

He glanced angrily at Kaye, then held out his hand to me. "Come here."

Reluctantly I let him lead me away from his truck, into the empty center of the parking lot. Pretty much all the football players had headed home, leaving only the vehicles of a few coaches, Kaye, Sawyer, and Brody. He looked at the fast-moving clouds in the overcast sky. Then he said, "You've felt like you were being daring to go out with me. I'm not safe like the guys you usually date."

He heaved a pained sigh. "But that wasn't it at all, was it? Going out with me was the *safest* thing you could do, because our class picked me for you. At least, you *thought* they did." He was very close to me now. "The second you find out I wasn't preapproved after all, I'm not worth the trouble!"

My heart was hammering, and I couldn't catch my breath. His words rang true. He was absolutely right.

Sawyer walked up beside us. "Larson. Can you take a step back?"

Brody faced him. "This is none of your business, De Luca. I'm not threatening her."

"You've got eight inches on her. It looks bad."

Brody blinked at me, as if he saw me for the first time. He stepped backward and put both hands up. "You're right," he said. "I'm sorry."

"It's okay," I breathed.

He laughed. "If we can apologize, this is nothing like my parents fighting."

"Mine, either."

Sawyer eyed me, then glanced back at Brody. "Don't make me come over here again." He sauntered toward Kaye, who still sat on Brody's tailgate.

"Anyway," Brody told me, "I don't know what else there is to say. Nice knowing you?" He followed Sawyer.

"What is that supposed to mean?" I called after him, irate for the first time.

He turned around and kept walking backward. "You broke up with me."

"Yeah, but . . ." I crossed the space between us. "You know, it was just a shock. I've been going crazy trying to figure out why we would be paired together. When I found out we weren't, that made so much sense that my gut reaction was we *shouldn't* be together. But . . ."

He shook his head.

"What?" I asked.

"It's not going to work," he said. "You'll always be on the verge of breaking up with me. You'll assume it won't work between us, and therefore it really won't, all because the senior class hasn't given you permission. We don't *look* right together, so we must be wrong for each other." He started backing up again. "I don't want to second-guess everything between us because you're too afraid to take a chance."

He walked swiftly toward his truck, pausing only to mutter something to Kaye and Sawyer. They slid off Brody's tailgate, and Sawyer slammed it shut. Brody cranked the engine and took off across the parking lot.

There were no screaming tires and burning rubber. That

would have made me feel better. I would have known he was angry, and therefore he cared. This calm acceptance meant he was really done with me. He wouldn't ask me to reconsider. He wouldn't make me jealous to try to get me back. Our entire relationship had been a mistake.

Kaye waited for me, leaning against her car next to Sawyer, tears streaming down her face. I could see them glinting in the sun even at this distance. I knew she felt awful, even though it wasn't her fault. I walked over.

"Kaye won't tell me what the problem is," Sawyer said. "It's some huge secret."

"It is," I said.

"Then I don't understand why *you* won't tell me," he said. "I am the *best* at spreading rumors. I could unburden you and let the whole school know in a matter of hours, and you wouldn't have to worry about people finding out anymore. You would feel so much better."

"Sawyer," Kaye bit out. "Damn. *It!*" Her last syllable echoed sharply against the school.

Kaye and Sawyer had picked at each other constantly since he moved to town two years ago. She often seemed exasperated with him, but she was rarely genuinely angry.

And I had never seen *him* fed up with *her*. He shouted back, "O-*kay!*" and stomped to his truck.

Watching him go, I leaned against Kaye's car in his place.

"I am so, so sorry," she said through her tears.

"It's all right, Kaye, really. It's better that we know. Brody's right. We never would have worked out."

"But you were having so much fun together," she protested. "You said you were happy. I could *see* you were happy. Your faces lit up at each other."

I shrugged. "It was only physical, I guess. I can always find another football player."

Kaye gave a big sniff. "You can tell yourself that. The problem with denial is, it's a bitch when it comes to a screeching halt. After that happens in a few hours, give me a call. I'm here for you."

I nodded. My heart was racing, but I felt strangely numb.

"You're good at keeping secrets," Kaye said.

"Yes, I am."

"Guess who the senior class *really* voted Perfect Couple That Never Was?"

I could tell from the look on her face. "You and Sawyer."

"And he hates me," she said. "I wish I'd never heard of these stupid titles."

"He doesn't hate you," I said. I would keep his secret. Besides, if I told Kaye that Sawyer had a crush on her, that would lead nowhere. Even if she wasn't with Aidan, there was no way she and Sawyer could get along as a couple. But I couldn't let her go on thinking he hated her when the opposite was true.

I could definitely agree with her on one thing: "These Superlatives titles are the worst idea ever." But I wouldn't say I wished I'd never heard of them. If it hadn't been for my title with Brody, I would never have shared last night on the beach with him. And though we'd probably been right to let each other go, I would cherish the feeling of understanding him so deeply, and the memory of his body on mine.

When I got back to the B & B, I found Mom sitting halfway up the grand staircase, oiling the newel posts. I asked her, "Where are the guests?"

"They're all out. What's up?"

I'd been doing deep-breathing exercises all the way home on my bike, so I was able to say calmly, "I would like to get on the pill."

It was dark in the stairwell, with only a little evening light filtering through the second-story stained-glass window. Even so, I could see every drop of blood drain from Mom's face. "Harper. Have you had unprotected sex?"

"No, Mom. I haven't had sex."

"Thank God!" She flopped backward on the staircase

with her arms sprawled out and her hair in her eyes, like she'd fainted. After this dramatic show, I waited for her to sit up again, but she stayed there. I patted her hand.

"Never scare me like that again," she murmured.

"That's the point. Brody and I broke up, but—"

"Oh, honey!" She sat up then, flipping her hair back over her shoulders. "I'm so sorry. You weren't dating him very long. What happened?"

"I broke up with him. And then I tried to take it back, and he broke up with *me*. Now I regret it."

"Why don't you try to make up?"

"He's really mad, Mom. *Really* mad. I don't blame him. The thing is . . . last night we fooled around. We didn't have sex, but we wanted to. It scared me. I think it scared me so badly that I pushed him away. I—" I stumbled over the rest of what I'd meant to say. Hearing myself verbalize the problem was what opened the floodgates, and all of a sudden I was bawling in Mom's arms.

Mom led me back to the house and actually cooked me dinner for once. We sat at the table and talked for an hour about Brody, and the Superlatives, and what all of it had meant to me. I explained that being named to the title with him had made me realize that my world was smaller than it needed to be, because I was mostly doing what other people wanted or expected, instead of exploring all my possibilities.

"The pill is just another part of it," I said with a loud sniffle. "I'm not sure I'll be able to get Brody back. Even if I did, I'm not saying we'd do it. For a while, at least. But I'm about to turn eighteen. I'll be at college soon. I think it's time I took care of myself. I'm tired of being afraid."

Mom nodded. "Those are all good reasons. We can definitely get you on the pill. And I know what you mean about being scared. It's a big decision. You should feel confident that you're protected." She eyed me. "But, Harper."

Uh-oh. "What?"

"If you're ever about to have sex and you're not a little bit nervous in a good way, you're not doing something right."

"That's wholesome, Mom. Thanks." I rubbed my eyes. I'd had to take my contacts out after the first fifteen minutes of bawling. "I *am* going to college, you know."

She shrugged and started to get up from the table. "You don't have to decide right now."

"No, Mom." I grabbed her hand and held it until she slowly sat back down. "I don't know why you want me to skip college and help you run the B & B. Maybe you see your relationship with Dad finally ending, and you're afraid to be completely on your own. There's no reason for you to feel that way. You're a successful businesswoman. You don't need me."

She smiled wanly. "Maybe I just *want* you."

"But I don't want *this*," I said. "I don't even want to help with breakfast anymore. I could really use more time in my day to expand my photography business, and that will help me pay for college. Plus, if you hire real employees, you could choose someone who's better company for your guests."

"Oh, honey!" she exclaimed. "You're lovely company."

"You're saying that because you're my mother. And as your daughter, there's another thing I'd like to do, too, if you'll let me."

She took a deep breath before she asked, "What's that?"

"I'd like to testify in court tomorrow and swear to the judge that you and dad don't need to go to counseling. Your marriage is irretrievably broken. Again."

She watched me for a long moment. "Wouldn't that make you sad?"

"No. I would be happy to help you both move on."

"I'll call my lawyer, then. Thank you, Harper." She reached across the table to stroke my hair out of my eyes. "Hey, do you have that pocket camera on you?"

"Yeah." I pulled it out and handed it to her.

She pointed it at me and snapped a picture before I could hide.

"Ugh," I said, putting my hands over my face.

"Uh-huh." She peered at the view screen, admiring the shot she'd taken. Satisfied, she handed the camera back to me. "Be sure to print that picture so you don't lose it as technology changes over the years. I promise you this: When you're my age, you'll look at it and think, 'I was gorgeous, with or without glasses, no matter what I wore or how I did my hair. Why did I waste my time worrying about how I looked?'"

I snorted. "God, Mom, that's something old people say."

"Listen to me," she said, patting the table for emphasis. "We old people are not making this shit up."

A few minutes later, I rang Granddad's doorbell and heard him walk to the door. He didn't open it.

"Granddad," I said.

"Who is it?" he barked.

"Three guesses."

"I'm busy." He took a few steps away.

"Granddad," I called through the door, "did you kill someone?"

"When?"

"Recently," I said. "Are you hiding a body in your house?"

"No."

"Let me in to see for myself."

"No."

"You know what? You're leading me to believe something is very wrong in there. If you don't open this door right now, I'm calling the police."

"Go ahead!"

I thought for a moment. "I'm calling Mom."

The door opened just the width of the security chain.

"All the way," I prompted him.

His face appeared in the opening. He glowered at me for a moment, then opened the door wide.

Before he could protest, I ducked under his arm and dashed for the back room he used as a studio. "Harper!" I heard him shout, but I'd already run though the studio doorway and seen what he didn't want me to see. I screamed.

"Eeek!" the naked lady squeaked.

"I am so sorry," I told her as I retreated into the hallway with my hand covering my eyes.

"It's okay, darlin'," she called. In a moment, she came through the doorway in a luxurious silk wrap. Her red hair was piled on top of her head, and she wore a lot of tasteful makeup. She was between Granddad's age and Mom's, I guessed, and her body was still beautiful. I could vouch for this, as I'd seen every inch of it. What hadn't been showing when I burst in on her was depicted in Granddad's paintings crowding the walls.

I extended my hand. "I'm Harper, the granddaughter."

She shook my hand. "I'm Chantel, the nude."

"Ha ha!" I said. "I beg your pardon. I was afraid Granddad was running an opium den or fight club or something back here. He's been so secretive."

"He's the strong, silent type." Chantel winked at me.

After backing out of that one, I returned to the front door, where Granddad was still scowling. "Granddad," I told him, "you're an artist. And you're a man."

"A *grown* man," he added.

"Well said. And you're within your rights to have Chantel pose nude in your studio. The only thing weird about this is that *you are being so freaking weird about it*!"

"I'm sixty-eight years old!" he shouted. "I'll do what I damn well please!"

I sighed, frustrated. Granddad was right—he'd been weird for a long time. The likelihood was slim that he would change because I complained. But it was nice to know that if I turned out to be an old curmudgeon just like him, maybe I would keep a few happy secrets.

"I actually came to make sure you're watching the weather," I said. "The hurricane's been downgraded to a tropical storm, but we're supposed to get rain and maybe tornadoes tomorrow."

"You think I don't have a smart phone?"

I heard my voice rising, despite myself. "I have never laid eyes on your smart phone. *You never let me in your house.*" I took a deep breath to calm down. "Also, may I borrow your car? I'll bring it back tomorrow after school."

"No," he said. "Same reason I didn't want you to borrow it on Labor Day. Chantel and I may want to get ice cream later."

I put my hands in my hair and pressed my lips together to keep from bursting into laughter, a yelling fit, or both. Granddad was being petty. But I was so relieved to find out it was because he was in love.

I cleared my throat. "May I please walk over and borrow your car before school tomorrow? I'll bring it back as soon as class is over. Mom and Dad have a divorce hearing. Mom needs to be at the courthouse a lot longer than I do because of meetings with her lawyer. I don't want to miss a whole day of school. I'm just testifying that their marriage is irretrievably broken."

Granddad grinned—the first time I'd seen him smile in a long, long while. "In that case," he said, "I'll deliver the car to your house."

*　　*　　*

The next day at noon, I sat on a polished bench in the marble-lined foyer of the courthouse in Clearwater, holding Mom's hand and waiting for the divorce hearing. Her lawyer was there. My dad's lawyer sat across from us, but my dad hadn't shown. Mom whispered that maybe he wouldn't, and the proceedings could go on without him interrupting them this time.

Thunder rolled outside.

Ten minutes before we were scheduled to appear in court, the front doors of the courthouse opened, and my heart sank.

But it wasn't my dad. It was Granddad and Chantel under an enormous umbrella. Outside on the street, their taxi pulled away.

I looked over at Mom. Her mouth was wide open. I wasn't sure what surprised her more: that Granddad had come to support her, or that he was guiding a glamorous lady friend by the elbow.

Granddad folded the umbrella and propped it up by the entrance, then brought Chantel over. Mom was all smiles as they moved away from the bench to make introductions and talk quietly.

I wanted to give Mom time alone with them. And I was too nervous to make small talk. I watched the clock and crossed my fingers.

Five minutes before we were scheduled to appear, the front doors of the courthouse opened again, and my heart sank all the way to the floor. My dad walked in, wearing his Coast Guard dress uniform, dripping from the downpour. He looked like a handsome, upstanding family man. I knew better.

He glanced around the foyer. His eyes skimmed across his lawyer and Mom's, lingered on Mom and Granddad, and landed on me. "Harper," he said curtly, like an order. He pointed to his feet.

Without even looking at Mom, I jumped up out of habit. It was only when I'd already hurried halfway across the room to him that I realized I was acting like his dog. But he was my dad, and I still had to do what he said—for a few more months.

He stared down at me sternly, trying to scare me. It was working. I considered crossing my eyes at him, because the tension was ridiculous.

He seethed, "If you testify against me in this court today, you are dead to me. Do you understand? I will pay child support until you turn eighteen because the law requires it, but after that, you don't exist."

Suddenly I realized how cold it was in the courthouse. I crossed my arms to warm myself and told my dad, "You've been dead to me since last Wednesday, when you shouted at me. I'm glad we've got that straight." I turned on my heel and walked back toward the bench.

Mom and Granddad looked over their shoulders at me.

I stopped in the middle of the foyer. This is exactly what I'd done yesterday: dumped Brody and regretted it instantly. Taking charge of my life was one thing. It was another thing entirely to throw important parts of it away.

I walked right back to my dad and put my hands on my hips. His jaw was working back forth, and he was blinking back tears.

I said gently, "I didn't mean that. You'll never be dead to me, no matter what. You're my dad."

No matter how I acted, I was still furious for what he'd said to me just then, and how he'd treated Mom for years. But I thought of him taking me to Granddad's beach when I was tiny, before we left for Alaska, and twirling me around in the warm waves.

I stood on my tiptoes and kissed Dad on the cheek.

17

ONLY A FEW MINUTES LATER, I WALKED OUT OF the courtroom as the daughter of soon-to-be-divorced parents, thank God. I hadn't even needed to testify after all. Dad hadn't contested the divorce this time or asked the judge to send my parents to counseling. Mom hugged me afterward and whispered that I deserved the credit. The way I felt, I expected a bright blue sky and a rainbow when I swung open the courthouse door.

Instead, the tropical storm had arrived. The rain was coming down so hard that an inch of water stood on the sidewalk. I opened my umbrella and waded back to Granddad's car.

Inside, I turned my phone on and checked my messages. I had a text from Brody, sent just a few minutes ago: *Where are you?* I hadn't told him or anyone in study hall that I would be absent.

He cared about me, in spite of everything. I felt myself flush, which meant I was very far gone.

I texted him back, *Parents divorcing, hooray! Driving back from courthouse.* I threw my phone into my purse and my purse into the back seat so I wouldn't be tempted to look at my phone again. Lately I'd been trying to embrace my daredevil side, but I wasn't dumb.

As I drove from Clearwater back home, I kept thinking I heard my phone beep with more texts. I suspected they were from Brody, and I was dying to know what they said. But I couldn't even be sure I'd heard the beeping. The rain was torrential, pounding on the car like a hundred high-pressure fire hoses. When I drove faster than thirty miles an hour, it was hard to keep the car on the road.

By the time I finally pulled into the school parking lot, the rain had stopped. I suspected the calm was only temporary, though. The air was thick with steam and the smells of rain and hot asphalt. The sky was light gray and swirling strangely.

Leaving all my stuff in my car except my camera and tripod, I hurried across the parking lot packed with cars but empty of people, into the football stadium. So quickly that my legs ached, I ran up the stairs to the highest point and looked over the guardrail.

Beyond the school campus stretched a residential section

of town. Roofs peeked above the lush canopy of palm trees and live oaks. Then there was a thin strip of white beach, and the ocean: an endless stretch of angry gray waves.

A waterspout—a tornado over the water rather than the land—snaked down from black clouds to dip its toe in the water elegantly, like a dancer. It glowed white against the sky.

I was glad I had lots of practice setting up my tripod, attaching the camera, and adjusting the settings. In seconds I was snapping photos, then switching the settings and snapping again, so I was sure to get at least one perfect photo out of hundreds.

Several minutes passed before it occurred to me that if there was one tornado, there might be more. We didn't have tornado sirens in Pinellas County, so I wouldn't know until it hit me, unless I saw it coming. But as I looked behind me at the landward side of town, I didn't see another twister. All I noticed was Brody standing way down at the stadium entrance.

"Lightning!" He pointed at the blinking southern sky.

I glanced back at my waterspout and snapped one more rapid-fire set of shots as it twisted up into the sky and disappeared. Then I swept up my tripod without pausing to detach the camera and hauled ass down the stairs.

"There's a tornado warning," he said, following me with his hand on my back as we hurried toward the school. "The rotation is close enough that everybody's crouched in the halls with their heads down, but I was afraid you wouldn't be able to get in because the doors are locked. Ms. Patel said I could come look . . . for . . . What are you doing?"

I sat down in Granddad's car. "Get in so we're not struck by lightning." I opened my laptop and plugged in my camera.

"You're getting online?" he asked, astonished.

"I photographed the tornado, and I'm about to sell the picture to the Tampa newspaper."

"Harper," he said as I typed. "Harper, remember when I told you that you should take risks only when you can get away with them? If that picture is published, the school will figure out you were on top of the stadium during a tornado. You might get suspended. Save it for your portfolio, maybe—"

"I hadn't checked in yet, so the school wasn't in charge of me." I finished composing my e-mail to the Tampa newspaper editor and attached the photo.

"You're not just trying to prove how daring you are to get me back, are you?"

"Hold on for a minute." The photo loaded, and I hit send. "What were you saying?"

"Nothing," he said, eyeing me across the car.

"I would love to date you again," I burst, riding the

adrenaline high I hadn't even registered until now. "We had so much fun, and I don't want to throw that away. The school is on crack for *not* pairing us together."

He grabbed me in a hug across the seat. I settled my head against his shoulder. He squeezed me gently and ran his fingertips through my hair.

Then he released me and sat up. "Yes, ma'am," he said, grinning. "Now let's go back, before we get in trouble."

We dashed across the parking lot. Inside the school, students lined the walls three people deep. As we were about to sit down too, the bell rang to cancel the warning. Everyone got up as one body and stretched.

"While we have a minute," I said, putting one hand on Brody's chest, "I've been thinking. Maybe if I told Mr. Oakley I would sign back on as yearbook photographer, he would make a few concessions. The Superlatives section isn't due to the publisher until Friday. I could ask to redesign Kennedy's ugly Superlatives pages and replace our Perfect Couple photo."

"Do you have an idea for it?"

I pulled my camera off the tripod, adjusted the settings, and handed it to Brody. "You take a selfie because your arm is longer. The camera's set to take five in a row, so just grin through it." We put our heads close together. "One, two—"

I smiled, and the camera flashed. By now we were getting pushed from all directions by the traffic in the hall. We moved over to the lockers and peered at the view screen. Both of us laughed. Brody looked happy and satisfied. I looked excited. Behind us, the hallway was filled with people, some photobombing us with their tongues sticking out, some ignoring us and absorbed in their own lives.

"I like this concept," I said. "See? The whole school is behind us."

"I like your glasses," he said. "You look sexy as hell. Come here." He looped the camera strap over my shoulder and wrapped his arms around me.

"This is against school rules," I said. "Talk about being in danger of getting caught—"

"I don't care," he whispered in my ear. "I was worried about you in the storm. I'm just glad you're safe." He squeezed me once more and let me go.

At the football game the following Friday night, the photographer for the local newspaper approached me on the sidelines with his hand out for me to shake. I was thrilled. I knew exactly who he was. I'd seen him snapping pictures of the games for years. I'd wanted to *be* him for years.

He asked, "You're Harper Davis, right?"

"That's right."

He introduced himself, then said, "Great shot of the waterspout in the Tampa paper."

"Thanks. That was just luck. And a tripod."

He shook his head. "You're a photographer. You make your own luck. Even now, look at you. Your eyes haven't left the game. You're scouting for a photo."

I smiled, because it was true. As we'd talked, I'd kept watching the field, determined not to miss a key play.

"You're still in high school?" he asked. "That's impressive work. I expect you'll go places."

We chatted for a few more minutes about my camera and his camera, and the best shots he'd taken of Tropical Storm Debby a few years ago. As I conversed with him, my eyes stole over to Brody, laughing with a local policeman who stood guard every game at the gate onto the field.

I wondered if Brody and I might be back here in five years or ten years or more, me photographing the game while he kept it safe. This wasn't necessarily *the* future, but it was *a* future. And a nice one to dream about. One I never would have considered if it hadn't been for a botched yearbook election mistakenly telling us who we were, and helping us find out the truth for ourselves.

The photographer moved off in search of a better angle

as the other team punted and Brody ran for the center of the field, tugging his helmet on as he went.

And then, on the first play, he got sacked. I had a tele-photo view, because I was shooting pictures of him when it happened.

I dropped my camera. The weight of it jerked the strap around my neck as I slapped my hands over my mouth in horror.

Five thousand people in the stadium hushed at one time. Every coach ran onto the grass. The entire football team and the visiting team took a knee. The paramedics from an ambu-lance parked beyond the end zone wheeled a stretcher onto the field.

I was sure he was paralyzed until Noah, huge in his hel-met and pads, jogged toward me. He put both hands on my shoulders. "Brody's okay," he panted.

"Brody's okay?" I shrieked.

"I mean, he will be. He didn't hit his head. Coach ordered a stretcher as a precaution because of Brody's concussion in the summer. This time he only got the wind knocked out of him."

"Thank you," I sighed.

"I couldn't let you freak out over here," he said.

"Thank you, Noah." I wrapped both arms around his wet jersey.

"And I didn't even fall on him this time." Noah put a

gloved hand in my hair. "I've got to go." He disentangled himself from me and ran back onto the field with the rest of the offensive line plus the second-string quarterback. Ten men surrounded the stretcher rolling off the field toward the ambulance. The stadium gave Brody a standing ovation.

Blinking back tears, I walked over to the ambulance and stood a few yards away, out of the commotion. Paramedics busied themselves around Brody. Coaches climbed in and out of the truck. Brody's mom appeared from the stands, the tracks of her tears visible through her makeup. I recognized her from a million elementary school parties, and from pictures of her in her own house at parties Brody had thrown when she wasn't home.

I waited, heart racing.

One by one, the coaches went back to the team on the sidelines. But I didn't believe Noah was right, and Brody was okay, until his mom jumped down from the ambulance, smiling and wiping her eyes. She walked around the fence to climb into the stands again.

I heaved one huge sigh of relief, then walked over.

"No pictures," said a paramedic sitting on the bumper of the ambulance, watching the game. He eyed my camera.

"I'm his girlfriend."

"Oh." He moved aside for me.

I climbed into the back of the ambulance, my heart beating harder and faster. No matter what Noah had said, it was terrifying to see Brody lying on a stretcher that wasn't quite big enough for his body, surrounded by sinister equipment. His helmet and jersey and shoulder pads lay heaped in a corner. He wore an athletic shirt with high-tech pads sewn into the sides. With his arms crossed on his chest, he looked slender and young and vulnerable. His long, wet hair had escaped from his headband and stuck to his forehead. His eyes were closed.

I took his hand and squeezed it.

He squeezed back, opening one eye to look at me. He closed his eyes again. "I'm okay. I couldn't breathe for a minute."

"Is that all?"

He laughed shortly. "Did you see the guy who got me? He must have weighed five hundred pounds."

The guy hadn't been that big, but football players probably looked a lot bigger to Brody when they were about to sack him. I decided to delete that series of pictures.

"I was just lying here"—he took a deep breath and exhaled slowly—"doing the relaxation exercise you taught me. I think I'm ready to go back."

"Are you sure?" I asked. The alarm from seeing him flat on the field, not moving, was too fresh.

"The paramedics already cleared me," he said. "I didn't hit my head."

"If you did," I said, "would you know?"

"Maybe not," he admitted.

I let go of his hand and held up seven fingers.

"Seven," he said.

"Who's your best friend?"

"Noah."

"How long have you played football together?"

"Since third grade." He answered every question with no hesitation. His brain was working fine.

"What are you doing after the game?" I asked.

"I'm going to the Crab Lab. With you. We haven't talked about what we'll do after that, but I was planning to get you to your granddad's beach again and show you what a perfect couple we are."

"Oh, really," I said archly. "Are you looking forward to that?"

He crooked his finger at me. I leaned closer. He whispered, "This is going to be our best night yet." His mouth caught mine in a sexy kiss.

Then he sat up slowly. "Goddamn, I'm going to hurt tomorrow. But right now, I feel great. Let's go play some football!"

I fished his pads out of the corner of the ambulance. "You're crazy, you know that? You definitely hit your head."

After we got him suited up, he jumped down from the ambulance. With a last salute to me, he jogged along the sidelines to rejoin his team and finish his adventure.

I brought up my camera and snapped a picture.

ACKNOWLEDGMENTS

Heartfelt thanks to my editor and favorite cheerleader, Annette Pollert. Every author of YA romance should be lucky enough to have an editor who draws little hearts on the manuscript.

To my brilliant agent, Laura Bradford. I would not be here without you.

And to my long-suffering critique partner, the best friend I could wish for, Victoria Dahl.

Don't miss Jennifer Echols's

the superlatives

most likely to succeed

I LEFT CALCULUS A MINUTE BEFORE THE BELL so I'd be the first to arrive at the student council meeting. Our advisor, Ms. Yates, would sit at the back of her classroom, observing, and I wanted her vacated desk at the front of the room. At our last meeting, Aidan had taken her desk in a show of presidential authority. But as vice president, I was the one who needed room for paperwork. A better boyfriend than Aidan would have let me sit at the desk.

A better girlfriend than me would have let *him* have it.

And that pretty much summed up our three years of dating.

The bell rang just as I reached the room. I stood outside the door, waiting for Ms. Yates to make her coffee run to the teachers' lounge and for her freshman science class to flood past me. A few of them glanced at me, their eyes widening as if I were a celebrity. I remembered this feeling from when I was an underclassman, looking up to my brother and his friends. It was strange to be on the receiving end.

As the last of the ninth graders escaped down the hall, I stepped into the room, which should have been empty.

Instead, Sawyer De Luca sat behind Ms. Yates's desk. He must have left his last class *two* minutes before the bell to beat me here.

Sensing my presence, he turned in the chair, flashing deep blue eyes at me, the color of the September sky out the window behind him. When Sawyer's hair was combed—which I'd seen happen once or twice in the couple of years I'd known him—it looked platinum blond. Today, as usual, it was a mess, with the nearly white, sun-streaked layers sticking up on top, and the dark blond layers peeking out underneath. He had on his favorite shirt, which he wore at least two times a week, the madras short-sleeved button-down with blue stripes that made his eyes stand out even more. His khaki shorts were rumpled. I couldn't see his feet beneath the desk, but I knew he wore his beat-up flip-flops. In short, if you'd never met Sawyer before, you'd assume he was a hot but harmless teenage beach bum.

I knew better.

I closed the door behind me so nobody would witness

the argument we were about to have. I wanted that desk. I suspected he understood this, which was why he'd sat there. But long experience with Sawyer told me flouncing in and complaining wouldn't do me any good. That's what he expected me to do.

So I walked in with a bigger grin on my face than I'd ever given Sawyer. "Hi!"

He smiled serenely back at me. "Hello, Kaye. You look beautiful in yellow."

His sweet remark shot me through the heart. My friend Harper had just altered this dress to fit me. I didn't need her beautifully homemade hand-me-downs, but I was glad to take them—especially this sixties A-line throwback as vivid as the Florida sunshine. After a rocky couple of weeks for romance with Aidan, I'd dressed carefully this morning, craving praise from him. *He* hadn't said a word.

Leave it to Sawyer to catch me off guard. He'd done the same thing last Saturday night. After two years of teasing and taunting me, out of the blue he'd told me he loved my new hairstyle. I always had a ready response for his insults, but these compliments threw me off.

"Thanks," I managed, setting my books down on the edge of the desk, along with my tablet and my loose-leaf binder for student council projects. Then I said brightly, "So,

Mr. Parliamentarian, what's procedure on letting the vice president have the desk? I need to spread out."

"*I* need to spread out." He patted the stack of library books in front of him: an ancient tome that explained procedure for meetings, called *Robert's Rules of Order*, plus a couple of modern discussions of how the rules worked. For once Sawyer had done his homework.

"Taking the parliamentarian job seriously, are we?" This was my fourth year in student council. We'd always elected a parliamentarian without fully understanding what the title meant. Ms. Yates said the parliamentarian was the rule police, but we'd never needed policing, with a charismatic president like Aidan at the helm and Ms. Yates lurking in the back. Nobody ran for parliamentarian during officer elections in the spring. Ms. Yates waited until school started in the fall, then pointed out that "student council parliamentarian" would look great on college applications. One study hall representative volunteered, got elected, and never lifted a finger during meetings.

Until now. "I have to be able to see everything and look stuff up quickly." Sawyer swept his hand across his books and a legal pad inscribed with tiny cryptic notes. "Last meeting, Aidan didn't follow parliamentary procedure at *all*. But I'll share the desk with you." He stood and headed for the back of the room, where a cart was stacked with extra folding chairs for the meeting.

Normally I would have told him not to bother retrieving a chair for me. His suggestion that we share a desk was the best way to make me drop the subject and sit down elsewhere. He knew I wouldn't want Aidan to think we were flirting.

But this week wasn't normal. Aidan had hurt my feelings last Saturday by dissing my hair. We'd made up by Sunday— at least, I'd told him I forgave him—but I wasn't quite over the insult. The idea of him walking into the room and seeing Sawyer and me at Ms. Yates's desk together was incredibly appealing.

Sawyer held the folding chair high above his head as he made his way toward me. He unfolded the chair behind the desk. I started to sit down in it.

"No, that's for me. I meant for you to have the comfy chair." He rolled Ms. Yates's chair over, waited for me to sit, and pushed me a few inches toward the desk, like my dad seating my mother in a restaurant. He plopped down in the folding chair. "Will you marry me?"

Now *this* was something I'd expected him to ask. In fact, it was the first thing he'd ever said to me when he moved to town two years ago. Back then I'd uttered an outraged "No!" He'd wanted to know why—he wasn't good enough for me?

Who did I think I was, a bank president's daughter?

After a while, though, I'd gotten wise to Sawyer's game. Every girl in school knew he wasn't exclusive and meant nothing by his flirtations. That didn't stop any of us from having a soft spot for this hard-living boy. And it didn't stop me from feeling special every time he paid me attention.

Something had changed this school year when he started practicing with us cheerleaders in his pelican costume as school mascot. He stood right behind me on the football field, imitating my every step, even after I whirled around and slapped him on his foam beak. When we danced the Wobble, he moved the wrong way on purpose, running into me. With no warning he often rushed up, lifted me high, and gave me full-body, full-feathered hugs. Because he was in costume, everybody, including Aidan, knew it was a joke.

Only I took it seriously. I enjoyed it too much and wished he'd do the same things to me with the costume off.

Then, last Saturday, he'd told me he loved my hair. My heart opened to him.

And *then* I'd found out the juniors had made a mistake tallying the Senior Superlatives votes. Each student could be elected to only one title. The girl and boy with the most votes won—except Perfect Couple That Never Was. This position was supposed to be tallied as the girl-boy pair that gained the most votes, not the girl and the boy individually. I wasn't allowed to say this to Sawyer or anyone, but he and I had been elected Perfect Couple That Never Was. Our class had paired us together.

My crush on him was now official and hopeless. He was toying with me, like he toyed with everyone. Plus, I was committed to Aidan.

"Yes, of course I'll marry you," I told Sawyer, making sure I sounded sarcastic.

The door opened, letting in the noise from the hall. "Hey," Will said, lilting that one syllable in his Minnesota accent. Lucky for him, derision about the way he talked had waned over the first five weeks of school. He'd started dating my friend Tia, who gave people the stink eye when they bad-mouthed him. And he'd made friends with Sawyer—a smart move on Will's part. Sawyer could be a strong ally or a powerful enemy.

Sawyer waited for a couple more classroom representatives to follow Will toward the back of the room. Then he turned to me again. "Would you go to the prom with me?"

"Yes." This was the game. He asked me a series of questions, starting with the outlandish ones. I said yes to those. Eventually he asked me something that wasn't as crazy, forcing me to give him the obvious answer: I had a boyfriend.

Here it came. "Will you sit with me on the van to the game tonight?"

A spark of excitement shot through me. A few weeks ago, Sawyer had passed out from the heat on the football field in his heavy mascot costume. Ever since, he'd ditched the suit during cheerleading practice and worked out with the football team instead, claiming he needed to get in better shape to withstand entire games dressed up as a pelican.

I missed him at cheerleading. I'd assumed he would ride with the football players to our first away game, but I wished he would ride on the cheerleader van. Now my wish was coming true.

Careful not to sound too eager, I said, "I didn't know you were riding with us. You've been more football player than cheerleader lately."

"I'm a pelican without a country," he said. "Some unfortunate things may have gotten superglued to other things in the locker room after football practice yesterday. The guys went to the coach and said they don't want me to ride on the bus because they're scared of what I'll do. The coach *agreed*. Can you believe that? I'm not even innocent until proven guilty."

"*Are* you guilty?" Knowing Sawyer, I didn't blame the team for accusing him.

"Yes," he admitted, "but they didn't know that for sure."

He settled his elbow on the desk and his chin in his hand, watching me. "You, on the other hand, understand I never mean any harm. You'll sit with me on the van, right?"

I wanted to. My face burned with desire—desire for a *seat*, of all things. Next to a boy who was nothing but trouble.

And I knew my line. "We can't sit together, Sawyer. Aidan wouldn't like it."

Sawyer's usual response would be to imitate me in a sneering voice: *Aidan wouldn't like it!*

Instead, he grabbed Ms. Yates's chair and rolled me closer to him. Keeping his hands very near my bare knees, he looked straight into my eyes and asked softly, "Why do you stay with Aidan when he bosses you around? You don't let anyone else do that."

Tia and my friend Harper grilled me at every opportunity about why I stayed with Aidan too, but they didn't bring up the subject while representatives for the entire school could hear. My eyes flicked over to the student council members, who were filling the desks and noisily dragging extra chairs off the cart, and Ms. Yates, who was making her way toward the back of the room with her coffee. Aidan himself would be here any second.

I told Sawyer quietly but firmly, "*You* would boss me around just as much as Aidan does. What's the difference?"

"That's not true." Sawyer moved even closer. I watched his lips as he said, "I wouldn't ask for much. What I wanted, you would give me willingly."

Time stopped. The bustle around us went silent. The classroom disappeared. All that was left was Sawyer's mouth forming words that weren't *necessarily* dirty, yet promised a dark night alone in the cab of his truck. My face flushed hot, my breasts tightened underneath my cute yellow bodice, and electricity shot straight to my crotch.

The many nights I'd pulled Tia away from Sawyer at parties over the past two years, she'd drunkenly explained that he had a way of talking her panties off. I'd heard this from other girls too. And he'd flirted with me millions of times, making me feel special, but never quite *this* special. Now I understood what Tia and those other girls had meant.

Abruptly, I sat up and rolled my chair back.

He straightened more slowly, smirking. He knew exactly what effect he'd had on me.

Bewildered, I breathed, "How did you do that?"

"It's a gift."

His cavalier tone ticked me off, and I regained my own voice. "That's what I would worry about. During study hall, you give me the 'gift'"—I made finger quotes—"but you've moved on to the next girl by lunch. No thanks."

His face fell. "No, I—"

Aidan sashayed in, greeting the crowd as he came, already starting the meeting.

Sawyer lowered his voice but kept whispering to me as if nothing else were going on and Aidan weren't there. He said, "I wouldn't do that to you. I wouldn't cheat on you, ever."

Aidan turned around in front of the desk and gave us an outraged look for talking while he was making a speech. Sawyer didn't see it, but I did. I faced forward and opened my student council binder, cheeks still burning.

Sawyer had complimented me, part of a strange new trend.

He'd dropped the playful teasing and blatantly come on to me, a brand-new pleasure.

And he'd gotten upset at my tart response, as if he actually cared.

I leaned ever so slightly toward him to give the electricity an easier time jumping the arc from my shoulder to his. His face was tinged pink, unusual for Sawyer, who was difficult to embarrass. I was dying to know whether he felt the buzz too.

Apparently not. I jumped in my chair, startled, as he banged the gavel on the block that Ms. Yates had placed on her desk for Aidan. "Point of order, Mr. President," Sawyer said. "Have you officially started the meeting? You haven't asked the secretary to read the minutes."

"We don't have time," Aidan said. Dismissing Sawyer, he turned back to the forty representatives crowding the room. He hadn't argued with us about who got Ms. Yates's desk, after all. He didn't need to. Instead of presiding over the council from here, he simply reasserted his authority by running the meeting while standing up. Sawyer and I looked like his secretarial pool.

"We have a lot to cover," Aidan explained to the reps, and I got lost in watching him and listening to him, fascinated as ever. About this time of year in ninth grade, he'd captured my attention. Previously he'd been just another dork I'd known since kindergarten. I'd preferred older guys, even if they didn't prefer *me*.

But Aidan had come back from summer break taller than before, and more self-assured than any other boy I knew. That's why I'd fallen for him. Confidence was sexy. That's also why, until recently, I'd felt a rush of familiarity and belonging and pride whenever I glimpsed him across a room.

After years with him, however, I was finally coming to understand he wasn't as sure of himself as he wanted people to believe. He was so quick to anger. He couldn't take being challenged. But as I watched him work the room like a pro, with the freshman reps timidly returning his broad smile, I remembered exactly what I'd seen in him back then.

Sawyer put his elbow on our desk and his chin in his hand, looking bored already. He glanced sidelong at me.

"We're entering the busiest season for the council," Aidan was saying, "and we desperately need volunteers to make these projects happen. Our vice president, Ms. Gordon, will now report on the homecoming court elections coming up a week from Monday, and the float for the court in the homecoming parade."

"And the dance," I called.

"There's not going to be a homecoming dance," he told me over his shoulder. "I'll explain later. Go ahead and tell them about the homecoming court—"

Several reps gasped, "What?" while others murmured, "What did he say?" I spoke for everyone by uttering an outraged "What do you mean, there's not going to be a dance?"

"Ms. Yates"—he nodded to where she sat in the back of the room, and she nodded in turn—"informed me before the meeting that the school is closing the gym for repairs. The storm last week damaged the roof. It's not safe for occupancy. That's bad news for us, but of course it's even worse news for the basketball teams. The school needs time to repair the gym before their season starts."

Will raised his hand.

Ignoring Will, Aidan kept talking. "All of us need to get

out there in the halls and reassure the basketball teams and their fans that our school is behind them."

I frowned at the back of Aidan's head. He used this bait-and-switch method all the time, getting out of a sticky argument by distracting people (including me) with a different argument altogether. Basketball season was six weeks away. The homecoming dance didn't have to die so easily. But hosting the event would be harder now, and Aidan didn't want to bother.

I did.

"Help," I pleaded with Sawyer under my breath.

Aidan had already moved on, introducing my talk about the election committee.

Out in the crowd Will called, "Excuse me," which hadn't happened in any council meeting I'd attended. "Wait a minute. My class wants the dance."

I couldn't see Aidan's face from this angle, but he drew his shoulders back and stood up straighter. He was about to give Will a snarky put-down.

Sawyer watched me, blond brows knitted. He didn't understand what I wanted.

"Complain about something in the book again," I whispered, nodding at *Robert's Rules of Order*. "Ms. Yates hasn't stopped Aidan from railroading the meeting. She obviously doesn't want the dance either, but they can't fight the book."

Everyone jumped as Sawyer banged the gavel. "The council recognizes Mr. Matthews, senior from Mr. Frank's class. Stand up, sir."

We'd never had reps rise to speak before. I was pretty sure the rules of order didn't say anything about this. But it was a good move on Sawyer's part. At Will's full height he had a few inches on Aidan, and when he crossed his muscular arms on his chest, his body practically shouted that nobody better try to budge him.

Before Aidan could protest, Will said in his strangely rounded accent, "I haven't been here long, but I get the impression that the homecoming dance is a huge deal at this school. Everyone in Mr. Frank's class has been talking about it and looking forward to it. We can't simply cancel at the first sign of trouble."

"We just did," Aidan snapped. "Now sit down while I'm talking."

Sawyer banged the gavel. I should have gotten used to it by now, but I jumped in my seat again.

Aidan visibly flinched. He turned on Sawyer and snatched the gavel away. Holding it up, he seethed, "Don't do that again, De Luca. You're not in charge here. I'm the president."

"Then act like it," I said.

Aidan turned his angry gaze on me. I stared right back at

him, determined not to chicken out. Will and Sawyer and I were right about this. Aidan was wrong.

As I watched, Aidan's expression changed from fury to something different: disappointment. I'd betrayed him. We'd had a long talk last week about why we couldn't get along lately. He understood I disagreed with him sometimes, but he wanted us to settle our differences in private, presenting a united front to the school as the president and his vice president.

Now I'd broken the rule. No matter what the council decided, he wouldn't forgive me for defying him in public.

And I didn't care. Keeping the peace wasn't worth letting him get away with acting like a dictator.

"We don't have *time* to debate this in a half-hour meeting," he repeated. "There's nothing to debate. The decision has been made. The school already canceled the dance because we don't have a location for it."

"We'll move it," I said.

"It's only two weeks away," he said.

I shrugged. "You put me in charge of the dance committee. It's our job to give it a shot."

Aidan's voice rose. He'd forgotten we'd agreed not to argue in public. "You're only pitching a fit about this because you're still mad about—"

"Give me that," Sawyer interrupted, holding out his hand for the gavel.

"No," Aidan said, moving the gavel above his head.

"Mr. President," Sawyer said in a lower, reasonable tone, like talking to a hysterical child, "you're not allowed to debate the issue."

"Of course I am. I'm the president!"

"Exactly. *Robert's Rules of Order* state that your responsibilities are to run the meeting and give everyone the opportunity to speak. If you want to express your opinion, you need to vacate the chair."

"I'm not *in* the chair," Aidan snapped. "*You're* in the chair."

"I mean," Sawyer said, rolling his eyes, "you need to step down as president while we discuss this matter, and let Kaye preside over the meeting."

"I'm not stepping down."

"Then you need to shut up."

"Sawyer," Ms. Yates said sharply. I couldn't see her behind Will, who was still standing, but her thin voice cut like a knife through the grumbling and shushing in the classroom. "You're being disruptive."

"On the contrary, Ms. Yates," Sawyer called back, "the president is being disruptive, trying to bend the entire council to his will. Ms. Patel's study hall elected me to represent them. The student council chose me as parliamentarian. It's my duty to make sure we follow the procedure set down in the council bylaws. Otherwise, a student could sue the school for a violation of rights and due process."

The room fell silent, waiting for Ms. Yates's response. Horrible visions flashed through my mind of what would happen next. Ms. Yates might complain to Ms. Chen that Sawyer was disrespectful. They could remove him from student council or, worse, from his position as school mascot. All because he'd helped me when I asked.

Underneath the desk, I put my hand on his knee.

"Sawyer," Ms. Yates finally said, "you may continue, but don't tell anybody else to shut up."

"So noted." Sawyer pretended to scribble this reminder to himself. Actually he drew a smiley face in *Robert's Rules of Order*. "Aidan, if you're really running the meeting, let Will bring up the idea of saving the dance, then put it to a vote."

Aidan glared at Sawyer. Suddenly he whacked the gavel so hard on the block on Ms. Yates's desk that even Sawyer jumped.

Sawyer didn't take that kind of challenge sitting down. I gripped his knee harder, signaling him to stay in his seat. If he could swallow this last insult from Aidan, he and I had won.

THE REMAINING TWENTY MINUTES OF THE MEET-
ing seemed to take forever. But Aidan followed procedure—
at least I figured he did, because Sawyer didn't speak up again.
By the time the bell rang to send us to lunch, the council had
agreed that I would lead the committee in charge of relocat-
ing the dance instead of canceling it.

On top of leading the committee in charge of homecoming court elections.

And leading the committee in charge of the parade float.
I didn't understand why Aidan opposed the council taking
on more projects when he simply passed all the work to me.

As everyone crowded Ms. Yates's door, Sawyer stood and
stretched. Then he leaned over and said in my ear, "We make
a good team. Maybe you and I got off on the wrong foot."

"For two years?" I asked.

He opened his mouth to respond but stopped. Aidan brushed past the desk on his way out the door. He didn't say a word to me.

Will was the last rep remaining in the empty room. He paused in front of the desk. "Thanks, you guys, for taking my side."

"Thanks for taking ours," I said, standing up and gathering my stuff, which was tangled with Sawyer's stuff. One side of my open binder had gotten caught beneath his books.

"For me, this wasn't just about the dance," Will said. "People have been talking about it, and Tia told me what fun it was last year. Of course . . ." He looked sidelong at Sawyer.

I knew what that look meant. Sawyer and Tia used to fool around periodically, up until she and Will started dating a few weeks ago. The homecoming dance last year had been no different. Too late, Will realized what he'd brought up.

"It *was* fun," I interjected before Sawyer could make a snide comment that everyone would regret. "Come on." I ushered them both toward the door.

"I was student council president back in Duluth." Will followed us into the hall and closed Ms. Yates's door behind us. Down at the end of the freshman corridor, a teacher frowned at us. Will lowered his voice as he said, "That is,

I was *supposed* to be president this year, before we moved. I know what the president is supposed to do, and Aidan's not *doon* it. Sometimes you have to stand up and tell somebody, 'You're not *doon* it right.'"

I thought Sawyer would make fun of Will's Norse *doon*. He might have stopped insulting Will behind his back, but he wouldn't be able to resist a comment to his face. Yet he didn't say a word about Will's accent.

Instead, Sawyer grumbled, "If the storm had destroyed the gym completely, the business community would rally around us, give us money, and solve the problem for us. They'd get lots of publicity for hosting our homecoming dance. Nobody's going to help us just because our roof leaks."

"Leaking isn't good PR," Will agreed. "I signed up for the dance committee and I want to help, but I'm the worst person to think of ideas for where else to hold an event. I still don't know this town very well."

"Doesn't the Crab Lab also own the event space down the block?" I asked Sawyer. "One of my mother's assistants had her wedding reception there. Could you sweet-talk the owner into letting us use it for cheap? Better yet, for free?"

"It's booked that night," he said.

"That's two weeks from now," I pointed out. "You've memorized the schedule for the event space down the block?"

"A fortieth class reunion is meeting there after the game," he said. "The owner asked me to wait tables. I said no because of the dance. I have an excellent memory for turning down money."

Sawyer waited tables a lot. While a good portion of our class was at the beach, he often went missing because he was working. Even though he'd helped me in the meeting, I was a little surprised the dance was important enough to him personally that he would take the night off.

And, irrationally, I was jealous. As we stopped in the hall and waited for Will to swing open the door of the lunchroom, I asked Sawyer, "Who are you taking to homecoming?"

He gaped at me. "You!" he exclaimed, like this was the most obvious answer in the world and I had a lot of nerve to joke about it. He stomped into the lunchroom.

Will was left holding the door open for me and blinking at us. He didn't understand the strange social customs of Florida.

"It would help if you could brainstorm over the weekend," I told Will, pretending my episode with Sawyer hadn't happened. "Ask around at lunch and on the band bus tonight. See if you can scare up ideas. Maybe we'll think of something by the next meeting."

"Sounds good," he called after me as I headed across the lunchroom to the teacher section.

Aidan, Ms. Yates, and I had eaten at one end of a faculty table after the last council meeting, discussing projects like the dance. Possibly the one thing worse than spending lunch with Aidan while he was mad at me was spending lunch with Aidan and Ms. Yates, who, judging from the expression on her face, hadn't liked how the meeting had gone down. But I was the vice president, so I straightened my shoulders and walked over.

They were deep in conversation. Trying not to interrupt them, I looped the strap of my book bag over the back of the chair beside Aidan. They both looked up anyway. I said, "Sorry. I didn't know we were meeting, or I would have gotten here sooner. I'll just grab a salad and be right with y—"

Ms. Yates interrupted me. "This is a private talk."

"Oh" was all I could think of to say. My face tingled with embarrassment as I slipped my bag off the chair and beat a retreat across the lunchroom to the safety of Tia, Harper, and the rest of my friends. By the time I finally sat down with my salad, they were spitting out and shooting down ideas for where to have the dance—led by Will, who repeated how angry he was at Aidan for what he'd been *doon* in the meeting.

I listened and waited for them to come up with something brilliant. For once I stayed silent. I still smarted from Ms. Yates telling me I didn't belong at the adult table anymore. And I wondered whether I deserved it. Lately I got so *furious* at Aidan, but I was probably going through an immature phase, like cold feet before a wedding. We'd known almost since we started dating that we were destined for each other. All summer we'd been planning to apply to Columbia together. Whenever Aidan annoyed me, I needed to take a deep breath before I spoke—as my mother reminded me each time I mouthed off to her—and make sure the problem was really with him, not me.

And I knew in my heart that the problem was mine, all because of the Superlatives mix-up. On the first day of school, the student council had run Superlatives elections for the senior class. We *thought* Harper and our school's star quarterback, Brody, had been voted Perfect Couple That Never Was. If I'd been in charge of the elections, as in years past, that mistake wouldn't have been made. Even though I was still the chair of the elections committee, Ms. Yates wouldn't let me count the votes. Since I was a senior this year, I had a conflict of interest.

But without me to watch over them, the wayward juniors had screwed up the whole election. They said I'd been chosen Most Likely to Succeed with Aidan. That sounded right. He was president. I was vice president.

Here's what didn't make sense: In reality I'd been elected Perfect Couple That Never Was with Sawyer.

When I realized the juniors' mistake, Ms. Yates had made me tell Brody and Harper they didn't really win the title since they'd started dating because of it. But I wasn't allowed to divulge the truth to anyone else. Each person in the class could get a maximum of one Superlatives position, so the single error had created a snowball effect. Almost every title was incorrect. And since Harper had already taken the pictures and sent them to the yearbook printer, Ms. Yates wanted to leave well enough alone. Not even Sawyer was in on this secret.

Definitely not Aidan.

I was thankful Harper and Brody had been able to work through their problems and keep dating after I told them the truth. They were adorable together, even if part of what made them fascinating was the fact that they were so obviously mismatched.

Now I was cycling through the same feelings Harper had when she believed she'd been paired with Brody. She'd seen Brody with new eyes and longed for a relationship with him because she'd mistakenly thought someone else had told her it could work. The only difference was, this time there was no mistake. I was *not* Most Likely to Succeed along with Aidan. Angelica, nefarious and cunning, had received that honor.

The senior class said Sawyer and I should be together.

I'd started to think so too.

Which was dumb, because the election was just a stupid vote for yearbook pictures. Aidan and I would attend Columbia University together, take a while to establish our banking careers in New York, and then get married. After three years of knowing that was my plan, letting a class election change my mind didn't say much about my decision-making skills.

Neither did obsessing about Sawyer. On the far end of my table he attacked his huge salad with the appetite of a seventeen-year-old, half-starved vegan. When he looked up and saw me staring, he tapped his watch, then splayed his hand, wiggling all five fingers. He meant he would meet me at the cheerleading van at five o'clock this afternoon, and we would ride to the game together, exactly as I'd promised (not).

I couldn't wait.

ABOUT THE AUTHOR

Jennifer Echols has written many romantic novels for teens and adults. She grew up in a small town on a beautiful lake in Alabama, where her high school senior class voted her Most Academic and Most Likely to Succeed. Please visit her at www.jennifer-echols.com.

3 1491 01166 3964

Niles
Public Library District

MAR 0 2 2015

Niles, Illinois 60714